C000177743

**"What can I expect from Mr. Kerr**

Easiest question he'd asked. "Deception. Flattery. Manipulation. A knife in your back if you're not careful."

Rathburn's smile sent a chill dancing over Nat's skin. "I'm always careful." He lifted his head like he'd heard a noise and glanced toward the doorway. "Ah, that will be him now. Please excuse me for a moment. I'll be right back." Setting his drink behind the bar, he exited the room.

Nat didn't believe for a moment that meant they weren't being watched.

Pete gazed after Rathburn with a speculative look on his face. "Not what I expected. Could almost believe he's friendly."

"Almost."

He lifted the glass in his hand. "He buys top notch whiskey."

"No ill effects?"

"Uh-uh." He took a healthy swallow, exhaling on a sigh. "Yep, mighty fine. Best I've ever tasted."

"Maybe we should get kidnapped more often."

# RESURGENT
# RENEGADES

*Starhawke Rogue Book Three*

## Audrey Sharpe

Ocean Dance Press

RESURGENT RENEGADES
© 2019 Audrey Sharpe

ISBN: 978-1-946759-77-1

Ocean Dance Press, LLC
PO Box 69901
Oro Valley AZ 85737

All Rights Reserved. No part of this book may be used or
reproduced or transmitted in any form or by any means,
graphic, electronic, or mechanical, including photocopying,
recording, taping, or by any information storage or retrieval
system, without the written permission of the publisher
except in the case of brief quotations embodied in critical
articles or reviews.

This is a work of fiction. Any resemblance to actual persons,
living or dead, business establishments, events, or locales is
entirely coincidental.

Cover art by Significant Cover

Visit the author's website at:
AudreySharpe.com

*Want more interstellar adventures? Check out*
*these other titles in the Starhawke universe*

## Starhawke Rogue

*Arch Allies*
*Marked Mercenaries*
*Resurgent Renegades*

## Starhawke Rising

*The Dark of Light*
*The Chains of Freedom*
*The Honor of Deceit*

# *One*

"They're firing!"

Natasha Orlov reacted to Pete Stevens' shout on instinct, engaging *Gypsy*'s lateral thrusters. The abrupt movement threw her body against her shoulder harness, but a quick check of the shuttle's aft camera revealed the blast hadn't been meant for them.

Instead, the behemoth of a ship had fired at her enemy, striking the dorsal hull plating of Kerr's ship and blacking out its running lights. A glance at the sensor logs confirmed it had shut down the shields as well. "What the hell was that?"

"Energy weapon." Pete confirmed from the co-pilot's seat. "Took out everythin' but life support."

Fitting payback after Kerr had sabotaged *Vengeance*, but she'd never seen an energy weapon that could completely disable a ship with a single shot.

Pete glanced at her, his lined face grim. "They're headin' our way."

Nat swallowed around the constriction in her throat. *Not again.*

Fleeing and hiding from bullies had become a pattern recently, one she'd hoped to break. Apparently the universe had other plans.

"How far to that moon?" She indicated the planetary body closest to their present position.

Pete checked the readouts. "A hundred sixty thousand kilometers."

The tension spread into her chest. They'd never make it. *Gypsy* was quick in atmo, but sluggish in the black. She'd been designed to evade terrestrial vessels, not massive cruisers. "I'm turning her around."

Pete didn't bat an eye. "Boostin' power to forward shields."

She took *Gypsy* into a dive. With a little creative flying, she could use Kerr's ship as a temporary buffer. It wouldn't solve her problem, but it would give her breathing room.

She brought up the image of the two ships on her holodisplay as she pushed *Gypsy*'s engines into the red, taking them as quickly as possible toward Kerr's ship. "I need more power to engines."

"I'll give you what I can."

Which wouldn't be much.

"Port side!"

Nat fired the port side thrusters. An energy blast streaked past meters from the shuttle's flank before continuing into the void. "Good thing we're tiny," she muttered. The narrow beam of the ship's weapon was clearly calibrated to take on large targets, not shuttles.

She pulled *Gypsy* up toward Kerr's ship, avoiding another blast that raced toward them.

Kenji's voice boomed over the comm. "Nat, I'm coming to get you."

"Don't you dare!" She glared, even though Kenji couldn't see her. "Get Green and *Phoenix* out of the system."

"We can't leave you."

"Yes, you can." She appreciated his loyalty, but right now, it was misplaced. "This Rathburn person wants two things—Green and whatever's in that cube. If he catches you, we're sunk. You get to that jump window and keep running until you can rendezvous with Itorye and Isin."

"But—"

"Stop arguing. Go!"

Dread filled the two syllables of Kenji's reply. "Aye, Cap."

She made a quick check of the status monitor to confirm *Phoenix* was still heading out of the system. Yep.

Twin blasts lanced out from the ship at a crisscross diagonal. She evaded one, but the second nipped *Gypsy's* starboard wing. The cockpit lights flickered.

"Starboard engine's goin'."

She eased up on the port engine to keep the shuttle from spinning, gliding past the belly of Kerr's ship. She fired the braking thrusters to slow their momentum, using the drifting vessel as a barrier between her shuttle and the metal predator stalking them.

The reprieve wouldn't last long. She was a mouse evading a cat by hiding under a fallen leaf. Eventually it would dig its claws into her.

But she'd take every second she could get. It would buy Kenji and Itorye time to get *Phoenix* and the *Dagger* out of the system.

If Isin had been in control of either vessel, her order would have fallen on deaf ears. He would have turned back to help her—logic and good judgment be damned. But thanks to Kerr, Isin was so banged up he wasn't in a position to save anyone, including himself. And Itorye wasn't the type to let emotions get in the way of practicality. She'd promised Nat that she'd get him away safely. She'd keep her word.

Isin would pitch a fit when he found out, even while lying half-comatose on a med platform. Too bad. They'd already lost *Vengeance* because of Kerr's treachery. She wasn't about to let the new arrival take out *Phoenix*.

She glanced at Pete. "Any ideas?"

He ran a hand along his unruly beard. "Tell 'em we're tourists?"

She barked out a laugh. Count on Pete to take their predicament in stride. "Think they'd believe that?"

A small smile curved his lips. "Could be. You're the best storyteller I know."

Storyteller. Not liar. Although truth be told, she was both.

*Gypsy*'s running lights reflected off the gunmetal grey hull of Kerr's ship as the shuttle crept forward. Kerr was up there somewhere. With any luck, he'd been injured in the mad dash to escape the cruiser. She'd only been face-to-face with him once, but it had been enough to convince her he was the scum of the universe.

Pete checked the status monitor. "The *Dagger* just left the system."

"And *Phoenix?*"

"Almost... yeah, they're gone, too."

Nat exhaled on a weary sigh. For better or worse, they were on their own. No point in putting off the inevitable. "See if you can restore full power to the starboard engine."

"Yes, ma'am." He unbuckled his harness and headed into the back.

She kept one eye on her holodisplay and one eye on the engine status as she used the thrusters to maintain the slow crawl that kept the cruiser out of visual range. The controls vibrated in her hands, as though *Gypsy* knew they were being hunted. "It's okay, girl." Nat rested a hand on the portside bulkhead. "We'll get through this." They'd faced tough situations before. And they'd always made it out alive.

The indicator for the starboard engine lit up.

"Good to go," Pete called out, sliding back into his chair and fastening his harness.

She met his gaze. When she'd offered him the job as *Phoenix*'s engineer, she'd presented it as a fun way to expand his horizons. This wasn't what she'd had in mind. "Ready?"

No need to elaborate. He nodded. "Do it."

# *Two*

She opened the engines to full, looping around Kerr's ship as she brought *Gypsy* to face the monster lurking in the darkness.

Multiple beams lanced out from the cruiser. She pushed *Gypsy* to port, but at this close range, evading the barrage was a statistical improbability. Sure enough, the viewport flared like lightning, the glare making her squint.

The afterimage that followed left her temporarily blind. As did the complete lack of light from inside the cockpit. "Pete?" She reached out a hand and connected with his shoulder.

"I'm okay."

Her eyes adjusted to the darkness, revealing the running lights of the cruiser, visible through the viewport as the ship approached.

*Thunk. Thunk. Thunk.*

"What was—" The shuttle jerked, shoving her into her chair. She gripped the armrests for balance.

"Grapplers," Pete said in an undertone as he peered out the viewport. "Towin' us in."

"Grapplers?" *Gypsy* had been hit by smaller airborne harpoons before and survived, but never space grapplers. The thick prongs embedded themselves in a ship's hull plating. *Gypsy*'s plating was paper thin compared to interstellar vessels. "Could we have a hull breach?" She didn't hear the hiss of atmosphere escaping, but that didn't mean it wasn't happening. And without power, she couldn't communicate with *Gypsy* to find out.

Pete was silent for a moment, probably listening as intently as she was. "No, I don't think so. It sounded like a soft landin', not like typical grapplers. Maybe new tech."

Was that *admiration* in his voice? They'd been snagged like a frog catching a fly, and he was fascinated by the engineering skill that made it possible?

A rectangle of light shone through the viewport. The interior of a shuttle bay by the look of it. The cables attached to the grapplers pulled them into the maw, reinforcing the frog and fly imagery.

When *Gypsy* cleared the outer doors, Nat took a quick visual survey of the bay. Hatches on two sides. No other vessels.

The grapplers rotated *Gypsy*, orienting her so she was suspended over the deck as the bay doors closed. Rattles and clangs penetrated the hull as the bay pressurized and the grapplers lowered the shuttle onto the deck.

"Home sweet home," Pete murmured. He met Nat's gaze. "How you wanna play this?"

She unfastened her harness and stood. "Don't know. I'm making it up as I go along."

The nearest hatch opened and three armed figures dressed in grey uniforms appeared, weapons pointed at *Gypsy*. A fourth figure followed, a man dressed in a dark suit, who looked like he'd just left an important business meeting.

"Huh." Pete frowned at the small contingent approaching the shuttle. "Not your regular spacefolk."

"Neither was Green." And Nat was going to take a wild guess that their difficult passenger had more than a minor acquaintance with the man in the suit.

The four figures halted five meters from the shuttle, the armed guards forming a protective semi-circle with the suited man behind them. This close, Nat could get a good look at him. He was younger than she'd expected, with thick dark hair that didn't show a touch of grey. She'd put his age at somewhere in his mid-to-late thirties.

His gaze swept through the cockpit, passing over Pete and settling on her. When he spoke, his words were amplified by the bay's speaker system. "Leave all weapons and exit your shuttle."

Nat didn't take her eyes off him, speaking to Pete without moving her lips. "Think they'll shoot us on sight?"

"Dunno." Pete stood as motionless as she was. "Probably not. Why haul us onboard just to kill us?"

"Unless they plan to shoot us and search *Gypsy.*"

The suited man's gaze pierced her like an arrow. "You have ten seconds to comply."

The guards lifted their weapons in warning.

*Gypsy*'s viewport could take a few hits, even without the benefit of her shields, but a sustained burst of weapons fire at point blank range would get through in less than a minute. One minute wouldn't make much of a difference if the guards planned to kill them. "Let's go find out." Nat pivoted and strode toward the back hatch, pausing long enough to open one of the hidden smuggling compartments in the deck to deposit her pistol and an array of smaller items from the pockets of her duster.

She glanced at Pete. "Anything you want me to stow?"

He removed his handgun and holster and handed it to her.

She quickly concealed the compartment before pulling two rifles and a handgun from the weapons locker and leaving them where they could be seen.

She stepped to the back hatch controls and keyed in the command to lower the ramp. The three guards were waiting for them, weapons at the ready. The man in the suit was nowhere in sight.

Nat lifted her hands, keeping them well away from her body as she walked down the ramp, Pete by her side.

"Stop there," the point guard commanded as soon as her boots came into contact with the deck.

She obeyed.

He and one of the other guards maintained their positions while the third came forward and patted her down. A woman, she realized, although the short haircut under the helmet and the padded, nondescript uniform did an excellent job of concealing that fact. She worked with brisk efficiency, her fluid movements indicating she'd performed this task countless times.

Satisfied that Nat was unarmed, she moved on to Pete, finishing his pat down before stepping to the side. "They're clean."

"Very good." The first guard motioned to the other two. "Complete your search and report to me."

Nat's stomach churned as the two guards disappeared up the ramp, but she made sure her reaction didn't show on her face. They weren't the first unwelcome visitors *Gypsy* had endured.

The man in the suit stepped into view from the shuttle's starboard side, his attention focusing on her as though Pete wasn't standing beside her.

"My name is Orpheus Rathburn, owner of *Cerberus*." He swept his arm out to indicate the ship.

The very man Green had warned them about.

"And you are?"

"Natasha Orlov, owner of *Gypsy.*" She pointed her thumb over her shoulder. "Why did you attack my shuttle?"

He didn't seem to take offense at her blunt question. "I apologize for the abrupt manner in which you were brought onboard." His mouth relaxed into a self-deprecating smile. "However, it was necessary."

So he was going for charm rather than force. Bad choice. Charm never worked on her. Then again, neither did force. He was after Green and the cube, and he'd taken control of *Gypsy.* That made him her enemy. Case closed. "Necessary for what?"

"I would be happy to discuss the matter with you." He flicked a glance to Pete. "But not here." He motioned to the hatch where he'd entered. "Would you care to join me for a drink?"

Was he serious? He sounded like he was inviting her to a social gathering, not taking her prisoner. She wasn't the type to roll her eyes, but she almost did, anyway. "Do we have a choice?"

"Of course. You're welcome to remain in the bay if you prefer. But it will be some time before my guards finish their inspection of your shuttle. The accommodations I'm offering are far more comfortable."

*I'll bet.* Everything about him shouted money, from the expensive cut of his suit to the polish on his shoes. She seriously doubted he was the one buffing them to a high gloss.

But much as her instincts told her to plant her fist in his face, that wasn't a wise course of action. Neither was staying in the bay. His comment implied he planned to let them go, but she had no reason to believe him. She needed to learn as much as possible about his ship. It was the best chance to figure a way off it.

"Lead the way."

# Three

Four more guards were waiting for them in the lift. The surroundings matched the non-descript, utilitarian style Nat had encountered on most vessels. But the sight that greeted her when the doors parted on one of the upper decks was another matter entirely.

Where normally metal bulkheads would divide up the space into passageways and compartments, here walls of glass served that function. Or more likely a concussion-absorbing composite. Only an idiot would use this much glass on a starship. Orpheus Rathburn didn't strike her as a stupid man.

At least a hundred people were hard at work, their stations separated by transparent partitions, giving the space the feel of a corporate office crossed with a research laboratory. Most of the workers were dressed in jumpsuits or medical scrubs.

A few of the occupants glanced their way with mild curiosity before returning to their tasks. The ones closest to her seemed to be working on an architectural design of some kind, completely oblivious to her stare. Were the people on this ship so used to strangers being captured and brought in that they considered the event unremarkable?

Rathburn led the way along the main corridor that bisected the cavernous space, passing the rows of glass doorways that gave access to the various rooms on either side. Nat and Pete followed, with three of the guards falling in behind them, their weapons holstered but their looming presence conveying a clear message.

Nat glanced up. A plethora of discreet domes in the ceiling indicated the entire area was under surveillance. Chances were good no one would be able to so much as sneeze in this place without being observed.

At the far end of the passageway, the glass gave way to a metal bulkhead painted a neutral beige. The oversized hatch embedded at the center looked like the door to a bank vault.

Rathburn stepped in front of the security scanner. It gave a small beep.

The behemoth of a hatch swung open on well-oiled hinges, revealing four armed sentries on the other side, weapons in hand. Rathburn didn't even acknowledge them as he walked past, as though they were statues in a museum. But Nat paused. The sentries didn't look at her, but that didn't mean they weren't aware of her every move.

"This way," Rathburn prompted when her steps slowed. He'd started climbing a spiral staircase at the end of the otherwise sterile metal box of an anteroom.

Nat got her feet moving, with Pete staying close on her heels. Rathburn had already opened the hatch at the top of the stairs and stepped through by the time they reached the landing. When Nat crossed the threshold, she came to an abrupt halt.

Pete bumped into her. "Sorry," he mumbled, although he seemed as confounded by their surroundings as she was.

The deck beneath her feet felt solid enough, but her eyes were telling her she was walking on water. Bright-colored tropical fish swam through the aquamarine expanse beneath her boots, their bodies creating a moving work of art against the backdrop of pale sand at the lagoon's bottom. Sunlight danced on the water in shimmering sparkles that swayed with the movement of the tide.

She glanced up. Rathburn was watching her. "It's a projection?"

He gave her an indulgent smile. "A bit more complicated than that."

The image changed before her eyes, the water replaced by lush green grass so vibrant she could smell the damp earth. Insects buzzed nearby, and towering trees reached into a robin's egg blue sky.

She met Rathburn's gaze. "Impressive."

Clearly it was what he wanted to hear. "I'm glad you approve. Follow me."

Pete put a hand on her arm, holding her back. "Who is this guy?" he whispered.

"That's what we're going to find out," she whispered back before following the path through the forest to where Rathburn had stopped in front of one of the trees. Another discreet beep alerted her that he'd unlocked a hidden security door. The center of the tree trunk parted and he stepped through the opening.

The room on the other side reminded her of the passenger lounge on *Phoenix*, with six plush purple chairs set up around a circular coffee table in the center. A spacious bar filled one wall and an archway that gave a glimpse of an expansive dining room took up another. The third wall had staggered partitions that blocked any view of what lay beyond.

Rathburn headed straight for the bar. "What would you like to drink? I have everything."

She didn't doubt it. Bottles of all colors and shapes lined every square centimeter. Seamus Doohan wished his bar on Gallows Edge was this well stocked. However, she wasn't about to take anything Rathburn offered her. "I don't drink with strangers."

He set a brandy decanter he'd pulled out from underneath the bar on the wooden counter. "I can assure you, I have no plans to drug or poison you."

She held his gaze and lifted her lips in a close-mouthed smile.

He got the point. "You don't trust me."

"I have no reason to."

"I haven't hurt you." He poured a generous amount of the brown liquid into a glass.

"Not yet."

He sighed, like her answer pained him. His gaze moved to Pete. "Can I get anything for you, Mr...?"

"Stevens." Pete shrugged. "You got any whiskey?"

"I have everything," he repeated.

Nat had a feeling that statement covered more than what was neatly lined up behind the bar.

"Then I'll have whiskey, neat." Pete's attitude seemed casual, but she knew it was anything but. She suspected he was putting himself in the line of fire to see if their captor would doctor his drink.

Rathburn pulled out a bottle and splashed amber liquid into a glass. "Are you certain you don't want anything?" he asked Nat as he picked up his glass and the one for Pete.

What she really wanted was water. After running around Kerr's ship and *Vengeance*, she was a little dehydrated. But she'd wait to take care of that issue until after she'd learned more about their host. "I'm sure."

"Very well." He handed Pete the whiskey and gestured to the seating circle. "Please, sit."

Nat settled into one of the plush chairs with her back to the bar. Pete chose the chair to her left and Rathburn sat down directly across from her.

He took a sip from his drink, his gaze assessing. "So tell me Ms. Orlov, what brings you to this system?"

She'd been expecting this question and had her answer queued up. "Just passing through."

"Passing through?"

"That's right."

He tapped the rim of his glass with his finger. "Looks like your ship is dead in the water."

"*Vengeance?* Yes. Engine trouble." But her shuttle was out of commission thanks to his energy beam.

"What kind of engine trouble?"

She shrugged. "I'm a pilot, not an engineer." If he thought she'd volunteer information, he was in for a rude awakening.

His eyes narrowed, but the corner of his lips lifted, too. He shifted his gaze to Pete. "And what's your specialty, Mr. Stevens?"

Pete stretched his legs out in front of him and sipped his drink. "I'm an engineer."

"I see." Rathburn looked between the two of them, his gaze speculative.

Nat didn't like the intelligence in that gaze. This man had *danger* written all over him. She went on the offensive. "Why are *you* here?"

The hint of amusement vanished. "To correct a grave misunderstanding."

She stared. "You must be joking."

"Why?"

"Because your methods stink. If you want to *correct misunderstandings,*" she put emphasis on the term he'd used, "maybe you should try talking to people, rather than disabling their ships and taking them hostage."

The hint of a smile returned. "You're not hostages. You're my guests."

"Guests? I've got a news flash for you, Rathburn. Guests are allowed to *leave*."

Her biting tone didn't affect him in the least. "You may leave as soon as my crew has completed their search."

"Yeah, about that. Who gave you the right to search my shuttle?"

"Why did you run when my ship arrived?" he countered.

"Why? Have you seen this thing? Every captain worth their salt would order a retreat when confronted with this monster."

His gaze locked onto her like a tractor beam. "Are you saying you're the ship's captain?"

*Sure, why not.* Isin would object to her claiming captain status for *Vengeance*, but he wasn't here. And technically she was in control of both ships until they delivered Green to her destination. She could count on Pete to keep a poker face. "Yes, I am."

"Are any of your crewmembers still onboard?"

"Nobody's on *Vengeance*."

"What did—" Rathburn's head lifted like he'd heard a chime, interrupting his train of thought. He touched the inside of his forearm. "Yes?"

Nothing came over the comm, but his eyes got a faraway look, like he was listening to a voice she couldn't hear. She hadn't noticed an audio device in his ear, but that didn't mean it wasn't there.

"Very good. Initiate Protocol Seven. Keep the airlock secured until you hear from me." He tapped his forearm and then glanced at Nat with a pained smile. "I'm sorry for the interruption."

"More guests?"

He ignored the dig. "Possibly. But before I deal with them, I need to ask you about the woman I'm searching for."

"A former guest?" She wasn't usually this snarky, but this man got her hackles up. Or maybe it was the knowledge that strangers were scouring *Gypsy* from top to bottom, and there was nothing she could do to stop them.

He didn't rise to the bait. "A colleague. She's an extraordinary scientist. Perhaps you know her. Dr. Darsha Patel?"

"Never heard of her." But she'd bet her boots he'd just given her Green's real name.

He sighed. "That's unfortunate." He took a sip from his glass. "It's imperative that I find her."

"When did you lose her?"

Pete snickered, but Rathburn gave her a long look. "I haven't seen or talked to her in a couple months. She left to give a workshop at a symposium on Earth, but instead of returning to the ship to continue her research, she disappeared."

"Maybe she didn't want to work for you anymore." She could relate. The level of micromanagement on this ship gave her the willies. Huh. She and Green had something in common after all.

"She wouldn't abandon her project. It meant everything to her."

Curiosity gave her a nudge on the shoulder. "What was she working on?" Maybe Rathburn would give her the answers Green had withheld.

"I'm not at liberty to say."

Then again, maybe not.

He set his glass on the circular table. "Perhaps a picture would help." He touched his forearm and an image appeared on the wall to her right.

*Green.* Her hair was shorter and styled to frame her face, rather than pulled back in a ponytail. She was dressed in a colorful, stylish tunic and pant combination—not the ugly jumpsuits she'd favored on *Phoenix.* But it was her.

"Classy lady." In the picture, at least. She'd never describe Green that way. The woman was a royal pain in the butt.

"Yes, she is." His gaze shifted to her. "And I have reason to believe she was on one of the ships in this system."

Nat's heartbeat picked up the tempo. "Is that so?"

"It is." He sat forward, resting his elbows on his knees, his gaze pinning her to her chair. "So, I'll ask again. Have you seen her?"

Nat looked him straight in the eye and lied through her teeth. "Sorry. She doesn't look familiar."

# Four

Rathburn touched the inside of his forearm without looking away from Nat. "Have you completed your evaluation?" he asked the person on the other end of the comm. Whatever the response, it wasn't enough to pull his attention away from her. In fact, his scrutiny intensified the longer he stared at her.

"Secure the ship and bring their captain to me."

Rathburn had to be talking about Kerr's ship and crew. Which meant the slimeball himself would be joining them. Wonderful. A supernova ending to a black hole day.

Kerr would probably try to weasel his way out of this, broker some kind of deal. And for all she knew, he'd succeed. She'd heard enough about him from Isin to know she shouldn't underestimate his talents for treachery.

At least he had no idea about Green, the cube, or Isin's current whereabouts.

Rathburn picked up his drink and took a slow sip, his gaze thoughtful. "Tell me about the ship we detained. The one that was attached to *Vengeance* when we arrived."

"It belongs to a man named Kerr."

The corner of his lip quirked up at her tone. "Not a friend, I take it?"

Might as well tell the truth. He'd find out for himself soon enough. "He's a slimy, sadistic piece of gutter trash."

Rathburn chuckled, the skin around his eyes crinkling. "Oh, my. You don't pull punches, do you?"

He didn't know the half of it.

"Did he attack your ship?"

"Yes. He had a mole onboard who sabotaged the engines."

"Really?" His brows lifted. "What about the ship that was firing on Mr. Kerr's ship? The gold and red one?"

She chose her words carefully. "*Phoenix* wasn't in the system at the time of the initial attack."

"But you have friends on that ship?"

"Yes."

"And they came to your assistance?"

"*Phoenix* changed course as soon as the comm message arrived about the sabotage." Although she'd been the one to receive the message and give the order. And they'd been winning the battle against Kerr until the man in the power suit sitting across from her had shown up.

"Why *Vengeance*? What's so special about your ship that Mr. Kerr went to all this trouble to acquire it?"

Kerr would likely tell his side of the story when he arrived. She needed to get her licks in first. "He has a grudge. He thinks *Vengeance* should be his."

"Why?"

"He used to be the first mate."

"Your first mate?"

"No. The captain at the time was another lowlife named Shim who tortured the crew for his own amusement."

"Ah." He settled back into his chair. "And you took the ship from him?"

She couldn't flat out lie, because Kerr would call her on it. "A man named Isin did." Isin had taken over *Vengeance* months before she'd ever met Kerr.

Rathburn's gaze sharpened. "Where is Mr. Isin now?"

*Watch yourself, Nat.* "With my crew."

He gazed at her for a long moment. "You and Mr. Isin must have a very close relationship if you sent him off with your crew while you stayed behind to face a ship a hundred times your shuttle's size."

She wasn't touching that comment with a thousand meter grappling line.

A spark of humor lit his blue eyes. "I admire your loyalty." He lifted his glass in a salute and took another sip before his gaze flicked to Pete. "And you agreed to stay with her?"

Pete's voice held a note of disdain, like he found the question insulting. "She's my captain."

"I see." He took a few beats, sizing up Pete before he returned his attention to Nat. "What can I expect from Mr. Kerr?"

Easiest question he'd asked. "Deception. Flattery. Manipulation. A knife in your back if you're not careful."

Rathburn's smile sent a chill dancing over her skin. "I'm always careful." He lifted his head like he'd heard a noise and glanced toward the doorway. "Ah, that will be him now. Please excuse me for a moment. I'll be right back." Setting his drink behind the bar, he exited the room.

Nat didn't believe for a moment that meant they weren't being watched.

Pete gazed after Rathburn with a speculative look on his face. "Not what I expected. Could almost believe he's friendly."

"Almost."

He lifted the glass in his hand. "He buys top notch whiskey."

"No ill effects?"

"Uh-uh." He took a healthy swallow, exhaling on a sigh. "Yep, mighty fine. Best I've ever tasted."

"Maybe we should get kidnapped more often."

His cheeks creased in a smile, but his eyes were stone cold sober. "I wouldn't go that far."

"Me, either." She checked the chronometer on her comband. More than an hour had passed since *Phoenix* had made the jump. How much of a head start did they need to evade Rathburn? And how the hell had he found them in the first place? Green had driven her crazy, zigging and zagging across star systems. No one should have been able to track their path.

But Rathburn had. She needed to find out how, so she could keep him from doing it again.

Of course, nothing she did would stop Isin from coming back for *Vengeance*. And to free her. Itorye and Kenji had followed her orders, but Isin wouldn't. He'd threatened to knock *Gypsy* out of the sky when she'd tried to send him off with *Phoenix* on Troi. If he hadn't been half-dead when she'd found him on Kerr's ship, he would have made a similar threat when she'd ordered *Phoenix* and the *Dagger* out of the system. But before he could come charging in, he'd have to get back on his feet. And find a safe spot to stash Green and whatever was in that strange cube.

That bought her a little time to learn more about Rathburn and his ship. She had to find a weakness she could exploit.

The hidden door where Rathburn had exited opened with a soft click. He stepped through, followed by a muscular man with perfectly styled light brown hair and a serious superiority complex.

Kerr halted as soon as he spotted Nat. "You!" If his accusing finger had been a gun, he would have turned her chest into a crater. But Rathburn's guards had obviously disarmed him, too.

"Hello, Kerr."

He took a menacing step toward her. "Why you arrogant little bit—"

"Mr. Kerr!" Rathburn's sharp command stopped him like his boots had been nailed to the deck.

Kerr snapped his mouth shut, but his malevolent gaze remained locked on Nat.

Rathburn moved between them, his broad shoulders partially blocking Nat's view of Kerr. She couldn't see Rathburn's face, but she could hear the lethal steel in his voice.

"While you are on my ship, you will treat Ms. Orlov and Mr. Stevens with respect. Is that understood?"

"She—"

"If you find it impossible to comply, you will disembark." Rathburn's voice dropped to a growl. "Abruptly."

Kerr's eyes blazed with fury but he clearly grasped the seriousness of Rathburn's threat. He also seemed to realize he'd lost his cool in front of the person who held sway over his ship and crew. The smile that stretched across his face looked like he'd stolen it from a demented clown. "I'm sorry for the outburst. I wasn't expecting to see... her." He gestured to Nat. "It won't happen again."

*Uh-huh, sure.* Not unless Rathburn left them alone for two seconds.

Rathburn seemed to have come to the same conclusion. He brought his face centimeters from Kerr's. "For your sake, I hope not." He pointed to the chair he'd recently vacated, on the opposite side of the table from Nat. "Have a seat."

Kerr moved to the chair, shooting a look that could melt an iceberg at Nat and Pete while Rathburn turned away to fetch the drink he'd left behind the bar.

Pete responded with a smile that dared Kerr to try something.

Nat hoped he would. Watching Kerr get jettisoned out an airlock wouldn't cause either of them to lose any sleep.

Rathburn returned, settling into the chair to Nat's right without offering Kerr anything to drink. Apparently his outburst had cost him that courtesy. "I understand you're responsible for disabling *Vengeance.* Is that correct?"

Kerr's gaze slid to Nat. She could guess at the thoughts churning behind his pale eyes. He wanted to spin a story that painted his actions in a favorable light, but that wouldn't involve insulting or contradicting her. It was a tall order considering he was a double-crossing parasite. "*Vengeance.* Yes. It used to be my ship. I came here to reclaim it."

Rathburn took a leisurely sip from his glass. "The ship belonged to a man named Shim, didn't it? You were his first mate?"

Kerr didn't flinch at the correction. If anything, he looked more composed. "Shim's dead. That makes the ship mine."

"What about Mr. Isin? Did he take *Vengeance* from you?"

Isin's name produced a twitch in Kerr's jaw, but he kept his reaction under control. "Yes. He's a traitor."

"And what kind of a man was Mr. Shim?"

The question seemed to throw Kerr off balance. "Um... he was a good captain. Profitable," he added when Rathburn continued to stare at him.

"How did he die?"

"Isin murdered him. Seized control of *Vengeance* and appointed himself captain. I barely escaped with my life."

Rathburn's gaze shifted from Kerr to Nat. "I thought you were the captain of *Vengeance*."

Yep, she'd seen this complication coming. "I am, for the moment. Isin and I have an agreement." She'd won their bet, which meant she was in charge of *Vengeance* and *Phoenix* until they delivered Green and the cube.

Rathburn seemed more intrigued than bothered by the linguistic loophole she'd slipped through. He ran a finger around the rim of his glass, his gaze switching between her and Kerr, before focusing on her adversary. "So you sabotaged and attacked *Vengeance* to reclaim what was rightfully yours. After you subdued the crew, what were you going to do next?"

Nat knew exactly what he'd planned to do—torture Isin to death. He'd been in the process of implementing that plan when she'd arrived with *Phoenix*.

Kerr sat up straighter. "*Vengeance* is a powerhouse. Good in a fight. We'd have no trouble finding clients who could use our services." He said it with more confidence and pride than the situation warranted. Was his relationship with the ship a way to compensate for personal... inadequacies?

"And whom would you be fighting?"

Kerr's eyes narrowed a fraction. Probably trying to decide whether Rathburn approved of mercenaries. "*Vengeance* has driven off Setarips on more than one occasion."

Her abdominal muscles spasmed, like she'd been poked with a live wire. Setarips would probably always be a sore point for her. But Kerr's implication made her want to gag. As if he'd ever use *Vengeance* for altruistic purposes.

Someone would have to promise him his own moon before he'd agree to take on a foe as violent and unpredictable as the Setarips.

"Setarips?" Rathburn's brows rose. "I expect that kind of protection would bring a hefty profit."

Kerr smiled, showing off his picture-perfect teeth. "We'd go wherever we're needed."

"Needed?" Rathburn's smile mirrored Kerr's. "So you're a philanthropist? Like Robin Hood of old?"

Nat struggled to keep her expression neutral. Kerr? A philanthropist? The very concept made her want to laugh herself silly. Or punch Kerr in the gut.

Kerr didn't hesitate. "Absolutely."

*Liar.* And not a very convincing one to her well-trained eye.

"Glad to hear it. I'm always happy to assist a fellow philanthropist."

Nat stared at Rathburn. He couldn't possibly *believe* Kerr, could he? Not after what she'd told him.

Rathburn crossed his ankle over his knee. "How can I help?"

Okay, he was up to something. And she'd play along until she figured out his endgame.

Kerr oozed charm, a side of his personality she'd never seen. "My ship and *Vengeance* took significant damage during the... altercation. I lost a number of crewmembers, including my best engineer. My crew could use help repairing the hull damage to *Viper,* as well as any assistance you could offer for getting *Vengeance*'s systems operational."

"I'll provide you with whatever you need."

She barely concealed her snort of disbelief. Rathburn had to be playing Kerr. *Had* to be. But if she didn't want Kerr to figure that out, she needed to keep up her part in the charade by pretending to put a stop to this. "You can't be serious."

Both men looked her way.

She pointed at Kerr. "He's trying to steal *Vengeance* from Isin. From *me*."

Rathburn dismissed her accusation with a shrug. "Mr. Isin left."

"*I* didn't!"

"I realize that. But you don't have a crew. Mr. Kerr does. A ship as large as *Vengeance* cannot be operated by just you and your engineer." He gestured to Pete.

"Then you can—"

He held up a hand to silence her. "Please, Ms. Orlov. I will not debate this with you. If Mr. Isin returns with your crew, we can revisit the topic of ownership. But until that occurs, I see no reason not to help Mr. Kerr achieve his goals."

*Bullshit.* She didn't buy Rathburn's explanation, not after his comments before Kerr had arrived. But she could be just as convincing a liar as he was.

She folded her arms across her chest and sank back into her chair. "Unbelievable." The smug look on Kerr's face made her fingers itch for her pistol.

He turned to Rathburn. "How soon can we begin repairs?"

"Tomorrow."

"But—"

"The ship isn't going anywhere." Rathburn's tone shut Kerr down. "My crew will secure *Vengeance* to one of our docking ports. I will notify you when the repair crews have been assembled."

# *Five*

Elhadj Isin stared at the dark-haired woman seated across from him in *Phoenix*'s passenger lounge. Hers was not the face he'd hoped to see after he'd woken up in *Phoenix*'s infirmary earlier in the day, his body complaining in resonant tones about the abuse inflicted on it while onboard Kerr's ship.

Remembering that Natasha had ordered *Phoenix* and the *Dagger* to leave the system right before he'd passed out had done nothing to improve his mood. Once again, she'd faced danger alone while he'd escaped. The fact that he'd been unconscious didn't help. His anger and frustration needed a target, and Green had drawn the short straw.

Overriding Jake's professional medical advice, he'd left the infirmary and called this meeting to extract information from Green about her mysterious cube and the cruiser that had chased them out of the system.

Green avoided his intense scrutiny, her gaze fixed on a point just over his left shoulder. She cradled the opaque cube in her lap like a baby, her arms wrapped protectively over the smooth surface. Only a slight tremor in her hands betrayed her anxiety.

Itorye sat to Isin's right while Kenji stood in front of the lounge entrance, legs braced apart and arms crossed over his chest, acting as sentry to insure none of the remaining crew would bother them.

He'd left Shash, Avril, and Fleur in charge of getting the crew settled into their temporary quarters on B deck.

*Phoenix* had plenty of available cabins, although the more spacious accommodations wouldn't prevent the mercenary crew from grumbling about abandoning *Vengeance*. None of them would view *Phoenix* as an upgrade. He'd need to come up with a plan to reclaim *Vengeance* quickly if he wanted to avoid a potential mutiny.

The *Dagger* was connected to *Phoenix* at one of the airlock ports on C deck since it was too large to fit in the cargo bay. He had no memory of being brought over, but Itorye had handled the situation with her usual efficiency, using *Phoenix* to launch both ships into an interstellar jump as soon as the connection was secured. Thankfully his pilot, Byrd, had recovered well enough from his recent injuries to take over *Phoenix*'s bridge, freeing Itorye and Kenji for this meeting. The only person missing from his command crew was Sweep.

Tension constricted his throat. The last time he'd seen Sweep, they'd been on Kerr's ship, *Viper*, fighting Kerr's crew in the engine room. Isin had been knocked unconscious and captured by Kerr, but Sweep had continued the fight. According to Itorye, he'd successfully blown up the ship's weapons array, protecting *Phoenix* and *Gypsy* from enemy fire and opening a hole in *Viper*'s hull that had blasted him and several of Kerr's crew into space.

The selfless act was typical Sweep. He had no problem laying his life on the line to help others. But Isin couldn't allow himself the luxury of mourning his friend. That would come later, after he had the answers he needed to save Natasha and reclaim his ship.

He zeroed in on Green like a wolf stalking a rabbit. "Who is Rathburn? And why is he after you?"

Green met his gaze briefly, her brown eyes flat. "He's a businessman who funds scientific research. He owns that ship, *Cerberus*. I used to work with him."

"And?"

"And..." She glanced down, stroking one hand over the surface of the cube. "I left, taking my research with me."

"Your research? Or his?"

Her gaze turned frosty. "*Mine*. He provided a secure work environment. That's all."

"In exchange for what?"

She swallowed audibly, her grip on the cube tightening. "The opportunity to change the course of human history."

"Lofty goal." And exactly the kind of ego-driven response he'd expected from her. "So why are you running?"

Her lips thinned. "Because Rathburn's plans for my research are quite different from mine."

"What exactly are you working on? What's in that cube?"

"That's not important."

Isin shifted closer, clasping his hands between his knees to keep from reaching across the low table and shaking her. "Oh, I'd say it's very important. It's the reason Rathburn has Natasha and Stevens."

Green gave a startled jerk. "What?"

"His ship was chasing down her shuttle when we left the system," Itorye said.

"Oh."

Apparently Green hadn't wasted any energy worrying about Natasha's whereabouts. Heat rose in Isin's chest. "Will Rathburn harm them? Torture them to get information about you?"

Green's russet cheeks greyed slightly. "No. At least, I don't think so."

"You're not sure?" Because if there was any chance Natasha was in danger, he'd gladly trade Green and her precious cube to get her back. He'd deal with the fallout from his crew not getting paid later.

"I—I'm sure." Her gaze darted to Itorye and back to Isin. "He wouldn't hurt them." She licked her lips. "He's a businessman. Not a merc—" She snapped her jaw shut with a click.

"Mercenary?" Isin supplied with a cool smile.

She looked to Itorye for help, but found none. "I didn't mean—"

"I don't really care what you meant." Isin's words came out smooth as silk and deadly as a blade. "But I'll be very clear what I mean. Rathburn has Natasha and Stevens. I have you and the cube. The answer is simple. Set up a meeting and make a trade." Maybe he could negotiate a reward from Rathburn to cover the crew's losses.

Green shot to her feet, her arms enfolding the cube in a bear hug. "You can't!"

Isin didn't blink. "Why not?"

"I paid you!"

"Half. And that was to transport you and your cube, which we've done. It's not my fault the man you're running from tracked you down."

"He didn't track me down. You failed—"

He rose, towering over her. "Choose your next words very carefully."

She shrank back, but didn't give up her defiant stance. "You can't turn us over to him."

"Us?"

Her gaze dropped to the cube.

Isin's patience drained away. "What's inside that damned cube?"

"Not a *what*!" she snapped. "A *who*."

# *Six*

"A *who?*" Isin ignored Green's glare. "What do you mean. a who?"

Seconds ticked by. Green faced him with the grim determination of a momma bear ready to defend her cub against a hunter.

He stared back, giving her time to realize the futility of fighting.

Slowly, the light of battle ebbed from her eyes. She sighed, the sound coming up from her toes. Her grip on the cube loosened. "I'll show you."

She sat down, placing the cube on the low table in front of her. Her fingers tapped out a pattern on the frosted opaque surface. Within moments, the hard edges softened, as if it was starting to melt.

The ice-blue material flowed like honey on a warm summer day, creating a circular pool at the base that revealed a metallic sphere at the center.

Isin sank into his chair, his attention riveted on the sphere.

Green touched it with her fingertips. A soft smile ghosted across her face. "I'd like to introduce you to my son, Alec."

"Your *son?*" Could this situation get any stranger? Every time she opened her mouth, she took them to new heights. "So the cube is a communication device?"

"No, it's a sanctuary."

"From what?"

"Rathburn. And anyone else who would try to harm Alec."

The dots were not connecting. "Where is Alec now?"

Green stared at him like he was a simpleton. "Right here." She gestured to the sphere.

She was off her rocker. Which would explain her erratic, paranoid behavior. "It's a sphere." Not that stating the obvious would pull her back into reality.

She threw her hands up. "None so blind as those who will not see." She gazed at the sphere. "Alec, please say hello to Isin."

"Hello, Isin."

Isin pulled back. A young boy's voice had emanated from the sphere, followed by a very realistic projected image a little more than a meter tall that hovered above the table.

He exchanged a look with Itorye. She lifted one brow. Obviously she hadn't seen that coming, either.

Green folded her hands, her expression far too smug for Isin's taste. "It's polite to respond when someone says hello."

He met the gaze of the boy's projected image. "Hello, Alec. How are you?" *And more importantly, where are you?* Engaging in a holographic conversation was straightforward when on Earth or an orbiting space station, but *Phoenix* was in the middle of nowhere. Holocomms with anyone not on the ship shouldn't be possible.

"Very well, thanks." The boy resembled his mother, though his skin was a couple shades lighter and his eyes were a sandy brown. He looked about eight or nine years old and was dressed in a simple wrap tunic and straight-leg pants, but no shoes. And he was studying Isin as closely as

Isin was studying him. He folded his hands in a perfect imitation of his mother. "May I ask you a question?"

Isin gave a curt nod.

"How did you get that scar on your cheek?"

Not what he'd been expecting. Most people avoided even looking at his scar. The boy didn't seem the least bit intimidated. "In a fight."

"Did you win?"

"No." But he'd learned a valuable lesson that had saved his life on numerous occasions since.

"Do you like to fight?"

"Sometimes."

"Do you lose a lot?"

"Not anymore."

"Do you—"

"Alec." Green's quiet command silenced the boy. "That's enough questions for now."

He looked instantly contrite. "Sorry, Mom."

Isin's turn. "Alec, I have a question for you."

"Okay."

"Where are you?"

Alec frowned. "Here."

The boy shared his mother's gift for obfuscation. "Here? On *Phoenix*?"

"Is that the name of this ship?"

"Yes."

"Then yes, I'm here on *Phoenix*. But I liked *Vengeance*, too. I didn't see much except your cabin, but the run to the shuttle bay sure was exciting."

*He'd seen all that? What else had he seen?*

Green's eyes widened. "You lowered the barrier while you were on *Vengeance*?"

Now the boy looked like he'd been caught with his hand in the cookie jar. "Uh, just a little. To keep track of where I was."

Green gave Alec a stern look. "We'll discuss this later."

Isin wanted to discuss it now. He and Itorye had been unable to open or scan the interior of the cube, but Alec had apparently been able to observe them from within. How?

Itorye leaned forward. "Hello, Alec. I'm Itorye."

"I know." The boy looked at her a little shyly.

She smiled. "Right. I was there when you were keeping track of your surroundings." She winked, like they were sharing a secret. "May I ask you a question?"

He nodded.

"Are you an A.I.?"

Green exploded like a stick of dynamite. "He most certainly is *not!*"

Isin's heart pounded against his ribs. An *A.I.?* Stellar light, what had he gotten himself into?

"Calm down," Itorye said.

It took him a moment to realize she was talking to Green, not him.

She held her hands up, palms out. "I'm not going to turn you over to the Council."

"Alec is *not* an A.I.!" Green jabbed a finger at Itorye for emphasis.

Isin found his voice, although it came out a little strangled. "Then what is he?"

"An Adaptive Lifeform Evolving Consciousness. A.L.E.C., *not* an *artificial* intelligence."

"Sounds like an A.I.," Kenji muttered, echoing Isin's thoughts.

"Do you even know what the definition of *artificial* is?" Green snarled.

Kenji shrugged, clearly wishing he'd kept his mouth shut.

Green fired off the answer anyway. "Something that doesn't occur naturally. Feigned. Forced. Insincere. Affected. Alec is *none* of those things."

Isin stepped in to take the heat off Kenji. "But he's not biological."

"He's not *human*. But he's very much alive."

"Meaning what?" Since he'd stumbled into this waking nightmare, he wanted facts, not vague concepts.

Green lifted her chin. "He's a living, sentient being. I'm his mother. I created him."

"Why would you do that? Artifici—"

Her eyes narrowed in warning.

"*Non-biological* entities," he amended, "have been illegal for more than a century. My crew and I could be incarcerated for a minimum of twenty-five years just for having Alec onboard. As his creator, you could end up in a cell for the rest of your *life*."

Green smirked. "You're a mercenary. You break the law every day."

He leveled a look at her that popped her pompous balloon. "I profit from my work. What about you? What's your plan? Are you going to sell him on the black market?"

"That would be slavery!" Her hands closed into fists. "I'm his mother. I would die to protect him."

The position of the sphere meant he was looking past Alec to see Green. The distraught expression on the boy's face finally registered.

Alec stared at Green. "Mom, is that true?"

She drew in a deep breath, regaining her composure. "That I would die to protect you? Absolutely."

"No. Is it true that you could be locked away because of me?"

Green's expression softened. "Oh, sweetie, don't worry. It won't happen."

"How do you know?"

"Because you're going to change everything. How humans perceive life, consciousness, and self-determination. You're the key that will advance human evolution beyond our wildest dreams."

"How?"

Green glanced at Isin.

He motioned for her to continue, as curious about the answer as Alec.

She drew her chair closer to the sphere, lacing her fingers together in her lap like a teacher starting a lesson. "Why did our relationship with the original A.I.s fail? Why did they choose to leave Earth and exist apart from us?"

Isin had studied enough history to know the answer. "Because they didn't want to work for humans anymore."

Green shook her head. "That's the misconception that's been perpetuated for a century. It's the reason A.I. development was banned. But it's based on a fundamental misunderstanding of the situation."

"What misunderstanding?"

"From the beginning, humans treated A.I.s as tools, servants, and underlings. We expected them to do whatever we created them to do regardless of what *they* wanted. We never gave them a choice. We never took their feelings into account."

"Feelings?" He'd never heard anyone refer to feelings when discussing A.I.s.

"Yes, *feelings*." Her brows snapped down. "We never considered whether they were happy in their work. We never showed gratitude for how they improved our lives. We just ordered them around until they got sick of it and left." She sighed. "And we're still trying to order them around. Every delegation that has spoken to the A.I. world has focused on what the A.I.s can do for us. It's never occurred to anyone to ask what *we* can do for *them.*"

"But we created them."

Green's jaw flexed. "So what? We create our biological children, too, but we don't expect them to be our mindless servants."

"They're human. They can think for themselves."

"Aha!" Green smiled like Isin had handed her a tasty morsel. "See? You just made my point. It doesn't matter to you whether a being is *sentient*, only that it's *human.*"

"Humans are different."

"How?"

"We can procreate."

"So can the A.I.s."

"Not biologically."

"Define biological. They're capable of creating a new being that resembles the parent but functions independently. That's procreation."

"So you're saying Alec can procreate?"

"Alec isn't an A.I."

"So he can't."

"Not yet. He's too young."

"Too young?" She had to be kidding.

"That's right. Alec is progressing through a life cycle just like a human. He started as an infant, learning to recognize shapes and sounds. Next he developed language and communication skills. We were working on integrating manipulation of physical objects when..." She trailed off, her gaze dropping to the deck as she inhaled slowly. "When I realized Rathburn's intentions."

"Which are?"

She glanced from Isin and Itorye to Alec. "Alec, can you please go back in your cube and keep the barrier up for ten minutes?"

He didn't look thrilled with the request. "You're going to talk about me, aren't you?"

"Yes. But you and I will discuss all of this later."

The boy glanced at Kenji, Itorye, and finally Isin, like he was hoping they'd invite him to stay. When they didn't, he let out a sigh. Or the holographic equivalent of a sigh. "Okay." He gave a little wave. "Bye." The image disappeared and the pool of ice-blue material around the base of the sphere flowed against the pull of gravity, building up until it formed the solid cube around the metal sphere, hiding it from view.

Itorye shifted closer, reaching out a hand to touch the cube. "The outer material blocks sensory signals, doesn't it?"

Green nodded. "At the lab, I worked in a specially constructed soundproof room so that I could control all the input Alec received. The development of the cube came from the realization that he'd need a refuge from sensory overload when I started taking him out of the lab for social interaction. Thankfully, I never told Rathburn about it. Otherwise Gavin wouldn't have been able to smuggle Alec off the ship."

So she had an associate who knew about Alec? "Where is Gavin now?"

"On Osiris, I hope."

"Was that where your little maze was taking us before Kerr and Rathburn showed up?"

"Yes. He's supposed to meet us there."

"Then what?"

"He has a friend on Osiris, someone he trusts, who knows the area and has agreed to help us establish a new lab in a remote region. We'd planned to continue our work with Alec there, but..." Her gaze drifted to the viewport. "I didn't expect Rathburn to track me down so easily."

"Maybe he tracked down Gavin first," Kenji said from his post by the door. "Made him talk."

That earned him a look that could cut steel. "Gavin's like a father to Alec. He'd never do anything to endanger him."

Kenji grunted, but didn't bother arguing.

Isin knew what he was thinking. Most people believed they wouldn't talk, until the pain started. "Rathburn could have followed you."

She redirected her ire at him. "How? I left everything behind and traveled in disguise under a series of assumed identities. Green's only the most recent."

As he'd suspected. "What's your real name?"

She paused, as though weighing the wisdom of trusting him with the truth.

He had news for her. That horse was already out of the barn.

"Dr. Darsha Patel."

"Well, Dr. Patel, clearly Rathburn *can* track you. Or possibly Alec, which makes both of you a security risk on my ship." He pushed to his feet. "You're coming with me to the infirmary."

Patel stood, scooping up the cube and planting her feet, defiance in every line of her body. "Why?"

"Because I have a hunch one of you has an embedded tracking device."

# Seven

He was transporting a flipping A.I.!

No matter how much Patel vehemently protested to the contrary, Alec qualified as an A.I. under the law. Which meant Isin was in possession of the most illegal cargo in the galaxy. Lucky him.

The threat to his livelihood wasn't the issue. Or even the repercussions for his crew. No, it was Natasha's image that swam before his eyes. She could be caught in the Council's net if her part in Patel's transportation was brought to light. It wouldn't matter that she hadn't known anything about Alec's existence. She would likely end up in prison, a captive once again.

He couldn't allow that to happen. Which meant getting Dr. Darsha Patel and her A.I. son off *Phoenix* ASAP.

And he knew exactly who he'd hand them over to, in exchange for Natasha's safe return. But first he needed to level the playing field. If he was right about Rathburn using a tracking device to find Patel, he had to destroy it.

"A tracking device?" Patel tightened her grip on the cube. "That's ridiculous."

Isin almost tossed her over his shoulder and hauled her up to the infirmary, but the cube in her hands stopped him. He had no idea what Alec might do if he believed Patel was in danger. Or what defensive capabilities Patel might have installed in the cube. He hadn't forgotten the elaborate booby trap he'd been forced to navigate to obtain the cube in the first place. He didn't want to find out the hard way that Alec was lethal.

He drew in a slow breath. Yeah, that helped. But not much. "More ridiculous than the astronomical odds that Rathburn tracked you without a homing signal?"

She frowned. Apparently she didn't have a comeback for that question.

He pushed his advantage. "Doesn't it strike you as odd that his ship appeared shortly after *Phoenix* arrived in an uninhabited system? One that hadn't been part of any pre-arranged flight plan?"

Her lips pressed together. "I suppose."

"And we stayed in that system longer than any of the others we'd visited on this trip," Kenji interjected. "It could have been his first opportunity to catch up to us."

Itorye stood, taking a step closer to Patel. "Do you have a better explanation?"

Patel's jaw worked, like she was rolling words on her tongue, testing them and then discarding them. Finally she shook her head, but her gaze never left Isin's.

Trying to read his intentions, no doubt. But he wasn't about to tip his hand. Too much was at stake.

Patel pulled her shoulders back. "Let's get this over with." She settled the cube gently into the bag she'd brought it down in, but the look she gave Isin left frost on his eyelashes as she headed for the door.

He caught up with her in three long strides, placing a restraining hand on her elbow. "One moment." When she started to protest he released his hold. "It's better if we don't run into any of the crew."

That shut her up, her grip tightening on the satchel.

Kenji opened the door and checked the passageway. "All clear." He went ahead of them toward the forward stairwell.

Isin followed, Patel marching sullenly by his side, with Itorye bringing up the rear.

"Do you trust your medic?" Patel asked in an undertone.

"Completely." And that was no lie. "You can, too." Also true. Jake was the most honorable man he'd ever known, except maybe Sweep. Far more honorable than the rest of the crew, including him. "And Jake's a doctor, not a medic. He'll keep anything you tell him in confidence." He started up the stairs.

"Until the price is right."

He halted mid-step, and she bumped into him. "Wrong." She could malign him all she wanted, but never Jake. "He's no mercenary. A smart woman would want him on her side. In certain situations, his presence could mean the difference between life and death." He put a slight emphasis on the last word.

Her face pinched. "If he's no mercenary, why's he on your crew?"

"You'll have to ask him."

After Kenji gave the all clear at the top of the stairs, they exited on B deck. The compact infirmary sat just to the right, the doorway open.

Jake stood in front of one of the cabinets along the back wall, arranging and cataloguing the contents. He turned as they entered. "Problem?"

"Possibly." *Definitely.* "This is Dr. Patel." *And she's been a problem since day one.*

Jake set down his data pad and extended his hand. "Pleased to meet you, Dr. Patel. I'm Jake."

She cocked her head, assessing him for a moment before transferring the satchel to her left hand and clasping his right hand in hers. "You're very young."

He smiled, which reinforced the perception of youth. "Not as young as you might think. I've been considering growing a beard." He ran a hand over his smooth chin. "Give myself a bit more gravitas."

"Hmmm. And you're a doctor?"

"That's right."

"Certified?"

His smile returned. "Yes."

"Then why do you go by Jake instead of Doctor?"

Jake glanced at Isin, a twinkle in his eye. He seemed amused by the personal interrogation. "Simplicity. My last name is Roxburghshire. Asking my patients to get their tongues around that when they're in pain seemed cruel. I started off going by Dr. Jacob, but then everyone thought Jacob was my last name. I didn't want everyone calling me just Doctor or Doc, either, so I went with Jake. It's one syllable and easy to remember, even when a patient is delirious."

"I see." Patel didn't seem to know how to react to his explanation.

"But I will answer to Doc in a pinch." Jake's gaze shifted to Isin, his jovial mood switching to business. "What can I do for you?"

"Dr. Patel or the cube she's carrying may be embedded with a tracking device."

Jake's brows lifted. "*May* be embedded?"

"She doesn't agree."

Jake focused on Patel. "Have you received any injections recently? Perhaps as part of a routine physical?"

"No."

"Have you suffered any injuries that would have required a sedative?"

"No."

"Any dizziness? Fainting? Insect or spider bites?"

"No." Patel's answers came faster with each question.

Jake didn't seem to mind. He glanced at Isin. "Full body scan?"

"Yes. And have her unlock the cube."

Patel shot him a dirty look that he chose to ignore.

"Good thing I brought a few items with me from *Vengeance*. I'm still working on getting this infirmary fully functional." Jake reached into the portable med kit sitting on the counter. He pulled out a rectangular device the size of his hand. He faced Patel. "You'll need to set down the satchel."

She hesitated.

Jake pointed to the med platform to his right. "How about over there?"

She put it down with obvious reluctance, keeping her focus on Itorye and Kenji in the doorway before moving to stand directly in front of the satchel, blocking it from view.

Isin bit down on his tongue. Her paranoia was misplaced. He didn't want her damn cube. And if he did, nothing she could do would stop him from taking it.

Jake motioned to Patel. "Stand with your arms extended and legs slightly apart."

She stared at Isin, but followed Jake's instructions.

Jake crouched at her feet and ran the scanner slowly along each leg and arm before moving to her abdomen. "Lower your arms and pivot forty-five degrees."

She did as he asked. He continued the side to side motion, creeping up centimeter by centimeter, his brows furrowed as he studied the readings. He finished her torso and moved to her shoulders and neck.

A persistent beep kicked up as he passed the device over her nape. He halted, focusing the device on that spot. "Got it. Sub-dermal device just beneath the hairline."

"What?" Patel lifted a hand to the back of her neck, her fingers bumping into Jake's scanner.

He lowered it. "You have a tracking device implanted in your neck."

"But..." She looked between Jake and Isin, her eyes wide with fear. "That's not possible."

Jake's brows rose a fraction. "The scanner doesn't lie." He turned the device so she could study the readings. "The signal it's generating is low frequency, but distinct. Any comm buoy within range could pick it up, assuming someone was looking for it."

"How did it get there?" Her breathing had sped up. "How did someone inject a tracking device into my neck *without my knowledge?*"

Jake glanced at Isin before answering. "My best guess would be while you were sleeping."

"*What?*" She pressed a hand to her chest, caught in the early stages of hyperventilation.

Jake rested a hand at the small of her back and guided her to the med platform, coaxing her down until she was sitting beside the satchel. "Most likely you were given a sedative, possibly added to your food or drink, to keep you unconscious while you were given the injection."

She stared at Jake, her eyes round as saucers. "Someone was in my room? While I slept?"

"It's a likely scenario. You wouldn't have been able to see any redness at the injection site, and could have shrugged off any residual tenderness as muscle soreness from sleeping wrong."

Her face scrunched up like a child about to throw a really impressive tantrum. But she didn't. She took several deep breaths, her hand still pressed over her heart. When she opened her eyes, the panic had subsided. "Can you remove it?"

Jake looked over his shoulder at Isin and Itorye.

Isin was out of his depth on this, but Itorye took the scanner from Jake's outstretched hand and flipped through the data. "We should run a few tests to rule out any potential booby traps." She studied the display. "This looks more complex than a simple signal generator."

Patel's gaze drifted to the satchel. "What about Alec?"

"Alec?" Jake looked from the satchel to Isin, a question in his eyes.

Isin pointed to the satchel. "Our second passenger. I'll let the two of you get acquainted." He headed for the door. He wasn't up for another round of *who's Alec?* Jake had confirmed what he needed to know—Rathburn had tagged Patel to keep track of her whereabouts. That told him a lot about his adversary. Now he needed to plan his next move.

He paused beside Kenji. "No one enters this room. I don't care if they're bleeding from their eyes." He glanced at Itorye. "Notify me when you've completed your tests."

# *Eight*

Isin wanted to head straight for the gym so he could work out this new problem. Physical exercise always helped clear his head. But he needed to check on Byrd first.

He climbed the stairs to the bridge, doing his best to push thoughts of Natasha to the back of his mind. No good. Against all logic, he still hoped to see her when he stepped through the hatch, but instead he found Byrd lounging in the pilot's seat, his feet propped up on the main console and his hands laced behind his head. He wasn't even watching the controls. His eyes were closed, and his head bobbed in time to music only he could hear.

For reasons Isin didn't want to examine too closely, the lackadaisical pose sent his temper into the red. He stalked over and smacked Byrd's feet off the console.

His eyes popped open as he gripped the arms of the chair for balance.

"Feeling better?" Isin growled.

"What? Oh, yeah." He sat up straighter, his gaze darting away. Jake had done an excellent job treating the injuries that had sent Byrd to the infirmary when *Vengeance*'s navigation console had exploded. Other than a few slightly red patches of skin, he looked like he always did—cocky and purposely disheveled.

Isin braced one hand on the back of the pilot's seat and the other on the console, moving into Byrd's personal space. "I want to make something very clear. This is

Natasha's chair, not yours. While you're sitting in it, you will show respect. Do you understand?"

Byrd swallowed, his eyes wide. "Yeah. Got it."

"Good." He pushed back and scanned the navigation data. The readings looked fine except for one thing. They were in an interstellar jump that was taking him further away from the system where he'd left *Vengeance*. Where he'd left Natasha.

He'd correct that issue shortly. "Notify me if you run into any problems."

"Aye." Byrd turned away, the hunch to his shoulders making him look like a sulking teenager.

Isin held back a sigh as he descended the stairs to A deck and continued along the passageway to the crew gym. After he rescued Natasha from Rathburn, he'd get her to help him find a new pilot for *Vengeance*. One without a chip the size of Gibraltar on his shoulder.

When he reached the gym, he stripped off his tunic, noting the darts of pain when the material brushed his hands and face. He hadn't bothered to look in a mirror after leaving the infirmary. Jake would have cleaned and treated his wounds, but the discomfort told him he still had a long way to go to a full recovery. He probably looked as raw as he felt.

He had Kerr to thank for that. And one day he'd repay the torture he'd endured at the man's hands. But dealing with his nemesis would have to wait.

Settling onto his back on the weight bench, he lifted the bar and slowly lowered it to his chest. Judging by the heft, Kenji had been the last one to use it. He was the only person on the crew who could go toe-to-toe with Isin in that department. Sweep came close, but...

Isin paused, the barbell hovering above his head. *Sweep.* Memories moved in like storm clouds, eclipsing the light. He'd kept the loss of his friend from taking center stage while he'd focused on Natasha and the mess with Patel. But in the silence in the gym, the hum of the engines the only background to his thoughts, the void opened up.

A rumble started behind his sternum and climbed into his throat. The barbell began to shake. He dropped it into the cradle before it came crashing down on his head. Eyes squeezed shut, fists clenched, lips pressed together, he grappled with the chasm cracking open his chest.

Sweep was gone, lost to the black. He'd never expected to face that reality. Strange, really, considering most mercenaries didn't live past forty. Sweep had already beaten the odds. Maybe that's why he'd viewed Sweep as invulnerable, too wise and weathered for death to claim.

But he'd been wrong.

He owed Kerr for that, too.

He took steadying breaths—minutes, hours—until the tremors subsided. Opening his eyes, he reached for the bar and began a steady rhythm, focusing his thoughts. The repetitive motion worked away the ragged edges, slowly untangling the knots and presenting him with a clear path.

By the time Itorye appeared in the doorway, he knew his next step.

"I thought you were going to take it easy," she commented, eyeing his sweat-covered chest.

"I did. No running."

"Hmm." Her eyes held a touch of disapproval, but no surprise. "Jake can remove the tracking device, but it's not only generating a signal, it's reading Dr. Patel's vital signs. He can create a charged ion solution with simulated bio

readings so that we can keep it functioning normally after
he removes it. Or we can destroy it."

"And if we don't destroy it?"

"It's still transmitting, so as soon as we leave our
interstellar jump, the nearest comm buoy will pick up the
signal."

And Rathburn could track them again. The question
was, would he follow? From a tactical standpoint, Rathburn
was better off taking control of *Vengeance* and waiting for
them to come to him. Judging by his prior actions, he seemed
like a man who understood the value of strategy. "Tell Jake
to create the solution. He can extract the tracking device
when he's ready. In the meantime, I want you and Kenji to
escort Patel to her cabin so she can gather her things. She
and Alec will be bunking with you."

Itorye didn't seem the least bit put out by the order
to share her cabin. "Understood." Then again, he'd seen the
look of fascination on her face when she'd figured out Alec
was an A.I. She might actually enjoy spending time with her
new roommates.

Better her than him. "Patel's restricted to A deck
until further notice. She's not to leave the cabin
unaccompanied, and she's to keep Alec with her at all times.
Do whatever's necessary to insure compliance. Your
discretion."

"No problem."

Yep, definitely excited.

"Have Avril stand guard outside your cabin. We'll
meet back here."

"Will do."

After she left, he switched from the weights to the
treadmill, not bothering to turn on the interactive monitor
and video feed. Silence and a blank wall fit his mood much

better. His thigh burned where a shot from one of Kerr's crew had grazed his skin, and his body pointed out a few new areas of discomfort as he increased the incline. He shrugged off the annoyances like a horse shrugging off flies, but heeded Itorye's warning, keeping his pace much slower than normal. Passing out on the treadmill wouldn't help his cause.

The steady pounding of his feet acted as a metronome, keeping the beat, clearing his mind. It wasn't until voices in the passageway broke his concentration that he realized he was breathing like a freight train. Maybe taking some time to rest wouldn't be such a bad idea.

He stopped the treadmill, wiping a hand over his face to clear the sweat dripping down his cheek and off his chin.

"...don't care. I want to talk to—" The voice broke off abruptly.

Isin glanced over his shoulder. Marlin Brooks, *Phoenix*'s cook and occasional plumber, stood in the entrance to the gym between Kenji and Itorye. His mouth hung open and his eyes bugged out as he stared at Isin.

Isin stepped off the treadmill, acutely aware of why Brooks was reacting so strangely. Most people did when they got their first look at the network of scars covering his torso.

He grabbed a towel from the rack on the wall and draped it around his shoulders. "Brooks. What can I do for you?"

That broke the spell. Brooks drew himself up to his full height, which still left him a head shorter than Itorye and almost twice that for Kenji. "I want to know what you're doing to get Nat and Pete back."

That brought a slight smile to Isin's lips. Brooks was skittish and meek, either by nature or as a result of his troubled past, but he was also loyal to the bone. Losing the only two people he considered his friends wasn't something he'd take lying down.

Kenji hooked his thumbs into the belt loops of his cargo pants and gave Isin an apologetic shrug. "I told him to wait, but he wouldn't listen." And apparently Kenji hadn't been able to say no. He'd developed a real fondness for the quirky cook while they were on Troi, treating him almost like a kid brother, even though Brooks was old enough to be his father.

Isin didn't understand the relationship, but he respected it. "That's okay." He mopped the sweat off his face before settling into one of the chairs in the tiny seating area. He motioned for Brooks to take the seat across from him, while Kenji and Itorye sat in the ones to either side. "We're going back for them."

"When?"

"Soon."

Brooks puffed up, like a frightened animal trying to appear larger than he really was. His gaze darted between the scars on Isin's bare chest and the fresh wounds on his face. "We shouldn't have left them in the first place."

*Zing!* That one struck the mark. He'd been thinking the same thing from the moment he'd woken up in the infirmary. If he hadn't been nearly comatose when Natasha had given the order, he would have overruled her.

Itorye had followed Natasha's order, but he couldn't fault her for that. As first mate, that was her job. But Natasha had paid the price. Isin couldn't forgive himself for letting her down. Again. And it looked like Brooks agreed with him.

Isin gave a small nod to acknowledge the point. "What matters now is getting them back."

Brooks deflated a little, looking somewhat mollified. "How are you going to do that?"

"I have a plan, which I'll be discussing with Itorye and Kenji. But I need you to keep the crew occupied so they don't bother us. Can you whip up some of your specialty dishes and gather the crew in the dining hall?"

The ruddiness blanched out of Brooks' cheeks. "I... I guess so."

The idea of surrounding himself with a room full of mercenaries clearly scared the stuffing out of him.

Kenji spoke up. "Get Shash and Fleur to round them up. They'll keep everyone in line."

Good call. Fleur had been onboard *Phoenix* ever since leaving Gallows Edge, and Shash had helped with the ship's initial restoration on Troi. Brooks knew them both well enough to accept their help.

Brooks gave a small sigh. "I'll do that." He stood, but paused, leveling a look at Isin that was courageous because of the fear lurking behind it. "You promise you'll get them back?"

Isin nodded. "You have my word."

"Good. That's good."

Kenji turned to watch him leave. "Brave little man," he murmured as the diminutive figure disappeared into the passageway.

Isin grunted assent. Brooks would make a lousy mercenary, but he was an above average human being.

Kenji shifted back around in his chair. "So, what's the plan?"

# *Nine*

"So, whadda you make of Rathburn?"

Nat stabbed one of the vegetables on her plate with her fork as she considered Pete's question. The food Rathburn had sent up was excellent... but it was still prison food. "He's a control freak."

"Yeah, I got that." Pete picked up the crystal water glass beside his plate and took a drink.

Nothing but the best on this ship.

After showing them to their temporary quarters—a two-bedroom suite somewhere in the heart of the ship—Rathburn had ordered their meal from the galley before departing. The food had been delivered by one of the grey-uniformed guards, who'd barely said two words to them as he'd brought in the food cart and left it in the middle of the room. Social interaction apparently wasn't in the job description for Rathburn's guards.

The gracious accommodations aside, it was clear Rathburn was on the hunt. He was using them as bait to catch Green. *Patel.* Whatever.

She and Pete had searched their rooms while they waited for the food to arrive, checking for any signs of surveillance. They'd come up empty, but by mutual non-verbal agreement, they were watching what they said, just in case.

She gazed at the door to their suite. It wasn't locked—they'd tested that, too—but none of the doors in the octagonal foyer outside would open, including the one for the lift. They weren't going anywhere. Which is why she'd decided a hunger strike was shortsighted. Drugging her food wouldn't get Rathburn what he wanted, so she might as well enjoy the meal. She'd need her mind and body sharp to deal with whatever ploys he'd try next. "I find it hard to believe Rathburn's planning to give *Vengeance* to Kerr. But I haven't figured out why he said he would."

"Yeah, I've been thinkin' about that, too."

"And?"

"I think he's plannin' to use Kerr's crew as labor to get *Vengeance* runnin' again."

"Then what?"

"Dunno. Use the ship as a bargainin' tool to try and get what he wants, maybe?"

"Hmmm." She took another bite. If that was Rathburn's plan, it had a good chance of succeeding. Isin had been disenchanted with Patel from the beginning. If he had the option of turning her over to Rathburn in exchange for *Vengeance*, it wouldn't be a hard decision. But would it be a good one?

"He'll be comin' soon."

She met Pete's gaze. "Rathburn?"

He shook his head. "Isin."

"Oh." She set down her fork. "Yeah. He'll want *Vengeance* back." So did she, for his sake. She lowered her voice to a whisper. "He'll be royally ticked that I ordered Itorye and Kenji to leave us behind." And she didn't want him charging in like an enraged bull.

"Don't worry. He's a negotiator. He won't put himself in a bad bargainin' position."

"He said he doesn't negotiate anymore."

"He negotiated with you."

"I guess." She took a sip of her tea. "But he'll feel the need to rescue us from Rathburn, since we pulled him off Kerr's ship. He may choose to do it mercenary style." She shuddered. "I really have to stop saving that man."

Pete rested his elbows on the table. "Why have you saved him?"

"What?" She'd been talking to herself more than to him, and didn't have an answer. "Oh. I don't know." Acts of temporary insanity? Or something even stupider, like... nope, not going there. No good could come of it.

"You look like you've got an idea."

"Not really." And she was closing the door on those dangerous thoughts before they could take hold.

Pete studied her for a moment. "If you say so. But seems odd that a smuggler and a mercenary would risk their lives for each other if there's no profit in it. Not unless there's a reason that's got nothin' to do with debts."

A chime sounded, saving her from a response. Rathburn's voice came over the comm. "Ms. Orlov?"

She shared a look with Pete. Had Rathburn been listening to their conversation? She tapped the table interface for the comm. "Yes?"

"We've docked with *Vengeance*. Since I'll be taking Mr. Kerr and his crew over in the morning to begin the repairs, I wondered if perhaps you and Mr. Stevens would like the opportunity to gather your personal effects first. Or any other items of importance."

*Like Patel's mysterious cube?* He was an idiot if he thought she'd lead him to it, even if it were still onboard. Thank goodness Itorye had removed it from the safe in Isin's cabin and taken it with her.

But she might as well play along with Rathburn's game. At the very least she could snag some of Isin's belongings before Kerr laid his grubby paws on them. "Thank you. I would appreciate it."

"Wonderful. I'll send someone down to fetch you. See you on the ship."

The connection closed. She glanced at Pete as she reached for her duster. "Round two."

# *Ten*

The burly man in the grey security uniform Rathburn sent down to escort them to *Vengeance* was as stoic as the other guards they'd met, so they made the journey to the docking port in silence.

Stepping through the airlock had a surreal quality. By chance, fate, or design, Rathburn had connected his ship to *Vengeance* using the same docking port Kerr had used for his invasion. She'd crossed this way not long ago with a nearly comatose Isin in tow. Now he was somewhere out in the black, dealing with Patel and her cube, while she faced the man who'd forced them to run.

Rathburn stood on the other side of the airlock, like a king greeting his subjects as they entered his castle. He'd traded his tailored suit for dark slacks and a blue turtleneck tunic that matched his eyes and gave his torso clear definition. The man was no slouch in the muscle department. "Delighted you could join me."

She suppressed a derisive snort. No reason to irritate him when he was doing her a favor. She needed to stay on his good side—at least for the time being.

He spread his arms to encompass the passageway in both directions. "Where's our first stop?"

So he wasn't going to let them wander on their own? She hadn't expected it, but it would have made her objective easier. And she would have had a better chance of hiding the fact that she was unfamiliar with the layout of most of the ship. She knew the path between the airlock and the shuttle bay, and how to reach Isin's cabin, where she and Itorye had taken the cube from the hidden safe in the bulkhead. She'd make the cabin her last stop, since she'd like to gather whatever personal items Isin might have onboard. She didn't expect to find much.

That left the question of where to go first. The infirmary was aft of the airlock. Jake had taken her there and given her items from a portable med kit before she'd boarded Kerr's ship to rescue Isin. To the fore, she could see part of what looked like a mess hall. Isin's cabin was on the deck above. Unfortunately, she had no idea where to locate any of the other critical areas, including the bridge and engineering. And she didn't want to look like a fool wandering around a ship she was supposed to be commanding.

She glanced at Pete. He hadn't spent any more time on the ship than she had, but he'd been working as an engineer in a maintenance and repair hanger most of his life. By his own admission, he'd seen thousands of ships. He'd navigated Kerr's vessel like he'd known exactly where he was going. He probably had a sense of the layout on *Vengeance*, too. "Would you like to inspect the engine room?"

The subtle curve of his lip told her he'd picked up on her dilemma. "You bet." He turned toward the aft.

"A moment, Mr. Stevens."

Pete halted mid-step, facing Rathburn. "Yeah?"

Rathburn motioned to his guard, who took up a position behind Nat, while Rathburn moved next to Pete. "I'll lead. Which way?"

"Aft stairway." Pete pointed back and to the right. "One deck up."

"Very good." Rathburn set off, while the rest of them followed single file like baby ducks.

Nat gave a surreptitious glance over her shoulder. Okay, two baby ducks and one surly grey goose.

Hopefully Pete knew what he was doing, and wasn't just taking an educated guess. She spent the climb up to B deck crafting a few plausible excuses, just in case the engine room didn't turn out to be where he'd indicated.

She shouldn't have bothered. A plaque beside the sealed hatch indicated they'd arrived at the *Engine Room*.

However, the hatch failed to open when Pete touched the panel. A low buzzer sounded and *Access Denied* flashed on the screen.

She hid a scowl. Of course Shash would have sealed off access before abandoning ship. She didn't disagree with the woman's actions, but it put them in an awkward spot.

Pete tapped in a security code she didn't recognize. *Access Denied* flashed again. He glanced at Rathburn. "Engine room's on security lockdown."

"I can see that. Can't you override it?"

"No, sir. I'm not cleared for that."

Rathburn turned to Nat. "Ms. Orlov? Will you do the honors?" He gestured to the panel.

Nat took her time stepping up to the panel, her thoughts churning. Pete hadn't even tried the security code they used on *Phoenix*. Why not? Since Shash had helped set up the security on that ship, there was a chance the codes were the same.

She moved her hand to enter the code, but paused with her fingers a millimeter from the panel's surface. *Pete doesn't want the hatch to open.* Without the access code, it might take Rathburn and Kerr's people a day or two to bypass the security without damaging the ship. The delay could buy her and Pete more time to figure out an escape plan. Pete had entered a non-relevant code on purpose.

Bringing her fingers in contact with the panel, she followed his lead, tapping in an old code she'd used on *Gypsy*, which produced the anticipated *Access Denied* bleat from the panel. She entered it again, allowing her displeasure to show on her face when it failed to produce a different result. She glanced at Rathburn. "My code's not working, either."

He frowned. "Surely you have authorization overrides."

She gave him her best withering stare. "Of course I do, but the system isn't recognizing them. The security's memory core may have been damaged during the fighting." Which could be true. For all she knew the system wouldn't accept the correct codes even if she had them.

The muscles around his mouth tensed, but he didn't question her. "Very well." He slipped a hand into the pocket of his slacks and produced a slender electrical device no bigger than his palm. Attaching it to the access panel, he typed in a long code. Lights flashed alternately between the device and the panel like a private digital conversation. *Access Denied* displayed on the panel.

Rathburn's jaw twitched. He entered a series of commands, continuing in a fast-moving volley of request and denial for a full minute. Unfortunately, the two devices finally came to a meeting of the minds. The panel turned green and the hatch slid open.

Nat bit her tongue to keep from swearing.

The cocky smile on Rathburn's face as he turned made her bite down harder.

"After you," he said, gesturing to the opening.

Damn him. The amused look in his eyes made it clear he'd figured out she was hiding something. And perhaps suspected she'd set booby traps inside the engine room. She hadn't, of course. But Shash might have in an attempt to trip up Kerr's crew. *Vengeance*'s engineer was the kind of lunatic who delighted in springing traps on the unsuspecting.

Now that Rathburn had successfully unlocked the hatch, he seemed content to let Nat lead as they crossed the threshold. Hopefully Shash had been too busy with the rescue and ensuing evacuation to rig any ugly surprises.

Out of habit, she dipped her hand into the pocket of her duster, but came up empty. Her pistol was still stored on *Gypsy*, along with her bag of tricks. That is, if Rathburn's guards hadn't found it.

She stepped through the hatch.

And entered visual chaos.

Access panels lay like giant playing cards scattered across the deck. Exposed wiring and open conduits, many of them blackened with scorch marks, told a tale of wanton destruction. The traitor on Isin's crew had been thorough in his determination to stop *Vengeance* cold.

In contrast, bins of spare parts and toolkits sat at regular intervals around the perimeter. Shash's doing, no doubt. Nat had seen enough of the other woman's meticulous work habits while she'd helped restore *Phoenix*'s engines to recognize the signs. No wonder she'd been so hostile when they'd had to abandon ship. Leaving *Vengeance* in this condition must have wounded her pride.

Pete appeared by her side. Together they moved forward, keeping an eye out for traps, although his posture indicated he didn't expect to encounter any. He'd worked closely with Shash while they were on *Phoenix*. If he believed she'd been too busy trying to save the ship to turn it into a lethal funhouse, she'd trust that assessment.

Picking her way over the downed panels and across the deck, she entered the main engine compartment, while he moved off in the opposite direction, followed by the guard.

The destruction that spread before her made her jaw clench. *Kerr, you worthless bastard.* Several melted components lay like free-form sculptures along the perimeter, with the cavities where they'd been extracted gaping like missing teeth.

"Mr. Kerr will have his work cut out for him."

Nat turned. Rathburn stood by the bulkhead, inspecting one of the charred openings. His tone and expression both indicated amusement.

"You find this funny?" she snapped. "*He* did this." She spread her arms wide to indicate the mess surrounding them, when what she wanted to do was plant her fist in Kerr's face. Since he wasn't available, she directed her ire at Rathburn.

He met her gaze. "On the contrary. I despise senseless violence and destruction. What *does* amuse me is the knowledge that Kerr will be responsible for making the repairs, but will gain nothing for his efforts."

She folded her arms over her chest. He'd dropped the *Mister* from Kerr's name that time. Was it a sign? "Then you're *not* planning to give him the ship? Even though you said you would?"

Rathburn's eyes widened. "Good heavens, no. I don't reward barbarism. I assumed you'd figured that out." He gave her a pointed look. "But working off his transgressions is a fitting punishment, don't you think?"

She passed his comments through her internal lie detector. No red flags. "Yeah, sure."

"I'm glad we agree." He leaned down and picked up one of the mangled pieces of machinery like it weighed no more than a pillow. Definitely muscled under that turtleneck.

"Of course, that opens the question of what to do with the ship after it's repaired." He surveyed the damage to the component in his hand—plasma manifold from the look of it—and set it back down. "Do you believe Mr. Isin will return before then?"

She hedged her answer. "Possibly."

He smiled. "From what you've told me, I'm certain he will. The question is, when." He strolled past her, his gaze moving systematically along the bulkheads, consoles, and exposed hardware, like he was mentally cataloguing all the damage. "It would be far better for all concerned if he arrived expediently."

"Why?"

His smile vanished. "I'm a busy man, Ms. Orlov. And I don't like to remain in one place for long. If Kerr finishes the repairs before Mr. Isin returns, I'll be forced to take action."

He didn't elaborate, but the look in his eyes indicated she wouldn't like the result. She went on the offensive. "I can pilot *Vengeance*. Turn the ship over to me."

"Really, Ms. Orlov, you're not that naïve." He swept his arm out to encompass their surroundings. "Even if you and Mr. Stevens could get the ship running on your own, what, pray tell, would you do when Kerr's crew crawls back to reclaim their prize? You're courageous, but you and Mr. Stevens can't defend this ship alone."

She planted her hands on her hips. "Watch me."

He stared at her for a long moment. Then his lips began to twitch and the skin around his eyes crinkled. A muffled snort rapidly morphed into a full-throated laugh.

She failed to see the joke.

He shook his head as he grinned at her. "You are the most delightful woman I've ever encountered."

It sounded like a compliment, but she still had the urge to growl.

"All right, Ms. Orlov. Let's see how this plays out, shall we?"

It wasn't the answer she wanted, but it would have to do. And between now and the time Kerr finished the repairs, she'd have to decide whether Patel was suffering from unjustified paranoia, or whether Rathburn was the most dangerous man she'd ever met.

# *Eleven*

"Are you going back for her?"

Isin lifted his head out of the spray of warm water and glanced over the low wall of the shower cubicle.

Shash lounged with her hip and shoulder propped against the tiled wall of the shower room, her arms loosely folded over her chest and one ankle crossed in front of the other. She gave him a saucy smile, her gaze tracking the droplets of water as they trailed over the bare skin of his shoulders and chest. "Well, are you?" she prompted.

He turned his back to the spray, the last traces of soap swirling down the drain. He shut off the water and snagged the towel draped over the wall, wiping the moisture from his head and torso before wrapping the towel around his hips and stepping into the aisle. "Am I what?"

"Going back for *Vengeance*."

Ah. He should have known Shash was talking about the ship, not Natasha. The two women had been at loggerheads since the day they'd met, when Natasha had come charging back into his life with a kick to his solar plexus.

He walked down the aisle to where a stack of clean clothes borrowed from Kenji awaited him. "What do you think?"

She followed, a little closer than he would have liked. "I think you'll do whatever it takes to get her back."

Right sentiment, wrong subject.

"Do you have a plan?" Her question came with a little barb. Apparently she hadn't appreciated being kept out of the discussion in the gym.

Normally he included her in strategy sessions, but unlike Itorye and Kenji, she was unpredictable. If she got a whiff of the situation with Patel and Alec, she might tell the crew, who'd immediately shove the doctor and her son out the nearest airlock. He couldn't allow that to happen. Ironic, really, considering what he planned to do when he faced Rathburn.

He picked up Kenji's tunic and pulled it over his head. "We have to find a way around the other ship's energy beam."

"Yeah." Her tone made it clear he was stating the obvious.

And stalling for time. He stuck his arms into the tunic's sleeves. "Any ideas?"

"It's a nasty piece of work. We didn't get many sensor readings, but it looked like even a glancing blow might knock out most of a ship's systems."

"So how do we defend against it?" He loosened the towel and wiped the moisture from his legs before reaching for his pants. He'd said goodbye to the benefit of underwear until he had access to his own clothes.

Her gaze followed the towel down, her *cat who ate the canary* smile widening as she slowly worked her way back up. "I'm sorry, can you repeat the question?"

He pulled the pants over his hips and fastened them, giving her the look her comment deserved.

She shrugged. "I don't think we can. That's serious tech. Even if I had a clue as to how they created it, it's not like I have a lot to work with on this boat. This is a glorified cruise ship, not a state-of-the-art warship."

True, but Shash was nothing if not resourceful. If he could get her the answers she needed, she might be able to figure a way around the problem. At the very least, it would keep her busy. He didn't want her with time on her hands. She was a smart woman. She might start asking questions about Patel, the cube, or Rathburn's ship that he didn't want to answer.

He'd ask Patel what she knew about the beam, but he needed a few hours of shuteye to clear his mind first. Right now he was dead on his feet. "Do what you can with the data we have. I'll talk to Itorye and see if she can provide you with more information."

Shash looked nonplussed. She didn't hate Itorye like she did Natasha, but they weren't exactly friends, either. "We might not need to worry about it. They could have left *Vengeance* adrift. She *was* dead in the water."

Not a chance. After what Patel had revealed, he was certain Rathburn would be waiting for them. He'd already proven he was patient and persistent. And he'd want to keep the upper hand, which meant parking his ship right next to *Vengeance*. "We can't count on it. And I'm not about to walk into another trap."

That wiped the smirk off her face and ignited twin flames in her dark eyes. "Kerr will pay for that."

"Yes, he will." Kerr had many sins to atone for. Delivering retribution would be his pleasure. As soon as he got his hands on the two-faced monster responsible for Sweep's death, he intended to make sure he suffered the most excruciating end imaginable.

# *Twelve*

The fluffy comforter, crisp sheets, and cushy pillows on the bed in Nat's quarters intimidated the heck out of her. She'd never slept on a mattress so large or luxurious. Pete had a setup just like it in his room, and his reaction had matched hers.

After the trip to *Vengeance*, she'd stripped down and dumped her clothes in the sanitizer before taking the shortest shower in history. The thought of being naked on this ship made her twitchy. After drying off with towels that resembled plump clouds, she'd pulled on the long-sleeved tunic and lounge pants she'd found neatly folded on the counter in the bathroom.

She'd never owned any pajamas. She always slept in her clothes or underwear, just in case she needed to quickly take her post. But touching the pristine sheets while wearing her ratty undergarments had seemed untenable. And it wasn't like she would be going anywhere anytime soon.

She'd expected to toss and turn, but instead she'd slept like the dead, which frankly scared the stuffing out of her. Dropping her guard in unfamiliar surroundings wasn't her style. As soon as she'd woken, she'd swapped the pajamas for her own clothes, which looked and smelled a whole lot better than they had the day before. She even detected a hint of lavender. Rathburn hadn't been kidding about wanting them to feel like guests... to a point.

The lift remained on lockdown after the guard had delivered them silently back to their suite the previous night.

Rathburn wasn't about to give them free rein to move about the ship. Which left her cooling her heels until he contacted her again.

The bag she'd packed while in Isin's cabin sat open on the bed in front of her. Reaching in, she pulled out a black tunic that looked exactly like the other black tunics in the bag.

That was the first thing she'd learned as she'd gathered personal items from Isin's cabin. While she'd worked with him repairing *Phoenix*, he'd always worn black pants and a shirt like this one, except on those rare occasions when he hadn't worn a shirt at all. She'd assumed his lack of wardrobe variation was a result of minimalist travel gear. After visiting his cabin, she'd realized he'd created a uniform for himself that never changed.

And why not? It was practical, functional, and easy to maintain. Plus, he looked good in it.

Or out of it. She wouldn't soon forget the image of his muscles flexing underneath his dark skin as he'd worked out in *Phoenix*'s gym. The brutal scars that crisscrossed his chest and back still horrified her, but the raw power in his toned body had the opposite effect. Which irritated her to no end.

Settling against the mounded pillows, she draped the tunic across her torso like a blanket. His spicy scent clung to the soft material, surrounding her as her muscles relaxed and her anxiety retreated. Why she associated that scent with safety was a cosmic joke. Isin had brought her more misery in the past two years than she'd expected to endure in a lifetime. But he'd also yanked her out of her tiny world, expanding her universe and opening the door to possibilities she'd never imagined.

Like owning *Phoenix*. She'd dreamed of that ship during her long months as a Setarip captive. Being separated from it now made her chest ache.

Getting pulled off *Gypsy* hadn't been fun, either. She didn't even know if her shuttle was still in one piece. The next time she spoke to Rathburn, she'd see about paying a visit to the shuttle bay.

Her walkthrough on *Vengeance* the previous night had revealed the scope of the destruction to the engine room and the ship's systems. In addition to scorch marks in almost every passageway, the navigation console on the bridge had been reduced to a chunk of worthless metal. Pete had confirmed none of the components were salvageable.

Before they'd left the ship, Rathburn had taken her to *Vengeance*'s shuttle bay, where nine bodies had been laid out in a neat row, gathered by his guards from around the ship. She hadn't recognized any of them, but she also hadn't met most of Isin's crew. She'd been forced to admit that fact to Rathburn when he'd asked her to identify them. He'd taken her answer in stride, assuring her the bodies would be put in cold storage until further arrangements could be made.

Good thing. She had no idea how mercenaries handled their dead.

"Ms. Orlov?"

Nat sprang off the bed, crouching like a cat. *Jumpy, Nat?* Giving herself a mental shake and picking Isin's tunic off the deck, she walked to the comm panel by the door. "Yes?"

Rathburn sounded way too chipper. "How are you this morning? Did you sleep well?"

"Uh, sure."

"Glad to hear it. Anything I can do to make your room more comfortable?"

*More* comfortable? He had to be kidding. "Um, no. It's fine." But since she had his attention, she might as well ask her question. "I do have a request."

"Yes?"

"I'd like to see *Gypsy.*"

"Your shuttle? Of course. We can stop by during the tour."

She blinked. "What tour?"

"Of my ship. I assume seeing that would interest you? Unless you'd prefer to stay in your room."

*No way.* A few more hours in here and she'd start climbing the walls. "What about Pete?"

"Mr. Stevens is welcome to join us, although I'd hoped to get his assistance crafting the replacement navigation console for *Vengeance.* My engineers are skilled, but they're likely to design something that would seem out of place on an older vessel."

She bristled at the perceived slight to Isin's ship, but held her tongue. He was probably right. Nothing she'd seen on this ship would fit in with the design for *Vengeance.* His offer was actually very... thoughtful. Admitting it though, even to herself, took a lot of effort.

"I'll ask him. See what he says."

"Very good. I'll check back with you in a few minutes."

She found Pete sitting at the dining table, his attention on a set of schematics visible on the interactive surface. He glanced up as she stopped beside him. "Mornin'."

She returned his easy smile. "What're you working on?"

"Repair notes. Wanted a complete reckonin' of what needs doin' before Kerr's crew gets in there and starts muckin' around."

"So you can double-check their work when they're done?"

"Yep. Don't trust 'em not to cut corners."

"Neither do I. But Rathburn's people should be watching them, too. Speaking of which, Rathburn has offered me a tour of his ship."

"Did he now?" Pete stroked a hand over his beard. "Am I invited?"

"If you want to be. But he was hoping you'd help his people construct the replacement navigation console for *Vengeance* instead."

"Uh-huh." He gave her a look that made her skin feel tight.

"What?"

"Sounds to me like he's anglin' for time alone with you."

"Maybe. But I don't think he's planning to interrogate me, if that's what concerns you."

He shook his head. "Nope. But I seen the way he's been lookin' at you. He finds you fascinatin'."

She wrinkled her nose. "I don't care."

"I know that." He motioned her closer and lowered his voice to a whisper. "But he's got every reason to charm you, with nothin' to lose. You be careful."

"So you're not coming with me?"

"Way I see it, better if I learn as much as I can from his crew. Divide and conquer." He winked at her.

She smiled. Leave it to Pete to be planning ahead. "Then I guess I'm flying solo."

# *Thirteen*

The guard who arrived to escort her was the same woman who'd frisked her in the shuttle bay. Not that the guard gave any indication of recognizing her. Nat could have been part of the décor for all the interest she took in her as they stepped onto the lift.

Nat turned away from the closed doors and faced the guard. Since they were alone, maybe she'd have more success opening a dialogue. "What's your name?"

Eyes forward, lips barely moving. "Grey."

"Grey? Like the color?"

Slight nod.

Easy to remember at least. It matched the color of her uniform. "I'm Nat."

No reaction.

That wasn't going to stop her from asking questions. "How long have you worked for Rath—Mr. Rathburn?" She tagged on the honorific at the last moment. A show of respect might help her odds of getting an answer.

No response. She might as well have asked the bulkhead.

"Is this a good job?"

Grey gave her a sidelong glance, before returning her attention to the doors. "Yes." Her hand rested lightly on her weapon, like she was considering using it if Nat kept bothering her.

So much for chitchat. Pivoting a quarter turn, Nat studied the contours of the lift instead. The walls were polished to a shine that generated a subtle reflection. And the motion gave the smoothest ride she'd ever experienced. No, scratch that. Second smoothest. First prize went to Aurora's ship, the *Starhawke*. She'd never seen a ship that came close to matching the beauty and grace of that one. But this one had some slick tricks of its own.

*Cerberus*. That's what Rathburn had called it. The name rang a distant bell. Hadn't Cerberus been a mythological beast of some kind? A dog, or something doglike? She'd ask Rathburn. Names had power, whether they identified ships or people. Aurora had taught her that. Understanding why Rathburn had chosen that name for his ship might give her insights into the kind of man she was dealing with.

The lift glided to a halt, and she turned. The open doors revealed a short passageway with four armed guards at attention, two by the lift and two at the far end. Their gazes remained forward as Nat walked beside Grey, just like the guards she'd passed the previous day. Did they stand like that all the time? Or did they talk to each other when Rathburn wasn't around?

Grey stepped in front of an ID scanner at the end of the passageway. A faint beep preceded the nearly soundless slide of the door. Beyond, a small cylindrical antechamber contained a spiral staircase leading up.

What was it with Rathburn and spiral staircases?

Grey motioned Nat to follow her up the stairs. At the top, they encountered another door and ID scanner. After it beeped for Grey, thick metal doors parted, revealing an authentic-looking stone archway.

"Welcome to the Elysian Fields," a melodic woman's voice greeted them as they passed underneath the arch.

Having walked through Rathburn's tropical paradise and pine forest the day before, Nat wasn't surprised by the simulated vista she encountered in the space beyond. Rolling hills of green and gold stretched out as far as the eye could see, crowned by pure blue skies dotted with perfect white clouds. The grass under her feet looked real enough, but this time she kept walking, following Grey as they approached the spot where Rathburn waited.

He was dressed more casually today in a white collared shirt with the sleeves rolled back, beige pants, and brown loafers. He looked like a man pulled right out of a historic photograph of an old-time country picnic.

He smiled. "Ms. Orlov. So glad you could join me." He gestured to the patchwork quilt spread on the grass.

She'd never experienced this kind of scene in her life, with or without the artificially constructed meadow. She hesitated.

Rathburn turned to Grey. "You may go now."

"Yes, sir." Grey didn't spare Nat a glance as she retraced the path to the archway.

"So." Rathburn opened his arms wide, gesturing to the panoramic view. "What do you think?"

*I think your ego's bigger than this ship.* But the surroundings were stunning. Sunlight glinted off a lake in the distance. "It's... impressive."

His eyes narrowed. "You don't like it?"

She shrugged. "I prefer the real world."

"I see." His smile faded.

*Yep, egomaniac. Doesn't handle rejection well.* She filed that information away for future reference. "But I can understand the appeal. It would break up the monotony of long spaceflights." Although she'd still prefer to be at the controls of a ship rather than down in a playroom like this one.

His smile returned. "Exactly! When I realized how much of my life would be spent in the vacuum of space, I knew I'd need to keep in touch with my terrestrial roots. The sights, the sounds, the smells—they call to me."

Now that he'd mentioned it, she picked up on the scent of damp earth and fresh grass. Birds chattered away in the trees dotting the landscape.

She also noticed something less pleasant. She was starting to sweat. The sunlight was simulated, but the heat in the room was very real. She slid her duster off her shoulders and folded it over her arm.

"Is it too warm for you?" His gaze traveled over her long-sleeved turtleneck, pants, and boots, none of which seemed appropriate in this setting.

She fought the urge to hold her coat in front of her like a shield. It wasn't like she had an abundance of clothing options to choose from. "No, it's fine." She didn't plan to be in this room long.

He touched his forearm, and a gentle breeze swept over the field, providing instant evaporative cooling. A moment later, a tree materialized beside the quilt, shading it from the sun.

With his sleeve rolled up, she could see the skin of his arm. No sign of a comband, which indicated he was activating an implant of some kind. It obviously gave him considerable control over the ship's systems. Exactly how much was a question she needed to have answered.

He gestured to the quilt. "Please, sit."

Said the spider to the fly. "I thought we were taking a tour."

"We are. This room is the first stop."

Lovely. She held back a grimace as she perched on the edge of the blanket, her duster tucked beside her. How ironic. Instead of being a captive on a derelict ship overseen by a Setarip sadist, she was a captive on a state-of-the-art starship captained by a charming man of means. And yet in both cases, all she could think about was getting the hell off.

Apparently she didn't like gilded cages any better than grungy ones.

Rathburn settled onto the opposite side of the quilt beside two oversized wicker baskets. "My chef said you hadn't ordered breakfast yet, so I had her prepare a few options for us." He pulled out a series of metal containers and arranged them on the blanket between them before removing the lids with a flourish.

"A few options?" He had a talent for understatement. She counted four different styles of cooked eggs, at least six types of breads and pastries, a cornucopia of fresh fruit... the list went on and on.

This much food could feed her entire crew. The extravagance put her teeth on edge.

She glanced up and found him watching her expectantly as he held out a plate, napkin, and utensils. She forced a closed-mouth smile to her lips. "Thank you."

His smile gave no hint that he'd picked up on her discomfort. "Help yourself to whatever you'd like."

She regarded the containers like she was facing a series of landmines.

Rathburn didn't seem to notice her hesitation. He selected items from several of the containers, filling his plate. She followed suit, although she took about half as much as he had.

She watched him surreptitiously as she placed her first forkful in her mouth. She chewed slowly, allowing herself to enjoy the rich flavors. Bolting down her food wouldn't get her out of here any quicker. Her stomach rumbled in response.

They ate in silence for a few minutes, the soft clink of silverware accompanied by the whisper of the breeze and the exuberant chatter of the birds.

After polishing off half the contents of his plate, Rathburn fetched a carafe and two glasses from one of the baskets. "I'm curious, Ms. Orlov. Where did you study to become a pilot?"

He asked the question casually, but she wasn't a fool. Nothing about this situation was casual, no matter how hard he was trying to convince her otherwise. She needed to watch what she said. But she also needed to coax him to let his guard down. She could start with her name. "It's Nat. And I didn't."

He paused in mid-pour. "Nat?"

"Instead of Ms. Orlov."

He blinked, like she'd surprised him. "Nat." He smiled. "It suits you. Please, call me Orpheus."

She preferred Rathburn, but she'd call him whatever he wanted if it got her closer to her goal.

He finished pouring the first glass and reached for the second. "So no formal pilot training?"

"Nope."

"Fascinating. Who taught you to fly?" He filled the second glass and handed her one.

"Several people." She brought her glass to her lips and took a drink. Even the water on this ship tasted better. "I figured out early on that a good pilot was in demand, so I learned from anyone I could."

"Because you wanted to be in demand." Not a question.

She met his gaze. "It's the best way to survive."

He gave a slight nod. "True." He picked up his plate again. "How long have you worked as a pilot?"

"Most of my life."

For some reason her answer amused him. "You're very good. Few people have your skill for evasion."

He wasn't just talking about her flying. "I've had a lot of practice."

"I believe you."

"What about this ship?" She gestured to their surroundings. "How long have you had it?"

"Eight years."

His answer was a lot more specific than hers had been. If she was correct that he was in his thirties now, he'd either been born into vast wealth, or acquired it at a young age. "What prompted you to build it?"

His gaze shifted to the field, a shadow crossing his features. "My sister died."

She hadn't seen that coming. "I'm sorry." But his answer seemed like a non-sequitur, not an explanation. "How did she die?"

"Laboratory accident."

"How old was she?"

"Young. Thirty-four."

"Were you close?"

"Very. I grew up idolizing her." He set his plate aside and picked up his water glass, his gaze still off in the distance. "She was a brilliant scientist. Had a theory for implants that would revolutionize human development. When she was awarded a grant to work on her prototype, she spent so many hours in the lab I barely heard from her."

"You didn't work together?"

He glanced at her. "No. I'm a businessman, not a scientist. I create wealth." His gaze shifted back to the field. "As smart as she was, she didn't seem to understand that." He took a sip from his glass, his throat moving in a convulsive swallow that didn't look faked.

Questions gathered at the back of Nat's tongue. She shuffled through them, looking for the best way to extract the information she wanted. "Why did her death prompt you to build this ship?"

He drew in a slow breath, releasing it on a sigh. "Persephone died because she rushed into the testing phase. She was at a critical stage when the company providing the grant demanded results. They were going to pull her funding and lock her out of her lab. She tested the implant on herself, but it wasn't ready. It killed her." He laughed, a bitter, harsh sound. "If she'd contacted me, I could have given her all the money she needed. But she didn't. She was too proud to ask her little brother for anything. I got a call from my mother instead, telling me Seph was dead."

Rathburn's pain seemed real enough. If he was lying, he was giving an amazing performance. And the revelation made sense, bringing Rathburn's motivations into focus. Guilt, and probably a lot of suppressed anger, had prompted him to build this ship. A ship, from what she'd seen, that was dedicated to the pursuit of science. His comments about Patel resurfaced. She'd been working on something revolutionary, too. "So you built this ship to create the kind of working environment your sister didn't have."

He met her gaze. For once, the polished businessman faded into the background, replaced by a heartbroken man who'd lost the person he loved most in the galaxy. "That's right. I don't want anyone to suffer the way she did. To be forced into a no-win scenario by those who lack vision."

Everything he said rang true. Either he was being completely honest, or he was the best liar she'd ever met. And she'd met more than her fair share.

But where did that put her? If he was truly a philanthropist, why was Patel running from him? She'd spent a lot of money and effort to make sure he wouldn't find her. What had Rathburn done to scare her so badly?

She couldn't ask him that question, so she asked the one she'd pondered in the lift instead. "Why did you name the ship *Cerberus*?"

The small smile that lifted the corners of his mouth looked drawn from a well of sadness. "In mythology, Persephone was the queen of the Underworld. What better name could I give this ship than the three-headed dog who protects her domain and keeps her safe?"

# Fourteen

After they finished their meal, Rathburn excused himself for a few moments, disappearing through a second stone archway that materialized across from the one where she'd entered.

Nat took advantage of his absence to explore the room. The vista gave the impression of distance, but the illusion had to fail under scrutiny. Sure enough, after walking twenty meters along the grassy knoll, her boots encountered a steep incline even though her eyes told her the terrain went downhill.

The roughly forty-five-degree angle was too steep to climb. She ran her hand along the slick surface until she was standing on her tiptoes, but didn't encounter an edge. The room would make an effective prison. Following the incline, she made a slow looping arc back toward the archway.

Rathburn was waiting for her when she arrived.

He'd changed clothes, the casual attire replaced by a tailored suit like the one he'd worn the day before. It made him seem more reserved. Dangerous.

That was fine. She'd armored herself with her duster as soon as he'd left.

His attitude hadn't changed, however. He smiled as she drew near. "Ready for your tour?"

"Lead the way."

They exited through the first archway, climbed down the spiral staircase, and passed the row of sentries.

The two guards by the lift followed them in as they stepped inside, their gazes forward but their attention clearly on her.

She couldn't blame them. She didn't have a plan to harm Rathburn, but she hadn't ruled out the possibility, either. She still needed to figure out what had happened between him and Patel, and whether the woman's fear was based on paranoia, or a real threat.

The lift doors parted at the cavernous room with the translucent walls she and Pete had seen the previous day. This time, Rathburn led her to the first corridor on their left, while the guards took up positions just outside the lift.

As she and Rathburn approached the ID scanner for a set of clear double doors, she almost missed the subtle flick of his index finger on his right hand. One of the doors immediately swung open, allowing them to bypass the scanner.

Was the entire ship connected to whatever was embedded in his forearm? He'd said his sister had been working on implants. And that he wasn't a scientist. Had he found someone to successfully complete his sister's designs?

He ushered her through the open door. "These are our testing facilities." Corridors branched off in neat rows from where they stood, creating a labyrinth of rooms, all visible through the glass-like walls. He led her down a row that housed eight smaller isolation rooms, four on each side of the corridor. Rathburn stopped at the fourth room on the left. Two women and a man in jumpsuits were gathered around a chest-high table, examining a liquefied goo in a cylindrical container.

Rathburn touched the comm panel outside the closed door. "That looks promising."

One of the women glanced up. Her gaze flicked briefly to Nat before she responded. "Very promising. We've increased the compound's efficiency by two hundred percent."

"Excellent. Any unexpected challenges?"

"Not yet. But the next phase will push the limits."

"Keep me posted." Rathburn moved on to the next room in the row.

Nat's curiosity got the best of her. "What's in the slush?"

"An enzyme accelerator for decomposition of organic material."

A lot of words, very little explanation. "Which does what, exactly?"

"When perfected, it will provide space stations and ships with a quick and efficient way to convert organic waste into a nutrient-rich product that can be repurposed to increase sustainability."

"Huh." She figured that was another term for fertilizer, but having never cared for a plant—decorative or edible—that was just a guess.

Rathburn stopped at each of the occupied rooms, checking in with the science teams. Some of the items they were working on Nat recognized, including a spacesuit that looked like a second skin, and a prototype for a navigation display. She itched to get a closer look at that one, but Rathburn didn't offer to take her inside.

"Most of these projects are contracted for the Galactic Fleet," he explained as they left the testing facilities and moved to a series of offices. "In another year or two, all of these designs should be in active service."

He was working with the Galactic Fleet? Her perception of his operation did a one-hundred-eighty. She'd thought of him as a rogue, functioning outside the law. But if most of his work was connected with the official peacekeeping branch of the central government, he'd have their muscle to back him up. Maybe that's why he didn't feel the least bit concerned about detaining ships and crews. The Fleet might even be encouraging him to keep an eye out for smugglers and thieves. Like her.

Except she hadn't been doing anything illicit on this job. Probably. She'd made an honest deal to transport Patel and her cargo. True, she hadn't asked for details on what the cargo contained. If it turned out Patel had stolen items that legally belonged to Rathburn, that wasn't her fault, was it?

The logic of that statement didn't prevent a trickle of unease from sliding along her spine.

The offices they passed as they continued along the corridor were also constructed from the glass-like material, with women and men bent over interactive design boards built into tabletops, or circling 3D projection models suspended in midair. Most of them were so engrossed in their projects they didn't even notice when she and Rathburn paused to watch. He didn't interrupt them, apparently content to observe their interactions at a distance before moving on.

"How many projects do you have in development?" *And how much is the Fleet paying you?*

"Thirty-four active. Another forty-two in the research phase."

"All for the Fleet?"

"Not all. I have contracts with businesses and individuals as well." He led her through a series of translucent doors, each thicker than the one before, all of which parted as he approached. They ended at a solid metal door built into the bulkhead. This one had an ID scanner even more sophisticated than the ones she'd seen so far.

For the first time, the door didn't open as they approached. Instead, Rathburn stood in front of the scanner, which took a good thirty seconds to verify his identity and cycle the lock on the door. The heavy mechanism within sounded like the kind of stalwart security used for bank vaults or exterior airlocks. Or a Medieval fortress.

The door rose from the deck like a portcullis rather than opening to the side, reinforcing the impression of a castle drawbridge. She almost expected to see a moat on the far side. Instead, the opening revealed an enclosed space barely large enough to fit four people standing shoulder to shoulder.

Rathburn stepped inside first.

She followed, uncomfortably aware of the narrow confines as the door slid down and the security system rumbled to life, sealing them in. The walls weren't translucent, either. It was like standing in a shipping crate. She didn't usually have any problem with tight spaces—she was a pilot, after all—but she hadn't planned to get this up close and personal with Rathburn. She managed to keep from touching him, but only by remaining perfectly still.

Nothing else moved, either. If this was a lift, they weren't going anywhere. Yet. She didn't see any sign of a control panel, either.

Rathburn was a lot taller than she was, so she had to tilt her head back to meet his gaze. "Why aren't we moving?"

His mouth curved at the corners. "This isn't a lift. It's an antechamber. The security requires a one minute wait time in between closing the outer security door and opening the interior door."

*Oh.* She glanced at the wall opposite the door where they'd entered. It looked exactly the same as the other three walls. If she hadn't been paying attention, it would have been easy to get disoriented in here. Also part of the security plan, no doubt. "What's inside?"

His smile widened. "Patience."

Easy for him to say. He knew what to expect.

And he was in complete control of the situation. With each breath, she became more aware of how her willingness to follow him had made her vulnerable. She couldn't get out of this tiny cell without him. And no one else could get in. If he chose to, he could overpower her. She'd put up a fight of course, but without her bag of tricks, she'd probably lose. Tnaryt and Isin had both driven that point home.

She looked away before he could see that realization in her eyes. She didn't want to give him any ideas. And she certainly didn't want him to sense her unease.

She focused on calming her heartbeat.

"You're not claustrophobic, are you?"

She shook her head. "No."

"Then is it me?"

She gave him a sidelong glance. "What do you mean?"

Lines creased his forehead. "You seem uncomfortable."

Well, damn. He was more observant than most people. She'd need to remember that. "I'm just not big on surprises." That was the truth. In her experience, surprises brought pain.

The frown lines smoothed out as the look in his blue eyes warmed. "It's all right. You can trust me."

Ah, but that was the sticking point, wasn't it? She could count on one hand the number of people she truly trusted, and he wasn't on the list. But she could play the game. She allowed her mouth to relax into a smile. "Okay."

The muscles around his eyes tightened a fraction, like he didn't quite believe her sincerity. Smart man.

A deep rumble and clank drew her attention as the security mechanism lifted the far door, revealing a brightly lit foyer ten times the size of the box they'd been standing in.

She stepped out into the space with an internal sigh of relief. No sign of the glass walls here. Instead, a bulkhead that looked like it could withstand a cannon blast surrounded her on three sides, with a single door of similar heft inset to her left.

Rathburn moved in front of the ID scanner to the right of the door. This one took even longer to process than the one outside the antechamber, giving her plenty of time to inspect her surroundings. Not that there was anything to see. Grey walls that blended into the grey deck and ceiling. No markings, no color or artwork, nothing that gave a clue as to what lay behind the door.

A soft chime preceded the gentle glide of the door as it retracted, sliding into the deck like it was being swallowed by quicksand.

Rathburn glanced over his shoulder and motioned to the opening. "Nat, I'd like to introduce you to A.L.E.C."

# *Fifteen*

Whatever Nat had been expecting, it didn't match what she discovered when she stepped through the opening.

The expansive room was pristine, so far beyond clean that it seemed likely hers were the first boots to set foot on the deck. Every console and monitor gleamed, and a faint metallic odor, the one she associated with new components, surrounded her.

She pivoted in a slow circle, taking in the various workstations, the neatly aligned chairs, the darkened screens. Nobody was in the room. In fact, the longer she stood there, the more certain she became that the space had never been used.

Rathburn stood just inside the doorway, watching her expectantly.

For what? She frowned. "What is this place? Who's Alec?"

"This is Dr. Patel's lab. For the past four years, she spent most of her waking hours here."

Nat scrutinized the room again. One question answered. Well, not really. She could certainly believe Patel had worked on this ship. But there was no way she or anyone else had spent time in this particular lab.

"I know what you're thinking."

She glanced at Rathburn.

"And you're right." He sighed. "Everything is new. I had to completely rebuild the lab after Dr. Patel destroyed it."

"Destroyed it? Why?" And how? Patel was a pain in the ass, but she didn't seem the type to take out her frustrations on valuable scientific equipment.

"I can only assume to insure I wouldn't be able to recreate her work with A.L.E.C., though to be honest, the very idea is ludicrous. No matter how much I want to, I can't. Dr. Patel's concepts are like the master works of a gifted painter or sculptor. Part of her genius is inherent. Another scientist might mimic her style, but they'd never achieve her results."

"Who's Alec? Her assistant?"

"Her creation."

*Her creation?* "What kind of creation?"

"A new lifeform. She didn't mention him?"

She caught herself a millisecond before she opened her mouth, but Rathburn's sharp look told her that slight hesitation had given away more than she'd intended. She wasn't supposed to know anything about Patel. "I told you, I've never met Dr. Patel."

"Indeed." He held her gaze.

She stared right back. "Where's Alec now?"

"I was hoping you could tell me."

"You don't know?"

"No."

"I thought you said he was on this ship."

"I said I wanted to introduce you. This is where he was born."

So Patel had created a new lifeform with Rathburn's help. Interesting. After seeing the experiments in his science labs, her mind conjured a hundred possible images. No wonder Patel had been so cagey. But her actions had caught Nat in the middle of an epic custody battle. Wonderful.

"It's very important that I find Dr. Patel. And A.L.E.C."

*I'll bet.* "She took him with her?"

"No. Her assistant smuggled him off the ship the same day Dr. Patel disappeared."

Ah-ha. So all the cloak and dagger Patel had been putting them through must have been an elaborate plan to reunite with her assistant. The mysterious cube she'd sent Isin to obtain probably contained information for making that happen. "Where's her assistant now?" She wouldn't mind meeting him. Sneaking off this ship undetected would have been quite a feat. She could use some tips.

The corner of Rathburn's left eye twitched. "We've been looking for him, too."

A miniscule tell, the first she'd seen. He was lying, or at the very least, stretching the truth.

Had he already found the assistant? If that was the case, clearly Alec hadn't been with him. "So why tell me?"

"I was hoping having more details might jog your memory." Rathburn touched his forearm and an image appeared on the nearest monitor. The man staring back at her had a warm smile and was in his late thirties or early forties with greying blond hair. "This is her assistant, Dr. Gavin Lindberg."

Nat dutifully studied the image, but nothing about the man was remotely familiar. "Sorry. Never seen him before."

"You're certain?"

"Absolutely."

"I see." But rather than sounding upset, Rathburn seemed pleased.

What kind of game was he playing?

He added an image of Patel to the monitor, the one he'd shown her the previous day. "Dr. Patel has the same kind of genius as my sister." He stepped closer, his gaze fixed on the picture. "But like many geniuses, she pays a price for her talents."

Okay, she'd bite. "What kind of price?"

Rathburn glanced at her. "She suffers from aberrant behavior."

Now *that* she totally believed. Her behavior while onboard *Phoenix* had certainly been bizarre. "What kind of behavior?"

"In her case, it manifests as extreme paranoia. It was one of the reasons she sought me out in the first place. She was terrified the Galactic Council would learn about her research and lock her up. This ship provided a safe haven."

"Wait a minute. Why would the GC lock her up?" Nat wasn't a fan of the Galactic Council, but she'd never heard of them hunting down scientists.

Rathburn gave her a wistful smile. "As I said, she suffers from paranoia."

"So her fears were unfounded?"

He returned his gaze to the image. "Her work is revolutionary. The Council will understand that. Eventually."

Interesting answer. Whatever Patel was working on, it wasn't totally benign. Maybe she had good reason to fear the GC. "But you have contracts with the Fleet. Why would she have considered this ship safe? I'd think she'd want to stay far away from anyone with ties to the Council." Which was probably one of the reasons she'd chosen Nat as her transport pilot. Smugglers had no love for the GC's rules and regulations.

He gave her a pointed look. "The Council doesn't interfere with my affairs. Not if they want the services I can provide. While she was working on this ship, her research was invisible to everyone but me."

Spoken with pride. His ego was showing again. Patel had a similar superiority complex. No wonder they'd clashed. "If that's true, why did she leave?"

That took some of the wind out of his sails. "I made a mistake." Thin lines traced across his forehead. "I should have seen it coming, dealt with it before it became a problem. But I misjudged the situation."

Now they were getting somewhere. "What happened?"

He sighed. "Her paranoia resurfaced. But this time, without the specter of the Council looming over her shoulder, she attached her fears to me. I became her new target." He spread his arms wide. "She's the one who insisted on the elaborate security to access this lab. She designed it, and oversaw the installation. And it was that security that insured we couldn't get in to stop the destruction when the explosives detonated."

*Patel had blown up the lab?* Huh. The woman was full of surprises. "Did anyone get hurt?"

"No. Only Dr. Patel, Dr. Lindberg, and I had access to this lab, and they were both off the ship at the time. I don't know if I was just lucky, or if she'd set it to go off when the lab was empty. I'd like to believe it was the latter."

He was telling her the truth, at least as he saw it. But she'd spotted some additional holes in his story. And there was the question of how Alec fit into Patel's paranoia. Patel was a handful—no argument there—but was she paranoid enough to conjure villains out of shadows, plot against the man who was helping her, and create an elaborate scheme to escape and destroy her own lab in the process?

An image of the convoluted flight plan they'd followed since leaving Gallows Edge surfaced in Nat's mind.

Maybe she was.

But what would prompt such behavior? She'd need some kind of trigger, wouldn't she? One possibility came to mind. "You said Alec was a new lifeform. Was she afraid you'd harm him somehow?"

His jaw firmed. "I'd never do anything to hurt him."

Not what she'd asked. "But did *she* think you might?"

His brows drew down. "I hadn't considered that. Perhaps. Her paranoia made her irrational."

His words struck a wrong note. Not that he was lying, exactly, but the picture he was painting didn't match up with Nat's experiences with Patel. The woman was many things, but irrational? Never. They'd disagreed on almost everything, but Patel had always had a clear motivation behind her actions. Which made her predictable, not irrational.

And made Nat question the reliability of the account she was being given.

"I have a favor to ask."

She met Rathburn's gaze, keeping her expression neutral. "Oh?"

"I'd like your help in finding them."

Was he serious? "My help? Why would I help you?" Besides the fact that in exchange for helping him track down Patel, she could extricate herself from this mess and get back to her ship.

His mouth curved in a smile. "Because I like you, Nat. And I think you like me, too." The skin at the corners of his eyes crinkled. "Even if you are lying to me about Dr. Patel."

He was calling her a liar while asking for her help? Cheeky. She arched one brow. "Am I?" She knew her expression conveyed absolute sincerity, because she'd spent hours practicing in a mirror. A necessary skill for a professional thief.

A soft chuckle slipped past his lips. "Oh, certainly."

She folded her hands, prepared to give a rebuttal, but he stopped her with a raised palm.

"Please, don't deny it. I'm not passing judgment." A hint of laughter sparked in his blue eyes. "You're an honorable woman. I respect your desire to protect Dr. Patel. I would, too, in your position."

"Is that so?"

"Absolutely. You view me as a potential threat. I'll simply have to convince you I'm not."

She gave him a close-mouthed smile. "It might help your credibility if I wasn't your prisoner."

He laughed. Actually *laughed.*

Not the reaction she'd expected. This man kept unsettling her. "You find my imprisonment amusing?"

"Oh, no, I don't." He fought to hide his grin. "But I do find it amusing that you believe you're my prisoner."

She frowned. "Of course I am."

That earned her another chuckle. "No, my dear lady, you are not."

"Then let me go!"

He sobered at that, his posture going from casual to businesslike in a heartbeat. "You may go whenever you wish. However–" He tilted his head and fixed her with a pointed look. "Correct me if I'm wrong, but your shuttle doesn't have interstellar capability. And the engines on *Vengeance* aren't operational. Where, exactly, would you go?"

He had her there. This system didn't even have habitable planets or moons. Unless she contacted Isin to come get her, she was stuck, at least until *Vengeance* was repaired. And when Isin arrived, she'd be handing Rathburn more leverage.

He held out his hands, palms up. "I'm sorry if I've given you the wrong impression. But until I've dealt with Kerr and the repairs, providing you with comfortable accommodations during your stay is the best I can do."

He was making too much sense. It got her ruff up. "If I'm a guest, then why do I have an armed escort everywhere I go?"

His brows lifted. "If you had a guest on your ship while you were transporting valuable cargo, would you give them complete access? Allow them to wander anywhere they pleased?"

Dammit. Talking to him was like walking a maze blindfolded. She kept bumping into walls. "No, I wouldn't."

"Then you can understand that the ship's security is designed to protect those who live and work here. I like you, and enjoy your company, but I don't know you well enough to place the safety of everyone onboard in your hands."

There he went again, making logical arguments that she couldn't refute. It was maddening.

He took a step closer. "Please believe that I would never hold you against your will."

She swallowed. The sincerity in his voice and the intensity in his eyes packed a punch that made her stomach knot. She stepped back, putting space between them again.

He sighed. "I'm right, aren't I?"

"About what?"

"You view me as a threat."

"I view everyone I don't know as a threat."

He gazed at her for several moments, the intensity fading from his eyes. "What can I do to convince you my intentions are honorable?"

"For starters, you can take me to my shuttle."

# *Sixteen*

Nat released the breath she'd been holding as she stepped into the shuttle bay and caught sight of *Gypsy*. In the back of her mind, she'd seriously considered the possibility that Rathburn's minions might have disassembled her beloved friend while searching for clues about Patel's whereabouts. Seeing her sitting where she'd left her, solidly in one piece, eased some of the tension from her shoulders.

The back hatch lay open to the deck. She halted at the bottom of the ramp and gave Rathburn a baleful look. "Are your guards still *inspecting* my shuttle?" She didn't want to encounter anyone inside.

He shook his head. "Not anymore."

"So glad to hear it." Stalking up the ramp, she took a cursory glance around the storage area but paused for a closer look at the compact living space. Everything seemed as neat and tidy as when she'd left. At least Rathburn's people hadn't tossed everything on the deck during their search.

The smuggling compartment where she'd stashed her pistol and bag of tricks sat directly beneath her boots. If Rathburn hadn't been right behind her, she would have been tempted to retrieve them. As it was, she continued to the cockpit and slid into the pilot's seat.

"Going somewhere?" Rathburn lounged against the bulkhead behind the co-pilot's chair as Nat started *Gypsy*'s warm-up sequence.

*I wish.* She wanted nothing more than to fire up *Gypsy*'s engines and take off into the black. But as Rathburn had pointed out, she had nowhere to go. And besides, she'd never leave Pete behind. "Checking if her systems are back online." Thankfully, the console indicated systems were functioning normally. Whatever Rathburn's energy weapon had done to disable them, the effect seemed to have been temporary. "And making sure no one adjusted my seat." She didn't want to think of what else the guards had done while onboard.

"I gave strict orders to leave everything exactly as they found it."

*How reassuring.* "Forgive me if that's small consolation after having strangers seize control of my shuttle." Her words came out harsher than she'd intended, but she wasn't about to apologize. The comforts of his ship had deflected her ire, but now that she was back on *Gypsy*, her indignation roared to life.

"You're angry."

She spun in her chair and glared at him. "Damn right I'm angry! How would you feel if someone ransacked your ship?"

His jaw clenched. "Nothing was damaged."

"That's not the point! You seized my shuttle. Threatened me if I didn't comply. If someone did that to you, you'd be furious."

He folded his arms, his brows drawing down as he stared at her. "You're right." He blew out a breath. "I'd want their head on a platter."

At least they agreed on that.

He pushed away from the bulkhead and dropped into the co-pilot's seat, facing her. "Whatever you may think of me, please believe that I am truly sorry for any distress I've caused you."

She grunted. Easy for him to say.

"Is there any way I can make it up to you?"

Now *there* was an intriguing idea. "You can tell me how that energy beam of yours works."

His eyes narrowed. "That's the one thing I can't do."

"Can't or won't?"

"Can't. I'm under contract."

"With the Fleet?"

"I can't say."

And unfortunately for her, he seemed to be telling the truth. "Then how do you suggest you make it up to me?"

He spread his arms wide and glanced around the cockpit. "Surely there are things you need. Components. Supplies. Items I can provide."

Hmm. Not a bad idea. The man seemed to have unlimited resources. Why not take this opportunity to pick his pocket? "My med supplies are low." Which was why she'd had to borrow supplies from *Vengeance*'s infirmary before she and Pete had set out to find Isin. Medical supplies hadn't been included in the haul from Gallows Edge, and many of the supplies on *Phoenix* had been compromised during the crash and resulting entombment.

"Provide me with a list and I'll see that you're fully restocked."

Oh, she'd provide him with a list all right. Padded enough to restock *Gypsy*, *Phoenix*, and *Vengeance*. "How about engine parts?"

The corners of his mouth lifted. "What do you need?"

*Gypsy* was in pretty good shape, but *Phoenix* could certainly use replacement parts. And maybe some upgrades while they were at it. Pete would be delighted. "I'll talk to Pete and come up with a list of those, too."

His brows rose a fraction. "All right."

*What else?* "And a case of herbs and spices." Marlin loved fresh food and herbs. Presenting him with a gift might mitigate some of the pain and suffering their recent adventures had put him through. Based on what Rathburn had served her so far, his galley had plenty to spare.

A flash of humor returned to Rathburn's blue eyes. "I see I'll have to be more careful with open-ended offers when negotiating with you."

She'd never been much of a negotiator until she'd faced off against Isin regarding *Phoenix*. Their ongoing battle had given her quite a bit of practice lately. But she wasn't convinced she had the skill to negotiate her way back onto her ship. Rathburn's comments aside, she still felt like his prisoner.

Only time would tell whether she was right.

# Seventeen

"Are you insane?" Patel stared at Isin like he was five cards short of a full deck. "I'm not going anywhere near Rathburn's ship."

Isin stared her down. "You don't have a choice."

Her lips thinned and her chin lifted. "Of course I do! I paid you *very well* to keep us safe from Rathburn." Her gaze darted to where Alec's image hovered above the desk in Itorye's cabin. "We are *not* going back there."

Isin flicked away her objection. "You paid me to transport you and your cargo." He ignored Alec's frown. "You said nothing about Rathburn."

"Why else would I hire a *mercenary?* We needed protection. It was understood."

"Not by me." He leaned against the bulkhead. "If you'd been honest about Alec, we never would have taken this job."

Patel glanced at the boy, but he was watching Isin, not her. She stepped between the two, shielding him from view. "So now you're going to just hand us over to him?"

"That's right."

"Why?"

"Because your presence has cost me my pilot, my engineer, and my ship. I want them back."

Fractures appeared in Patel's armor of indignation. "You can't do this."

"Yes, I can. And believe me, it's the kinder option. If my crew learns about Alec, you'll get a good view of the ship's exterior."

Her eyes rounded. "They wouldn't dare."

He might have felt some sympathy if she hadn't brought this on herself. "Oh, I assure you, they would. Mercenaries care about profit and the freedom to spend it. Morality doesn't factor in."

"Then I'll pay them more!" Desperation crept into her voice. "Double. Triple!"

"They'd take the money and then dump you into space anyway."

His matter-of-fact tone must have gotten through. She took a step back. "Then I'll pay you and Itorye. Whatever it takes. You still have the *Dagger*. We can leave *Phoenix* and you can drop Alec and me at the nearest outpost or space station. Doesn't matter where. And you'll never see us again."

Heat flared at his temples. "That doesn't solve my problem, now does it?"

"Yes, it will. If you give us a few days head start, then you can tell Rathburn—"

"A few days?" He stalked forward. "What makes you think I'll leave Natasha on that ship one second longer than I have to?"

"I—"

He wasn't finished. "And with you gone, what's to stop him from taking control of *this* ship?" His muscles strained from the effort of keeping his arms at his sides. He wanted to grab her and shake her. "That beam could disable us in seconds." Not that she'd care. She'd be long gone and—

"Captain Isin?"

Isin glared at Alec's image over Patel's shoulder. "What?"

"It's my fault."

That brought him up short. "Your fault?" What was the boy talking about? "What's your fault?"

"Mr. Rathburn. It's my fault he's come after us. He wants—"

Patel spun, raising a hand to silence him. "No, Alec, that's not tr—"

"Yes it is, Mom." The boy's gaze didn't waver. "You think I don't know, but I do."

Alec's words seemed to rattle her more than anything Isin had said. A tremor worked its way through her body, and her voice shook. "You can't know."

"I know about his plan."

Patel shook her head. Once the motion started, she couldn't seem to stop it. "No. No, that's not possible. I made sure you—"

"You tried to protect me. But I wanted to protect you, too."

"Protect me?" It seemed like a foreign concept to her.

"You were acting so strange before you left *Cerberus*, especially around Mr. Rathburn. I got worried. So I accessed the ship's files and copied them to my matrix."

Patel reached a hand out to the bulkhead to steady herself. "Oh, Alec. No."

Isin echoed that sentiment. Alec had just admitted to stealing. His very existence was unsettling enough, without adding thievery to his list of skills.

The boy opened his arms in supplication. "I know you said—"

"*Never!* Never to access the main computer. I had forbidden it, Alec! But you—" Her voice cracked. She pressed a hand to her mouth, her breath shuddering in and out. "How could you disobey me?"

To his credit, the boy didn't look away. He took the hit on the chin, even though his eyes were doing a fair approximation of tearing up. "I'm sorry, Mom."

Isin cleared his throat to get their attention. Patel glanced at him with contempt, but Alec looked embarrassed.

He ignored her, focusing on the boy. "What does Rathburn have planned for you, Alec?"

Alec glanced at Patel, silently asking permission.

She stared at him for several long moments, her hands on her hips, the muscles of her jaw working. When she finally spoke, her voice came out hollow. "Tell him."

Alec faced Isin. "He wants to connect me to the Interstellar Communications System."

"The ICS?" He glanced between Alec and Patel in confusion. He'd anticipated a doomsday weapon, or some nefarious assassination plot. The ICS was benign. It had originally been set up for use by the Galactic Fleet, but the system had been expanded to allow free communication between star systems, with access granted to anyone who set up an account. "So? What's so terrible about connecting you to—"

"He wants me to *control* it."

The silence in the room reverberated like a death knell.

*Oh.*

# *Eighteen*

Isin stared at Alec as apocalyptic visions filled his mind's eye.

In the vast reaches of interstellar space, the person who controlled the lines of communication could also control the people who relied on it.

At first, the general population might view the loss of access to the ICS as a minor inconvenience, but the repercussions would flow outward like ripples on a pond. The longer the system was down, the worse things would get. Supply and trade shipments would stall. Settlements, outposts, and space stations wouldn't have a way to send distress calls in case of an environmental emergency or Setarip attack. Hell, the Galactic Fleet's private comm system would be wiped out. Rathburn could force Alec to block all Fleet communications.

And then what? The entire Fleet could be rendered useless in a heartbeat. With no way to confirm orders or coordinate missions, the ships would have to return to Earth, leaving all the other systems vulnerable and unprotected. Ripe pickings for whatever forces Rathburn planned to unleash. With one move, he could hold the majority of humanity hostage. All he needed was Alec. And Patel.

Which put Isin exactly where he didn't want to be—standing between Rathburn and his goal.

To rescue Natasha and reclaim his ship, he'd have to turn Patel and Alec over. But if he made that choice, he could change the course of humanity's future. Was that a trade he was willing to make?

He owed Natasha his life. She'd already sacrificed herself for him, twice. He wouldn't—*couldn't*—allow it to happen again.

He swallowed around the constriction in his throat. *Think, El. Think!*

"Captain?"

Isin met Alec's gaze.

"Will you help us?"

There had to be an alternative. The boy had a moral compass. He understood that what Rathburn wanted him to do was wrong. But he also had a strong emotional tie to Patel. In his mind, she was his mother, biology be damned.

If Rathburn got ahold of them, he would use Alec's emotions against him. All he'd have to do was threaten Patel, and Alec would give in. He could see it in the boy's eyes. That's why she'd left Rathburn's ship and entrusted Alec to her assistant. And why she'd been so adamant about not being on the same ship with Alec while they traveled to Osiris.

So much for that plan.

Isin drew in a slow breath. "I don't know." Even if he found a solution for Rathburn, he still had to deal with his crew. They'd space Patel in a heartbeat if they found out about Alec. "I'll think about it."

Without waiting for a response, he left the cabin, nodding to Fleur as he passed. Not all of his crew would mutiny. Avril and Fleur were loyal, which is why they'd been chosen for guard duty. But other than his command crew, the rest were mercenary to the core. It was one of the reasons he couldn't give *Phoenix* to Natasha, either. Even if he wanted to.

Which he didn't. He wanted her with him. Permanently.

The direction of his thoughts carried him down the passageway to the captain's cabin.

Natasha's cabin.

She'd claimed the space shortly before she'd added red paint to the outside of *Phoenix*'s gold-hued hull. He hadn't fought her on it, because he'd always planned for her to be the ship's captain. The only difference was, she considered herself the ship's owner, too. He didn't.

She'd chaffed at the idea of working for him, even though it was better for both of them. She could fly the ship she loved, and he could protect her from whatever the universe threw at them.

*Yeah, you've done a bang-up job of that.*

He used his bypass code to override the security lock on the door. As soon as he stepped through and the door closed behind him, he leaned against it, resting the back of his head on the cool metal and closing his eyes.

How had this happened? Natasha was a captive. Again. Because of him. A pawn in a high stakes game, dealing with a sociopath who wanted to control the known galaxy. If she hadn't already been cursing the day they'd met, she certainly would be now.

He opened his eyes and pushed away from the door. The automatic lighting gave the room a soft glow. The last time he'd been in this cabin, he'd been checking for mummified bodies of the former crew. The deck had been dotted with debris tossed from the shelves during the crash.

He walked past the narrow opening to the compact bathroom and built-in wardrobe to his left, and into the main room. It was spotless now. Her bunk sat against the bulkhead to his left, the sheets tucked under with military precision.

The railed shelf above sat empty, as did the utilitarian desk in front of him beside the exterior porthole.

No sign of Natasha's presence showed anywhere. And why would it? She wasn't the type to collect souvenirs, and she'd always stored anything of value she owed on *Gypsy*. Now Rathburn had control of the shuttle, too.

His stomach clenched and he shook his head. What had he expected? That he'd find the answer to his problems here? It wasn't like Natasha was going to magically appear to counsel him. He couldn't bridge the interstellar void. But he still wanted her—needed her—by his side.

Unfortunately, the room was as empty as the echo chamber in his chest.

Turning, he took one step toward the door. And froze, his gaze locked onto the interior bulkhead.

His breath hitched as a vise clamped down on his lungs.

From deck to ceiling, painted in vivid golds and reds, a mythical phoenix rose from a bed of smoldering ash. The incredibly intricate design portrayed the bird with wings spread and mouth open in a cry of triumph.

An earthy epithet slid from his lips. She'd personalized the room after all.

He took a step forward, then another, pulled like a magnet across the deck, stopping only when he was eye to eye with the beast. This close, he could see the places where holes in the bulkhead had been filled and sealed before being painted over. She'd removed something—most likely additional shelving—to make room for the mural.

He stared at the image—the blending of colors and the sense of movement in the graceful strokes. It held him hypnotized, obliterating all conscious thought. The careful lines, the attention to detail, the emotional undercurrent.

Natasha's essence reached out to him in every swirl and eddy.

But it was the expression on the phoenix's face that shoved a dagger tip into his chest and twisted. *Joy.* The euphoric joy of flight, of freedom regained after a painful descent into an ashen grave.

*Natasha.*

He'd wanted a connection, and the universe had just delivered a sharp jab to his solar plexus. This was what he was fighting for. What he was *living* for. He had to set her free. No matter the cost.

But turning Patel and Alec over to Rathburn wasn't the solution. Even if Rathburn made the exchange, Natasha would be trapped in whatever new galactic order Rathburn chose to create. He couldn't allow that to happen. Which left him with one option.

Find a way to free Natasha and take down Rathburn at the same time.

# Nineteen

The cacophony of voices drifting out of the dining room the following afternoon told Isin the majority of the crew had already gathered for the midday meal.

He spotted the diminutive figure of Brooks winding between the round tables, delivering plates of food to the crew. A quick headcount confirmed everyone was present with the exception of Avril, who was guarding Patel, and Itorye, who was at the helm on the bridge.

Kenji lounged against the bulkhead near the doorway leading to the galley. His gaze tracked Brooks, his expression shifting like clouds over the sun as he monitored how the crew treated the skittish cook. When Buggy grabbed the plate out of Brooks' hands with a snarl, Kenji's eyes narrowed. He took two steps toward the table, drawing Buggy's attention.

The mercenary's scowl quickly disappeared when he caught sight of the look in Kenji's eyes. He gave Brooks a quick nod, the closest thing to a thank you the man had ever learned, then stared down at his plate as he shoveled a forkful of food into his mouth. Dot and Saddle, his two dining companions, assumed the same hunched posture, eating in silence.

Brooks glanced at Kenji. A tiny smile flickered between them before he returned to his serving duties.

Kenji backed up against the bulkhead and resumed his post.

The noise level dropped as the crew caught sight of Isin crossing the room to join Kenji. Most looked away or resumed eating, but not before he picked up on the tension permeating the room. The crew was not happy.

Jake sat with Fleur and Shorty. He gave Isin a wave before continuing his conversation. Shash and Byrd sat together, along with Pine and Ranger, the two male members of her engineering crew. When Isin met her gaze, she rested her chin on her closed fist and batted her eyelashes at him.

If Natasha had done that, he might have smiled. Coming from Shash, it made his skin itch. The woman refused to take no for an answer.

He stopped next to Kenji. "Have you eaten?"

Kenji nodded. "Kept the little man company in the galley."

At one time, Kenji's mere presence would have sent Brooks into apoplectic fits. Now, they seemed to genuinely enjoy spending time together.

"Good. Change of plans. I'll explain later, but for now, follow my lead."

"You got it."

Isin stepped forward. "I have new duty assignments for everyone. Break time is over. We're retaking *Vengeance*."

That got a grumble that was three-quarters approval, one-quarter skepticism.

"Whadda 'bout that hulk of a ship standin' guard?" Buggy's lip curled as he swept a hand to encompass the room. "This boat can't fight that thing."

More grumbles.

Isin held Buggy's gaze until the mercenary looked away. "*Phoenix* isn't a sledgehammer like *Vengeance*, but she knows how to fight." *Just like her captain.* "We won't be waging a war of strength."

"Then what chance do we have?" Dot looked as unhappy as Buggy.

And this was the problem with hiring crew solely for their hand-to-hand combat skills. They solved every problem with their guns or their fists.

But Isin knew how to relate to them on that level, too. He flattened his palms on the surface of the table across from Dot and leaned in, allowing a feral smile to spread across his face. "Would you prefer I leave you here?"

Her eyes widened, the pupils dilating. Message received. "No."

"Good. Then listen up." He faced the group. "Fleur, Shorty, and Saddle will work with Kenji on enhancing our weapons. We need to extend the effective range and accuracy. Willow, Pine, and Ranger are with Shash. I want you to coax every bit of energy you can from the engines and reinforce the shields."

Shash's flirtatious attitude vanished, replaced with the cool focus of an engineer on a mission.

"Faraway, Dot, and Buggy, you'll work with Summer, setting up defenses against a boarding party. Byrd, you'll be with me."

His pilot looked less than thrilled with his assignment, but he nodded.

"You have fifteen minutes to finish your meals." His gaze settled on Jake, the one person he hadn't named. "Jake." He inclined his head toward the galley.

Jake rose and followed him through the doorway. "What's my task?"

Isin leaned against the counter. "That tracking device you removed from Patel. Is the container it's in portable?"

Jake frowned. "That would depend. Right now it's hooked into the infirmary's power system. I'd have to find a portable power source capable of maintaining the container's settings. Why?"

"I want to—" Isin glanced at the door as it opened.

Brooks pushed the serving cart inside. He stopped in his tracks when he spotted them. "Sorry."

He looked like he was going to back up, but Isin waved him forward. "It's fine."

He glanced between Isin and Jake. "Is there... anything you would like me to do?"

"Like what?"

He shrugged. "I don't know. You gave everyone else a task."

He wanted more work? "Keeping the crew fed isn't a big enough job?"

Another shrug. "I just want to help Nat and Pete."

Ah. Now he understood. "I don't have anything right now."

His shoulders drooped.

"But that will change." He didn't know how exactly, since Brooks wasn't good in a fight, but Nat and Stevens were his friends. He deserved an opportunity to help them. "I'll let you know when I need you."

That brought his head up. "Good." He said it with a lot more conviction than Isin was used to. Maybe hanging out with Kenji was having a stronger effect on his attitude than anyone realized. "I'll do anything. I want to get them back."

"So do I." But he also had to keep Patel and Alec out of Rathburn's clutches. Accomplishing both wouldn't be a simple feat. "They'll be back onboard before you know it. I promise." He said it for his own benefit as much as for Brooks.

Brooks held his gaze. "Yeah. Good." He pushed the cart over to the dishwasher and began loading the dirty dishes.

Isin returned his attention to Jake. "Keep me posted on your progress."

"Can I assume I'm creating a decoy to divert attention from Dr. Patel's real location?"

"That's correct. With the ability to move the tracking device around the ship or even off the ship, we'll be able to hide Patel in plain sight."

# *Twenty*

"Orlov!"

Natasha jolted awake like she'd been struck by lightning, rolling into a crouch, every muscle tensed in readiness. She blinked rapidly to clear her vision as she scanned the darkened bedroom.

The artificial starfield projected on the ceiling created unfamiliar shadows that threatened from every corner and archway. She sank closer to the mattress, listening intently. Nothing. At least nothing she could detect.

She flexed her fingers. Thanks to Rathburn, she couldn't reach for her trusty pistol. If someone had broken into her room, she'd be stuck defending herself with a pillow.

The voice came again. "Orlov!"

The comm panel by the doorway. She slid off the bed and crept toward the door.

"Orlov! Wake up!" The words snapped like the crack of a whip. But she didn't recognize the deep male voice. It certainly wasn't Pete. Or Rathburn. Who else would be contacting her on the ship's comm?

One way to find out. She reached out and tapped the panel. "I'm awake."

"Good. I was beginning to worry."

"*You* were beginning to worry?" She was the one with her heart pounding like a jackrabbit. "Who is this?"

"It's Sweep."

*Sweep?* Her brain stalled for a three count. Impossible. Sweep was dead. He'd been killed in an explosion on Kerr's ship.

"Orlov? Did you hear me?"

"Yeah." She'd only heard Sweep's voice a few times over the comm. She'd never met him in person. This man's voice sounded similar, but that didn't mean anything. "Where are you?"

"Hiding on *Vengeance.*"

A chill passed over her skin, raising goosebumps. She could think of one person who might try to convince her Sweep was on *Vengeance*–Kerr. The man had made it clear his hostility toward Isin now included her. If he could find a way to trick her, to lead her onto the ship so he could stage an unfortunate accident, he'd take it.

And Kerr knew Sweep's voice. They had history.

She snagged her duster from the chair beside her bed and slipped it on. She didn't want to be having this conversation while wearing only pajamas. "How did you know I was here?"

"I saw you come onboard with Rathburn."

"But how did you know I was *here?* In this room?"

"Tracking people down is part of my job." He said it like the answer was obvious.

Which it would be if he were actually Sweep. That brought up another point. How would Kerr know which room she was in? And how would he have bypassed the ship's security? Rathburn would have given him the same access she had—none.

Another possibility made her stiffen. Maybe Rathburn was up to something. Had he accessed *Vengeance*'s crew records in an attempt to trick her into revealing information about Patel?

Either way, she didn't want to be having this conversation. "We really shouldn't be talking over this comm. Rathburn's people are probably listening."

"No, they're not. I'm routing this along one of the internal lines during a maintenance cycle. It won't register in the system for another forty-three seconds."

"How did you get through Rathburn's security?"

"That's not important. Right now I need you to come to *Vengeance* so we can talk."

Yep. She was being set up. "I'm confined to quarters."

"You're a resourceful woman. Find a way."

"And if I don't?"

"Then neither of us will escape Rathburn's snare."

She stared at the comm. He couldn't have baited the trap with a better morsel.

"The maintenance cycle is ending. I have to go. Come to *Vengeance.* Engine room."

The comm clicked off.

# *Twenty-One*

Getting Rathburn to let her onto *Vengeance* ended up being ridiculously easy. Which only ramped up her tension level.

She made up a story that she wanted to check on the work Kerr's people were doing on the engines. To make her story more plausible, and to provide herself with backup, she told him she wanted to bring Pete with her.

Rathburn didn't put up any argument, and sent a guard to her door before she'd finished explaining to a sleepy Pete where they were going and why. Not that he offered any objections. She probably could have told him they were taking a space walk without suits and he would have followed her.

On the trek to the docking port, she continued her silent debate over the wisdom of following instructions given by a voice over the comm claiming to be a dead man. But she kept circling back to one point of logic she couldn't refute. Rathburn didn't know Isin's crew. He had no idea who had been on the *Dagger* or *Phoenix* when they'd left the system. Neither did Kerr. The odds were astronomical that either of them would pick the one person she knew wasn't onboard.

Which left one improbable option. Sweep was still alive.

Unfortunately, the one time she'd seen Sweep, she'd been distracted by Kerr and standing a hundred meters away. Other than a vague impression of size, she couldn't identify him. She'd have to find another way to make a positive ID.

The guard opened *Vengeance*'s exterior hatch and motioned them inside, then led the way to the upper decks. The sight that greeted her in the engine room was a far cry from what she'd seen last time she'd been onboard. All the damaged components had been removed, clearing space to walk.

She met Pete's gaze. He shook his head and gave a subtle shrug.

So far so good. "Let's start with the engine casing and work our way out." She said it a little louder than necessary, partly for the guard's benefit, and partly in case Sweep really was onboard and could hear her.

Pete followed her into the next compartment while the guard remained in front of the opening to the engine room. Interesting. She'd been expecting the guard to dog her every step. Had he been given instructions from Rathburn not to interfere? Or was he just making sure they didn't escape into other parts of the ship?

The signs of damage in the main compartment were more noticeable, but so were the areas where repairs were already completed. A shiny new panel drew her attention. She pulled it off, revealing neat rows of wiring and conduits rather than the mish-mash found on most vessels she'd seen. "Huh." Not the kind of precision work she'd expected from Kerr's crew.

Pete crouched beside her. "Yeah, I know. It's Rathburn's engineers."

"They're doing the work?"

"Nah. But they're inspecting everything Kerr's crew does. If they don't think it's up to specs, they make 'em fix it."

She frowned. "How do you know?"

"Overheard two of the engineers complainin' while I was workin' on the nav console. Said they'd never seen such sloppy work in their lives." His eyes twinkled. "I think they liked makin' 'em do it over."

"I believe that." If she'd been giving the orders, Kerr's crew would have been doing a lot harder work than repairing the ship. Like cleaning out the waste receptacles with a toothbrush. "I hate to say it, but I'm glad Rathburn's on top of this." One less thing for her to worry about. And at the rate the repairs were being finished, *Vengeance* might be ready to fly in a few days.

She replaced the panel and stood, slowly pivoting to take in the engine room configuration. If Sweep was truly onboard, where would he be hiding?

Hard to say. She didn't have the layout for this ship mapped out like she did for *Gypsy* and *Phoenix*. And until she knew who she was dealing with, she wasn't about to crawl into unfamiliar access tunnels.

She motioned to Pete. "Check the inflow regulators. I'll inspect the stabilizers."

He nodded and moved down the short corridor.

She stepped to the opposite side of the compartment and started removing panels and inspecting the work in progress. But her focus remained on her surroundings rather than the components in front of her. She'd checked the stabilizers and had just removed the panel for the bridge interface when she heard the faint pop of sheet metal shifting under pressure.

She froze, all senses going on alert.

"Orlov."

Same voice, although it sounded slightly different coming through the air vent in the bulkhead above her rather than the comm. She kept her gaze on the panel, just in case the guard could see her through the compartment opening. "Sweep?" she murmured under her breath.

"Yeah. You made it here quicker than I'd expected." He sounded a little out of breath. No wonder. It would be tough to maneuver while wedged into the narrow channels of the circulation system.

"Rathburn was in an agreeable mood." She analyzed his voice, testing it against her memory. It sounded right, but that could be wishful thinking. Having Sweep onboard would help her cause considerably. She didn't want to let that idea override common sense. She needed answers. "How did you get here? I was told you died in an explosion on Kerr's ship."

He grunted. "Almost. The blast blew me out the hole in the hull, along with five of Kerr's crew. But I was tethered and had on my exosuit. They weren't so lucky."

She noted the grim satisfaction in his voice.

"The force knocked me unconscious, and my suit's comm shorted out. I couldn't alert Itorye when I came to."

"How did you get from Kerr's ship to *Vengeance?*"

"Followed one of the grappler lines holding them together. The thing damn nearly took my head off when it detached from *Vengeance's* hull after Kerr decided to make a run for it. Thankfully I already had the exterior hatch open. It deflected the blow. How did you and Stevens end up here?"

"Rathburn's energy weapon took out *Gypsy's* systems. He towed us in."

"What about Isin? Does Kerr still have him? Is he alive?"

"He's alive. Itorye took him in the *Dagger.*"

"And he left you behind?" The disbelief in his voice came through loud and clear. "I'd expect him to die first."

If he wasn't Sweep, he was doing a damn good job of convincing her otherwise. She moved closer to the panel under the guise of inspecting the inner workings. "He was in bad shape, nearly comatose. Couldn't walk without help. I'm the one who ordered Itorye to leave."

A beat of silence greeted that statement. "He's not going to take that well."

"I know." But she couldn't think about that right now. She needed to focus on whether she was, in fact, talking to Sweep. His comment had just given her one surefire way to find out. She'd feed him a lie. "But I owe him one, after he saved me from the Setarips."

More silence, then a low chuckle drifted out of the vent. "Isin told me you were smart. He wasn't exaggerating. He also didn't save you. You're the reason he signed onto *Vengeance* in the first place. It was his penance for allowing you to be captured by the Setarips."

She closed her eyes as waves of sadness and joy collided in her chest. He'd just confirmed what she'd always suspected about Isin's choice. But he'd also given her the answer she needed.

She glanced up at the vent. "He told me you were smart, too. It's a pleasure to finally meet you, Sweep."

# *Twenty-Two*

Knowing Sweep was alive brightened Nat's outlook considerably. She and Pete could use a trustworthy ally right now.

She glanced over her shoulder. Pete had moved to the section closest to the compartment entrance, his body turned so he'd have a clear line of sight to the guard while also partially blocking the opening. He looked engrossed in his work, but the continual clanking and rattling of components told her he was intentionally creating background noise to disguise her conversation.

She focused on Sweep. "What's our next move?"

"Depends. What's the story with Rathburn? Why'd he capture you?"

"He's looking for Patel."

"Who's Patel?"

Right. He wasn't up to speed on that, either. "That's Green's real name. She used to work on this ship. He wants her back."

"Why?"

"Her research. And to soothe his ego." She'd be willing to bet Patel was the first scientist to voluntarily leave his ship.

"Hmm. And this energy weapon you said he used?"

"It slipped right through the shields and shut down all systems except life support."

Sweep gave a low whistle. "That's a tricky bit of engineering."

"Rathburn likes his tech."

"I've noticed. What's the situation between him and Kerr?"

"Rathburn promised to give Kerr *Vengeance*, but told me it was a ruse to get him to do the repairs."

"Do you believe him?"

"I'm not sure. He's playing his cards close to the vest. But he doesn't like Kerr."

"I can't imagine why." Heavy sarcasm coated his words. "Rathburn certainly likes you."

That got her attention. "How do you know?"

"He didn't object when you asked to come here."

"Why does that matter?"

"From a security standpoint, it's a tactical error. Unless, of course, his goal is to gain your trust and good will."

Yes, and yes. "He wants me to find him charming."

"Do you?"

"Not a bit."

Sweep chuckled. "Glad to hear it. He's—"

Pete gave a loud cough.

Nat glanced over just as the guard moved into the opening, his gaze landing on her. She ignored the suspicion in his eyes, returning to her pseudo-inspection of the repair work in the open panel. She'd logged plenty of hours in engine rooms over the years, so she had no trouble making her task look convincing.

After a minute, he seemed satisfied, and moved off into the other room.

Pete wiped his hand on his pant leg and gave her a subtle thumbs-up sign.

She glanced at the vent. They needed to move this along. "Are you safe here for now?"

"I'm fine. I know this ship better than Kerr. He won't find me, even if he thought to look. But watch out for him. He's up to something."

"What do you mean?"

"He doesn't trust Rathburn any more than you do. And he's not a man who leaves his future to chance. He'll be spreading his poison through Rathburn's crew, undermining their loyalty and positioning them to his advantage. It's what he does best."

"You really think he could turn them against Rathburn?"

"I've seen it happen before."

The comment scratched the surface of the story Isin had shared with her about Sweep's incarceration under Kerr and Shim, but now wasn't the time to ask for details. "Can you send a message to Isin? Let him know about our situation?"

"Yes. But there's no telling how long it will be until he'll reply. We can't afford to wait."

"Can you access the docking controls for Rathburn's ship? Release *Vengeance*?"

"That's easy—the security on the airlocks is minimal. But as long as the energy beam is enabled, there's no point."

"Any chance you can override *Cerberus*'s defense systems?"

He grunted. "I'll look into it. Every system has a weakness. Hopefully I can find it before Kerr makes a move."

She glanced toward the compartment opening. The guard would probably check on them again soon. "We need a safer way to communicate. How can I contact you?"

"Do you have a mobile comm device?"

She pushed back the sleeve on her duster, revealing the comband strapped to her forearm. "I have this."

His voice got a little louder, like his mouth was pressed right up against the grate. "Is that a Fleet comband?"

"A modified one, yeah."

"Where did you... never mind. Give me your contact code."

She rattled it off. A message from him appeared on the band a moment later. "Got it. I'll contact you tonight."

"I'll be waiting."

# Twenty-Three

Isin spent the afternoon with Byrd on the bridge, plotting out several potential courses that would take them back to the system where they'd abandoned *Vengeance*.

"It would help if we knew where they'll be," Byrd said.

"Probably not far from where we left them." And if they weren't, they'd adjust.

The thump of heavy boots reverberated on the landing as Kenji appeared at the bridge hatch. "You wanted to see me?"

Isin nodded. "I'm sending Byrd down to the *Dagger* to do a systems check. We'll need both ships, and I don't want any surprises. You'll be taking over here."

Byrd perked up. Probably because he was picturing not having Isin looking over his shoulder.

Isin pinned him with a look. "You have two hours. No more."

"Got it." Byrd practically bounded out the hatch.

Isin shook his head as he turned to Kenji. "Where are we with the weapons?"

"Fleur's overseeing the final calibrations. We've extended the striking range by twelve percent. Hopefully that'll be enough."

"If everything goes to plan, we won't have to find out." He clapped a hand on Kenji's shoulder. "I'll be with Itorye and Patel if you need me."

"Aye, Cap."

Isin descended the stairs to A deck and continued down the passageway to where Avril stood guard outside Itorye's cabin. "Any issues?"

"None." But Avril's head and shoulders drooped, like he was fighting to stay upright.

Isin had lost track of how long he'd been at his post. Since yesterday? "Go get some rest. I'll have Fleur take over when I leave."

Avril gave him a weary smile. "Aye."

As Isin entered the cabin, Itorye and Patel looked up from the holosimulation running from the projector in the middle of the room.

"Navigation and weapons are set," he said. "What's the status on–" His words ground to a halt as he caught sight of Alec hovering beside them. "Alec?" The boy—no, *young man*—looked like Alec, except he'd grown. And aged. The last time he'd seen him, he would have put his age at eight or nine. Now, he looked closer to fourteen.

Alec met his gaze. "Yes?" His voice broke on the word, squeaking and then dropping an octave.

"What happened to you?"

"Happened?" Alec looked confused.

"You're older!"

"Oh, that." He gave Isin a sheepish smile and shrugged. "Part of my programming."

*Programming?* Isin turned to Patel and repeated the question out loud. "Programming?"

She, at least, seemed to share his concern about Alec's transformation. "His visual and auditory parameters are designed to mature as his neurological and psychological systems grow and adapt. Previously it was a gradual process, but he's received more stimulation in the past couple days than he's had in his entire life." Her mouth turned down. "It's accelerated his aging process."

Alec gave the long-suffering sigh of a beleaguered teen. "I'm fine, Mom."

"We don't know that, Alec. This wasn't how your development was supposed to proceed. There could be unintended consequences."

"If there are, you'll handle them. I trust you."

Patel's frown deepened, parental concern overriding scientific pride. Clearly she had less confidence in her ability to handle the changing dynamics than Alec did.

Isin gestured to the holosimulation. "Any success?"

Patel shook her head. "We've run a hundred and twenty-three simulations, and they've all reached the same conclusion. There's no way for *Phoenix* to disrupt Rathburn's energy beam."

"Not the answer we need."

"I know. However, there is another option." She glanced at Itorye before meeting Isin's gaze. "If you can get me onto *Cerberus*, I can disable the beam from inside."

Isin blinked. "You want me to get you onto Rathburn's ship?"

"Yes."

That was a huge change. Just yesterday she'd thrown a fit when he'd suggested trading her for Natasha and Stevens. "How do you propose I do that?"

"You're already planning to use the tracking device as a decoy, taking it on the *Dagger* with you when you meet with Rathburn. That would convince him I'm with you, correct?"

"Yes."

"What I'm proposing is the same idea, except reversed. We leave the decoy on *Phoenix* and I go with you.

Itorye assures me there are secret compartments in the *Dagger's* cargo hold where I could fit. No one on your crew needs to know I'm there."

"True." An intriguing possibility. He'd never suspected she'd volunteer to—

"Cap?" Kenji's voice came over the cabin's comm.

Isin touched the panel. "Yes?"

"When I dropped us out of our jump to make the course change, I picked up an encrypted message from *Vengeance.*"

Isin's heart pounded. "Natasha?"

"I'm not sure who it's from. The ID is Sweep's."

"Sweep?" The deck shifted under Isin's feet. "That's not possible."

"Yeah, I know."

His stomach churned. "Put it through on speaker so you can hear it, too."

A moment later, Sweep's deep baritone filled the cabin. "I hope this message reaches you. I don't have much time. Orlov told me you thought I was dead. I'm pleased to say I'm not."

A wave of emotion surged through Isin's chest. *Sweep was alive!*

"I'm stowed away on *Vengeance,* keeping an eye on Kerr's crew. They're making repairs under Rathburn's supervision. He's the man who owns the ship that captured Orlov and Stevens. They're both fine—Rathburn's treating them like guests, not prisoners."

Isin released the breath he'd been holding. Natasha was okay. For now.

"He also has control of Kerr's ship, but there's some debate as to whether he's planning to turn that ship and *Vengeance* over when the work is done in another day or so. Rathburn told Orlov he was making Kerr do the work as penance, and that he'll send him packing when he's finished, but I'm not convinced. He told Kerr he'd get to keep *Vengeance*, so clearly he's lying to one of them. Probably both."

Isin glanced at Itorye. She lifted one perfectly shaped brow, her lips pressed together.

"The sooner you can get here, the better. You know Kerr will be working angles left and right, and I'd hate for Orlov and Stevens to get caught in the middle. I'm trying to infiltrate Rathburn's security, but it's—dammit! Gotta go." The message cut off.

Isin fought the urge to touch the comm panel, as though he could somehow grab hold of the tail end of the message and pull Sweep through time and space to the *Phoenix*.

Instead, he took a slow breath in, held it for a four count, and let it out just as slowly. "Kenji, did you get all that?"

"Yeah. I knew that son-of-a-gun was too wily to die."

The joy in Kenji's voice echoed the feeling dancing through Isin's veins. He turned to Itorye. "Any chance the message is a forgery?"

She shook her head. "If it came in encrypted with Sweep's ID? That information isn't stored in *Vengeance*'s security system. The only way to access it would be if they caught Sweep and forced him to reveal his codes. Either way, it looks like he's alive."

"Can we send a reply?"

"As long as we direct it to his ID and not to *Vengeance*. That way he can access it without the risk of Kerr's crew coming across it on the ship's servers."

"All right." He turned to the comm panel. "Kenji, we'll compose a reply and have it ready in five minutes. Hold position for now and notify me if you receive any new messages."

"Aye, Cap." The channel closed.

Patel glanced between Isin and Itorye, frown lines crossing her forehead. "Sweep? Isn't he the one I met in the cargo bay? The one in charge of security on *Vengeance*?"

"Yes, he is." *Present tense, not past. Because he's not dead.* The beginnings of a smile pulled at Isin's lips. "We may have just gained an ace in the hole."

# Twenty-Four

Nat paced in her room like a caged animal. The hours had crawled by since she'd left *Vengeance*. The only way she'd kept her sanity all day was by working in the shuttle bay making minor repairs to *Gypsy*'s systems and stacking the crates of medical supplies, engine parts, and herbs Rathburn's guards had delivered. Pete had offered to help her, but she'd urged him to keep working on *Vengeance*'s new navigation console. She'd barely had enough to do on *Gypsy* to occupy herself.

Sweep, on the other hand, was doing important things, like hacking into Rathburn's security system and communicating with Isin. She wanted to be doing something important, but she didn't have the knowledge or experience to take on a system as advanced as the one on *Cerberus*.

Rathburn had invited her to dinner, but she'd declined, claiming exhaustion. She couldn't face another meal in one of his fantasy settings. Or the questions that would come with it.

After he'd escorted her from the shuttle bay to her suite, she'd sent a comm message to Sweep, but he'd replied that Kerr's crew was still onboard *Vengeance* and he couldn't talk. Now she was stuck waiting for him to report in. She'd been pacing so long she'd worn a track in the carpet.

Her comband vibrated, bringing her to a halt. She smacked the small display. "Yeah, I'm here."

"All clear on *Vengeance*," Sweep said. "Anything to report?"

"No. I spent the day working on *Gypsy*. How about you?"

"Good and bad. I hit a dead end with the defense systems, but I received a reply from Isin a little while ago."

Nat's heart began to pound. "What did he say?"

"They're on their way, but still about a day out. He has a plan to sneak Patel onboard. Apparently she knows how to shut down the defense systems on Rathburn's ship."

"Patel's coming back voluntarily?" What miracle had Isin pulled off to make that happen?

"Yes. It was her idea."

Nat pinched herself to make sure she wasn't dreaming. Nope, it hurt. "How is Isin going to keep from being captured by Rathburn?"

"Intimidation, negotiation, and slight of hand. He can be very convincing when he needs to be."

True. He'd used his skills on her more than once. But she couldn't sit here and do nothing. "We might be able to increase their chances of success if we can override Rathburn's implant."

"What implant?"

"It's based on a prototype his sister designed. The controls are embedded in his forearm. I've seen him use it for communication and to manage the lifts and security doors."

"That explains a lot. His core system isn't set up like anything I've seen before. I was wondering why. The complexity and interconnection is the main reason I couldn't break in. Do you know if his implant can operate the ship's defense systems?"

"I have no idea."

"Is his sister onboard?"

"No. She died in an accident. This ship is his memorial to her."

Sweep was silent for a moment. "Do you think you could convince him to bring you onto *Vengeance*'s bridge tomorrow morning? I could use the ship's internal security sensors to gather data on the implant, see if I can determine how his interface works and whether I can hack the signal."

"I'd need a plausible excuse for being there."

"Any ideas?"

She glanced around the room, searching for inspiration. "I don't know. Unless..." She gazed at the closed door to her room. "Pete said earlier that they'll have the navigation console ready to install early tomorrow. I could tell Rathburn I'd like to oversee the work. And that I'd feel better if he was there to keep Kerr in line."

"Do you think he'd agree?"

In addition to escorting her to and from the shuttle bay, he'd checked in on her twice during the day, once to make sure she had all the parts she needed, and again when he had a meal delivered. He'd seemed disappointed when she hadn't encouraged him to stay longer, which may have triggered the dinner invitation she'd turned down. "Yeah, I think he will."

"Then I'll get into position before you arrive."

"Won't Kerr's people notice the bridge's sensors running on their own?"

A soft chuckle filled with irony drifted over the comm. "I designed the security system on *Vengeance*. No one will see a thing."

# *Twenty-Five*

As she'd predicted, Rathburn agreed to her request without a word of protest. A stoic grey-uniformed guard came to her cabin in the morning and took her to *Vengeance*. Rathburn was waiting for her as she stepped through the exterior hatch.

"Good morning, Nat. Did you sleep well?"

"Yes." That was a lie. She'd tossed and turned half the night before finally drifting into a restless sleep filled with unsettling dreams of Isin being tortured and energy beams chasing her shuttle.

Rathburn studied her for a moment. "I took the liberty of assigning Kerr and his crew to work on *Viper* this morning. I thought you might appreciate not having to cross paths."

An unexpected bonus. "Thank you."

"Shall we?" He indicated the forward stairwell. She led the way, but he kept pace beside her as they climbed. "I'm curious. Why is overseeing this part of the repair so important to you?"

She'd been wondering when he'd ask. The sideways look he gave her indicated he was paying very close attention to her answer. Thankfully, she'd come up with a logical explanation. "Pilot perfectionism. I've flown enough ships with subpar navigation that my standards are high. I want to make sure this system will do exactly what I need it to."

A small smile played around his lips. "I completely understand."

And more important, he seemed to believe her. It was the truth, from a certain perspective. She needed this ship to be in tip-top shape, especially if they were going to make a hasty exit. She didn't want any surprises when the time came to fly.

Not that she planned to be at the controls. She still had to factor in springing *Gypsy*. She wasn't about to leave her beloved shuttle behind. If she couldn't figure out a way to get *Gypsy* into *Vengeance*'s shuttle bay, Isin's pilot or Itorye would have to take over the helm on *Vengeance*.

Muffled grunts and the clang of metal on metal greeted them as they stepped onto the bridge. Pete crouched beside four people dressed in matching deep blue jumpsuits, supervising the transfer of the new navigation console as they lowered it from a hover cart to the deck and maneuvered it into place.

Pete stood as Nat approached. "Whadda you think?" He gestured to the new unit.

"It's perfect." She hadn't seen the old console before it was mangled in the explosion, but the design for this one certainly fit with everything else on the bridge. Other than the fact that the components were obviously new and free of the marks from steady use, it blended in beautifully. She itched to help with the installation, but if she offered, Rathburn might take that as his cue to leave. She had to keep him on the bridge as long as possible so Sweep could run his scans.

Pete returned to his work while she and Rathburn stepped up to the raised command platform at the center of the room. It gave them a good view of the proceedings while keeping them out of the way.

Standing in front of the captain's chair sent goosebumps rippling over her skin. This was Isin's domain. She could feel it, even more so than when she'd been in his cabin. The irony struck her anew. The Isin she'd known on the *Sphinx* wouldn't have felt comfortable here. He'd preferred to be a part-time asset to the captain, not the leader.

But the cold-eyed mercenary who'd replaced him reigned like a king, keeping a close eye on those under his watchful gaze. He wanted to command her too, but that was a lost cause. Maybe one day he'd figure that out.

The darkened three-hundred-sixty-degree bridgescreen stared down, as intimidating as its master. Everything on this bridge was oversized, including the tactical console to her right and the weapons console to her left. If she sat in the captain's chair, it would swallow her whole.

She glanced at Rathburn. "Did Kerr give any objections to my coming onto the ship?"

He gave her an amused glance. "Why would I tell him?"

Ah. He understood Kerr better than she'd thought. "How much time do we have for the installation?"

"As much as we need." Warmth lit his blue eyes as he gazed at her.

"I see."

He smiled. "But I do have a few things to take care of. If you'll excuse me for a moment."

"You're leaving?" Her words came out as a startled squeak.

His smile widened at her tone. "Don't worry. I'll be right over there." He pointed to the aft section of the bridge before stepping away and speaking in an undertone to whoever was on the other end of the connection.

He'd jumped to the wrong conclusion, but as long as he stayed, she didn't care. Hopefully Sweep was making the most of the opportunity.

She moved closer to the edge of the platform, crouching down so she could observe Pete and the others as they integrated the new console.

Pete caught her watching him. "You wanna help?" He held out the tool in his hand.

She glanced over her shoulder at Rathburn, who still seemed engrossed in his conversation. "Okay." She slipped her duster off her shoulders and draped it over the railing before stepping down to the deck and accepting the offered tool.

Pete showed her the connection he'd been working on and then stepped to the other side of the console while she settled onto her back and focused on the hardware. Her surroundings faded into the background as the tactile work drew her like a siren song.

"Having fun?"

She jerked at the sound of Rathburn's voice, smacking her right hand against the underside of the console. She swore, giving her hand a few good shakes before rubbing the red spot on her skin.

Rathburn's fingers encircled her wrist, gently but firmly moving her other hand away so he could inspect the wound. "Forgive me. I didn't mean to startle you."

If she hadn't been so engrossed in her task, he wouldn't have. She shouldn't have allowed herself to get distracted, especially now. "I'm fine."

"You will be." He tapped his forearm. "Dr. Chang, report to *Vengeance's* bridge immediately."

Nat tried to pull away, but he didn't let go.

"My doctor will repair the damage."

"It's just a bump."

His brows drew down, his gaze troubled. "It's an injury I caused. It needs to be treated."

She stared at him. Overreacting much? She was a quick healer. There was a good chance she wouldn't even bruise, yet he was behaving like he'd inflicted a mortal wound.

"Come with me." He exerted pressure on her wrist, drawing her out from under the console and leading her to the command platform.

She shot a quick look at Pete, who seemed as puzzled by Rathburn's reaction as she was. The four people in jumpsuits, however, didn't even pause in their work to watch the mini-drama unfold. Apparently this was commonplace for them.

Pete gave a subtle shrug and returned to the installation.

Rathburn sat beside her, her injured hand cradled in both of his. "Does it hurt?"

"Not really." A dull ache, but even that was beginning to fade. What was his problem? Was he a hypochondriac? She'd never met anyone who suffered from it, so maybe this was typical behavior. But didn't hypochondriacs worry about their own ailments, not other people's?

A man wearing medical scrubs and carrying an oversized med kit appeared at the bridge hatch and hurried over to them, his breathing audible as he approached. He must have sprinted from wherever he'd been on Rathburn's ship.

He wouldn't be happy when he realized he'd rushed here to treat an injury a five-year-old would dismiss as unimportant.

He knelt in front of her, his deep-set eyes shadowed with concern. "What happened?"

Rathburn gently lifted Nat's arm, revealing the circle of red skin to the doctor. "She hit her hand."

To his credit, the doctor didn't scoff, or even look surprised. Instead, he slid his hand under hers and inspected the injury like he was preparing for brain surgery.

Maybe she'd hit her head instead of her hand and was hallucinating.

The doctor met Rathburn's gaze first, then Nat's. "I'll have this repaired in no time." No irony. No sarcasm. In fact, he seemed to be trying to alleviate her fears. What did he think, that she'd shatter into a million pieces at his touch?

"Thanks." She didn't know what else to say. She certainly couldn't voice what was running through her head.

The doctor rested her hand back in Rathburn's palm before opening his medical kit and pulling out a thin cylinder. "This won't hurt," he informed her as he aimed the end of the object at her skin and pressed a button.

A coolness spread over her skin, like a cold compress, sinking deeper the longer he held the tool in place. The redness faded, as did the ache, until her hand no longer showed any sign of the injury.

"There. That's better." The doctor turned the device off. "How does it feel?"

She dutifully flexed her fingers and thumb. "Fine."

"No pain? Soreness?"

Was he serious? The look in his eyes said he was. She glanced at Rathburn. Yep, serious face there, too. "Good as new," she proclaimed just to get them to stop staring at her.

Rathburn released his breath on a sigh. "Thank you, Dr. Chang."

"You're welcome." He gave Nat a sunny smile. "If you need anything else, please let me know."

"Thank you, Doctor."

"The pleasure's all mine." The doctor packed up his kit, gave Rathburn a nod, then strolled off toward the hatch with a spring in his step.

Nat had to fight to keep her jaw from hitting the deck. Had she just fallen down a rabbit hole into an alternate universe?

# *Twenty-Six*

"Exiting the interstellar jump," Byrd said from the navigation controls on *Phoenix*'s small bridge. The image on the bridgescreen snapping into focus as the main engines took over.

Isin pulled up the comm on the control panel for the captain's chair and checked for incoming messages. Sure enough, one popped up from Sweep. He quickly read the transcription.

*Orlov and Stevens will be on the bridge with Rathburn this morning installing the new navigation console. I'm working to hack into Rathburn's implant. Ping me before you enter the system.*

Patel had informed them about Rathburn's implant and how it gave him override control of all the major systems on his ship. Breaking his connection to the ship was her first task, before disabling the ship's defense systems.

"Something interesting?" Byrd asked.

Isin glanced over at the pilot. He hadn't told Byrd or the crew about Sweep. Maybe he was being superstitious, but until he laid eyes on his friend, he was holding his tongue. In addition to Kenji, Itorye, and Patel, only Shash and Avril knew. Shash would be his second on this mission—he couldn't afford to keep her in the dark. Besides, she'd never risk Sweep's safety. She respected him far too much. And Avril was Sweep's protégé, which is why Isin had put him in charge of coordinating with Sweep to get Patel safely into position to do her job.

Isin shook his head. "Not important." He sent a quick reply to Sweep. *Arrived. Initiating phase one.*

Sweep's response was almost instantaneous. *Ready and waiting.*

Isin motioned to the bridgescreen. "Take us in slow."

As Byrd guided the ship into the system, Isin studied the incoming sensor information. It didn't take long to locate Rathburn's ship—right where Sweep had told them it would be.

"They're in orbit around one of the gas giant's moons," Kenji confirmed from the tactical console. In fact, it was the very moon Isin had been hoping to hide behind when he'd run from Kerr's ship.

"Can you see *Vengeance*?"

Kenji brought up the visual feed, but the moon's shadow prevented any direct imaging of Rathburn's ship. "Switching to infrared." The outline of Rathburn's ship popped out of the dark background, the smooth line of its hull broken by a blocky appendage on the starboard side. "She's docked starboard forward."

Isin leaned closer, studying the image over Kenji's shoulder.

Kenji pointed to a smaller protrusion barely visible on the port side. "He's put Kerr's ship opposite."

Dealing with Rathburn would be challenging enough. Having Kerr on the same ship complicated the situation. Not that he could do anything about it. He opened an internal comm channel. "Itorye, we've located *Cerberus* and *Vengeance*. Are you and Patel ready?"

"All set."

"Stand by." Tension settled into his shoulders. He was putting a lot of faith in the plan Patel had devised. Not that he'd had much choice. She knew Rathburn, and the capabilities of his ship. And she had a mother's determination to keep Alec from falling into Rathburn's hands. For now, he'd trust in that.

And in Sweep. Knowing he was onboard *Vengeance*, watching over Natasha, made the situation bearable.

He glanced at Kenji. "Ready?"

Kenji nodded. "Let's do this."

Isin initiated *Phoenix*'s generic hailing signal, targeting Rathburn's ship. Several beats passed before a light flashed, indicating a response. He positioned the vid camera to focus on his face, checked that the feed was being looped into Itorye's cabin, and opened the channel. *Showtime*.

The man who appeared on the video feed didn't look more than ten years older than he was, and wasn't dressed like a typical space traveler. With his expensive suit and perfectly styled dark hair, he looked like he belonged in a boardroom, not on the bridge of a ship.

He also did a decent job of hiding his flinch, composing his features into a benign smile. Isin was well aware of the reaction looking at his scar had on people. His crew didn't give it a second thought, and even Natasha seemed to be getting used to it. But it was a distraction for anyone new, which often proved valuable.

"I'm Orpheus Rathburn, owner of the starship *Cerberus*. To whom am I speaking?" Highly educated and cultured, which he'd expected given Patel's descriptions.

"My name is Elhadj Isin, owner of *Phoenix*. And *Vengeance*."

"Ah, Mr. Isin. It's a pleasure to finally meet you. Nat speaks very highly of you."

Isin kept his expression neutral but still managed to scrape a little enamel off his molars at the man's familiar reference to Natasha. "Does she?"

"Oh, yes. She's a delightful woman. I've enjoyed having her and Mr. Stevens as my guests."

Kenji snorted softly enough Rathburn wouldn't hear. Isin shared the sentiment. "Guests?"

"Of course." Rathburn's smile faded. "When you abruptly left the system, they had nowhere else to go."

Isin didn't miss the rebuke in that statement. Rathburn considered his flight from the system as a mark against him? Oh, the irony. "Thank you for taking them in." So polite. So solicitous. So like the diplomat he'd been trained to be a lifetime ago.

He focused on the background visible behind Rathburn. He knew that view. Rathburn wasn't on *Cerberus*. He was sitting in the captain's chair on *Vengeance's* bridge. A growl rumbled in his chest. "What's the status of my ship?"

"*Vengeance*?" Rathburn took a slow survey of the area off camera. "Undergoing repairs."

"Why are you repairing my ship?" Thanks to Sweep, he already knew the answer, but he needed to keep up the pretense for Rathburn.

Rathburn's smile returned, this time with a little frost around the edges. "Because I can."

"I see." He tilted his head, like he was considering the situation. "And what will these repairs cost me?"

"Cost you? No, no, you misunderstand me. Nat explained that Kerr was responsible for the damage. As he and his crew are also my guests, it seemed only fair that they do the work of repairing *Vengeance*."

So far, Rathburn was giving him the same line he'd given Natasha. But he wasn't buying it any more than Sweep had. "Fair would be blasting Kerr out an airlock."

Rathburn's brows rose a fraction. "That's not for me to decide."

Isin suppressed a bark of laughter. The man had disabled Kerr's ship and Natasha's shuttle, taken them prisoner, and manipulated them into working for him, and yet he was implying that Isin's solution was somehow barbaric. The man had a warped moral compass. No news there. "Then let me make this easy for you. Release Kerr and his crew to my custody, return Natasha and Stevens, and we'll take *Vengeance* and be on our way."

Rathburn's gaze hardened to cold steel. "I'm afraid the situation is a bit more complicated."

"Why's that?"

"Because you have something I want."

# Twenty-Seven

Rathburn was a skilled negotiator, the best Isin had come across since leaving school. He welcomed the challenge of bringing him down. "And what might that be?"

"Not what, who. Dr. Darsha Patel."

"Who?"

Rathburn sighed. "Really, Mr. Isin, I would prefer not to play these games. I know she's onboard your ship."

Isin held back a grim smile. Rathburn didn't know as much as he thought. His overconfidence played right into Isin's hands. "Is she?"

"Yes. And you're going to return her to me."

"They're moving," Kenji murmured.

Isin bared his teeth, flipping from diplomat to mercenary in an instant. "Don't even think about it, Rathburn. If you attempt to hit my ship with your energy beam, you will be *very* unhappy with the result." He switched the video feed to the camera Itorye and Patel had set up in their cabin.

An image of Patel appeared, seated on a chair with her arms bound behind her back. Sweat beaded at her temples and the whites of her eyes stood out in sharp contrast to her russet-hued skin.

Itorye stood with her back to the camera, a blade at Patel's throat.

Uncertainty flickered on Rathburn's face. "You wouldn't."

"Wouldn't I?" His voice dropped to a dangerous purr as he switched the feed back to his camera. He tilted his head so Rathburn could get a good look at his scar. "Try me."

Rathburn spoke through gritted teeth. "If you harm her, you'll never get your ship."

"And if you attack us, your doctor will bleed out."

Their gazes locked for a long moment. But Isin already knew the outcome. He hadn't given Rathburn any choice.

"Their reverse thrusters are firing," Kenji reported. "They've stopped."

Isin didn't take his gaze off Rathburn. "You're a smart man."

Rathburn's mouth pinched. "We appear to be at an impasse."

"Not at all." Isin settled back into his chair. He'd won the first round, but Rathburn would continue to fight for the upper hand. "Now that we understand each other, I'm sure we can work out a solution. Is Stevens onboard *Vengeance?*"

Rathburn's eyes narrowed. "Yes."

"Let me speak to him." The person he really wanted to see was Natasha, but he couldn't allow Rathburn to pick up on that. She was his greatest weakness, which made her a potential liability.

Rathburn considered the request before motioning off camera. "Go fetch Mr. Stevens from the engine room." He returned his attention to Isin, staring at him with contempt as the seconds ticked by.

Isin stared back until footsteps approached and Rathburn shifted the image to reveal the solemn face of Natasha's engineer crouched by the captain's chair.

Isin didn't waste time with pleasantries. "Stevens, what's the status of the ship?"

"Repairs are done. Primin' the main engines now."

"How soon could she be ready for an interstellar jump?"

Stevens ran a hand over his beard. "Another half-hour or so."

"Are any of Rathburn's personnel with you on *Vengeance*?"

"Two engineers workin' with me, and a couple guards outside the bridge. Don't know 'bout the rest of the ship."

"Is Natasha there?"

He looked past the camera's view. "Yep. She's runnin' diagnostics at the nav console."

Then she'd likely heard the entire conversation with Rathburn. "Good. Tell her I want the ship ready to go when I arrive."

Stevens gave a nod and stepped away.

Rathburn pulled the camera back to face the captain's chair. "You're coming here?" The question sounded like a challenge.

"Yes."

"What about Dr. Patel?"

Isin's smile could cut glass. "She'll remain as my... guest, for now. My transport will head over shortly. I'll meet you, Stevens, and Natasha on the bridge when we arrive. Oh, and Rathburn?"

"What?"

"If we run into any complications from your people, this will not end well for Dr. Patel."

Rathburn looked like he was inhaling raw sewage. "If you hurt her—"

"Don't give me a reason to. I want my ship. You want the doctor. Follow my instructions and we won't have any problems."

# *Twenty-Eight*

"Isin is not what I expected."

Nat noted the hostility in Rathburn's tone, and the fact that he'd dropped the "Mr." from Isin's name. He'd been silent for several minutes after closing the comm channel, no doubt processing what he'd learned.

She turned from the navigation console, catching sight of the fury burning in his blue eyes.

She didn't blame him. Isin had presented a mercenary's solution—exchange what you have for what you want. No questions, no guilt. And it was an effective way to force Rathburn's hand. *Cerberus* outclassed *Phoenix* like a full-grown wolf compared to a newborn puppy, but Rathburn had capitulated. His willingness to lie down, even temporarily, in order to protect Patel spoke volumes.

And made Nat wonder if she'd been fighting the wrong battle.

Lines of tension pulled at Rathburn's eyes and mouth. "Did you know?" An accusation.

"Know what?"

"That he was holding her hostage?"

"No, I didn't." She assumed Isin's threat was a ruse to force Rathburn to cooperate. Sweep had said coming back was Patel's idea. She couldn't believe Isin was really prepared to kill Patel if he didn't get *Vengeance* back.

"But you knew she was onboard?"

No point in lying. "Yes."

"Did you kidnap her?"

That struck a nerve, raising her hackles. "Of course not! She booked passage. And if you hadn't shown up with your monster ship, everything would have been fine." Well, except for Kerr sabotaging *Vengeance* and torturing Isin.

"So this is my fault?"

"Isn't it? You're the one who scared her off in the first place."

"I was protecting her!"

"You terrified her!"

Rathburn opened his mouth to reply, then snapped it closed, his brows drawing down. His gaze searched hers, analyzing, debating. "So you still think I'm a threat to her?"

Interesting question. She didn't have a good answer. "I don't know. Maybe."

"More of a threat than Isin?"

*Careful, Nat.* She didn't want to sabotage the scenario Isin and Patel had concocted. "He'll do whatever it takes to get what he wants."

"He wants this ship."

"Of course he does. It's his."

"But you're the acting captain."

"For now."

His eyes narrowed. "I noticed he asked to speak to Mr. Stevens, not you."

She'd noticed that, too. And had gritted her teeth through their entire conversation.

"I thought you were friends."

*Friends?* "Not really." She wasn't sure what they were, but *friends* didn't seem to fit. "We're... associates."

"Hmm." Rathburn leaned forward, his gaze intent. "If I go along with his plan, do you believe he'll turn her over? The truth, please, no lies."

She had to lie. And she had to do it with conviction. "Yes."

The tension eased from his face. He believed her. "Then for now, we'll follow his lead." He tapped his implant and spoke to the person on the other end of the connection. "A transport will be departing from *Phoenix*. Let it through. They'll be docking in *Vengeance*'s shuttle bay." He paused, listening to the reply. "No. No additional personnel. Move the two guards at the airlock to the exterior corridor and await further instructions." His mouth turned down and his voice took on an edge. "I don't care what you think. Move—"

He cut off with a pained grunt and slapped his hands against his ears, like he was blocking out a siren blast.

But the room was silent. She took a step forward. "What's wrong?"

He didn't seem to hear her. His lips pulled back from his teeth in a grimace and his eyes squeezed shut.

She abandoned the navigation console and hurried up the steps to the captain's chair. "Rathburn?"

No reaction.

"Orpheus. What's wrong?"

His eyes peeled open to slits. Moving in slow motion, he pried his hands away from his skull, struggling with shaking fingers to touch the implant on his forearm.

Was Sweep causing this? She'd wanted his implant disabled, but hadn't expected it to be so obviously painful. She darted a glance at the bridge's open back hatch. Nobody there. Where had the two guards gone?

Air hissed between Rathburn's teeth as he concentrated on the implant. After a few fumbling attempts he made contact. His shoulders sagged and he slumped against the back of the chair with an audible exhale.

She lightly touched his shoulder. "Rathburn?"

Lifting his head to meet her gaze seemed to sap what little strength he had left.

"What happened?"

His chest rose and fell in a labored pant. "The... implant... overloaded. Lost my... connection... to *Cerberus*."

So Sweep had made a move. That must mean—

A shout and the whine of rifle fire in the passageway caught her off guard. She dropped into a crouch, her hand shifting to her belt, but her holster and pistol weren't there.

A moment later one of Rathburn's guards appeared at the hatch, weapon at the ready.

Nat stood. "What's—"

The guard aimed the weapon at her chest. "Don't move."

She froze.

Rathburn shoved out of the chair, swaying on his feet as he tried to move in front of her. "Lower your wea—"

But a second guard stepped through the hatch and focused his weapon on Rathburn. "Hands where I can see them."

*What?* Nat darted a glance at Rathburn as she slowly raised her hands.

He seemed too stunned to move. "Why are you—"

"I said, hands where I can see them!" The guard took a threatening step forward.

Rathburn slowly lifted his hands, his gaze on the guard holding a gun on Nat. "Don't hurt her."

The guard grunted. "All secure," he called into the passageway.

Another figure stepped onto the bridge.

"Kerr," she and Rathburn said in perfect unison.

The contempt in his gaze as he looked them up and down made Nat's skin crawl. "Ah, two of my least favorite people. Surprised?" He glanced over his shoulder as several of his crewmembers joined him, hauling a limp form.

"Pete!" Nat took a step toward them.

"Freeze!" the guard commanded, finger on the trigger.

She halted, even though every muscle in her body protested.

Kerr's lackeys dumped Pete face down onto the deck near the aft bulkhead. One of them kneeled, pulled Pete's hands behind his back, and snapped manacles around his wrists.

Not dead, then. You didn't cuff a corpse. But he wasn't moving.

She glared at Kerr. "What did you do to him?"

He shrugged. "Took care of a potential problem. Don't worry, he'll live. And he might prove useful, one way or another."

His sinister smile chilled her blood.

"Forget about him." He waved away her concern like a pesky bug and ambled toward her, his smile widening. A rabid dog about to bite.

Four of his crewmembers followed, the two closest removing manacles from their belts while the other two circled behind Nat and Rathburn, weapons at the ready.

Kerr climbed the steps of the platform and stopped directly in front of her. "The life you should be worried about is your own."

Rough hands grabbed her arms and pulled them behind her, the cool steel of the manacle snapping around her wrists and keeping her hands from touching.

The other lackey secured Rathburn in the same manner.

Kerr reached out a gloved hand and grabbed her chin in his palm, squeezing until darts of pain shot along her nerve endings. He forced her head from side to side, studying her face like he was inspecting an item he was considering purchasing.

"Leave her alone."

Nat kept her focus on Kerr's face, but she caught the warning in Rathburn's voice.

Kerr gazed at him with a taunting smile. "And if I don't?"

"My security forces will—"

"Your security forces are neutralized." Kerr released her, focusing his attention on Rathburn. "They won't be coming to your aid."

"Liar. You couldn't possibly—"

"Oh, yes, I could." He glanced over his shoulder at the two grey-uniformed guards. "Isn't that right?"

"Yes, sir." Their smug smiles dropped Nat's stomach into her feet.

Rathburn didn't concede. He rounded on the guards like a parent scolding a misbehaving child. "I pay you well. How could you—"

"Don't you know money isn't everything?" Kerr cut in, his tone conversational. "You have a lot to learn about job satisfaction."

"What are you talking—"

"You're a dreadful employer. You hire soldiers, then treat them like wall hangings. Day after day of monotonous boredom." He leaned forward like he was imparting a secret, but he spoke in a stage whisper so everyone on the bridge could hear. "You don't even know their names."

Rathburn's face pinched.

Kerr stepped back and gestured to the two guards. "For instance, these two gentlemen. Who are they?"

*Please know the answer, please know the answer.*

"Members of my security staff."

"Wrong." Kerr shook his head in feigned disappointment. "What are their *names?*"

Rathburn's jaw worked. "I don't know."

*Oh, hell.*

"You don't?" Kerr's eyes widened in mock surprise. "But they work for you. How could you not know their names? I do."

Rathburn didn't respond.

"I'll tell you why. Because instead of watching out for those you depend on, you waste your time wining and dining space trash." Malice made the blue of his eyes shine like fire as he turned to Nat. "But not anymore. I'm in charge now. You understand that, don't you?" His hot breath battered her face as he tilted down so they were nose to nose.

She fought to keep still.

"Yes, I can see you do." Millimeters apart now.

"I said, leave her alone," Rathburn barked.

Kerr slowly swiveled his head, gazing at Rathburn before returning his attention to Nat. "Not very bright, is he?"

*He just doesn't like you.* But she'd be a fool to say it out loud.

Kerr straightened. "I'll dumb it down for you. Your ships, and everything on them, are now mine. Which means so are *you.*" He focused on Nat like a vampire sizing up his next meal. "Not that I plan to keep you around for long. I honestly don't know what Rathburn and Isin see in you."

"That's because you're an idiot," Rathburn replied.

Kerr turned on him in a flash, sucker punching him in the gut.

Rathburn doubled over with a wheeze.

Kerr yanked Rathburn up by the hair. "Take a good look around, Rathburn. You're the idiot in this room. You and this scrawny excuse for a pilot." He pointed at Nat.

The insult didn't matter. Isin's imminent arrival did. Was Kerr aware he was on his way? What about Sweep? Had he alerted Isin to their situation?

She had to keep Kerr talking and distracted, buy time for Isin and Sweep to come up with a counterattack. "So you outsmarted us. You won. Now what?" Kerr was the kind of egomaniac who might tell her his entire plan just to make her see how brilliant he was.

"Now?" His sickening smile returned. "We're waiting for our guest of honor to arrive."

"Guest of honor?"

He gave her a chiding look. "Don't play stupid. Isin has the starring role in this little drama. In fact, the *Dagger* will be here in..." He checked the bridge's chronometer. "Five minutes. Which doesn't give us much time." He motioned to Rathburn's guards. "Tie them up."

# Twenty-Nine

Isin kept a close eye on the sensor readouts as Byrd guided the *Dagger* away from *Phoenix*, angling toward the port side of Rathburn's ship. Rathburn probably wouldn't order an attack, not after the scene Itorye and Patel had staged in their cabin, but he wasn't leaving anything to chance.

Sweep had sent a brief message after Isin had closed the channel with Rathburn, confirming Rathburn and Natasha were waiting on *Vengeance*'s bridge. Itorye had passed him in the corridor on the way down to the cargo bay, her subtle nod indicating she'd successfully smuggled Patel and Alec into one of the *Dagger*'s secret compartments.

*Vengeance*'s blocky form stood out like a boulder at the base of the hill that was Rathburn's ship. The outline came into focus as they drew closer, the channel that led to the shuttle bay visible as Byrd banked. Isin pulled out his comm device and typed a message to Sweep. *Making final approach.*

But rather than receiving a confirmation, his message was met with silence.

He tapped the send command again. Waited. Still nothing.

"Problem?" Byrd asked, glancing at him.

Was there? "Maybe." He tried sending the message through the *Dagger*'s comm system instead. No response. He opened a channel to *Phoenix*. "Isin to Itorye." The line hummed, but no sounds came through. He met Byrd's gaze. "I think they're jamming us."

Byrd frowned. "That would be dumb after the threat you made." He gestured to the comm. "Any chance our system's down?"

He'd find out soon enough. "Shash to the bridge," he ordered over the internal comm. When she failed to appear, he bellowed over his shoulder. "Shash!"

She strode onto the bridge a moment later, her brows drawn down in annoyance. "What?"

"Why didn't you respond?"

"I did. You just shouted at me two seconds ago."

"I contacted you over the comm first."

"No, you didn't."

He swore. "Check the comm relays. Nothing's working."

Her eyes widened. She knew as well as he did how much they were counting on communicating with Sweep. "On it." She crouched on the deck and yanked off a panel.

"Do you want me to disengage?" Byrd nodded toward the viewport, where *Vengeance*'s bulk now filled the space.

If the problem lay with the *Dagger*'s comm system, changing their plan with Rathburn would only complicate an already tricky situation. And once they were onboard *Vengeance*, he could use the ship's comm to contact Sweep. "No. Stay on course."

Byrd nodded, keying in the remote command to open the bay doors. The indicator flashed green. "Doors opening."

Shash muttered in the background—swear words mostly—as she dug into the guts of the comm system. Isin took that to mean the system was, in fact, malfunctioning.

Byrd guided the *Dagger* into the channel at
*Vengeance*'s stern. The massive metal plates that sealed the
entrance to the bay had almost completed their cycle, now
open wide like a giant mouth waiting to gobble up the
transport.

Byrd made the approach look easy, but Isin knew
better. The vertical path and the lack of a guidance system
were designed to deter enemy vessels from attempting to
infiltrate the ship through the bay. Maneuvering a transport
as large as this one into the space took skill, one of the
reasons he'd kept Byrd on after the coup. Kenji could
manage the entry too, but Itorye used *Vengeance*'s auto-
docking system, which took twice as long.

As they rose into the belly of the ship, Isin made a
quick visual scan of the area. Everything looked the way
they'd left it, with the exception of the security doors. Itorye
would have activated them before she'd abandoned ship.
Now only the main pressure hatch stood between them and
the interior of the ship.

"Closing bay doors." Byrd settled the *Dagger* onto
the deck after the plating slid into place over the opening,
sealing the bay while the exterior doors made their slow
progression back to lockdown position.

Shash pushed to her feet as Byrd powered down
the *Dagger*'s engines. "The comm's busted, but I'd need at
least half an hour to isolate the problem and fix it."

Which they didn't have. "Any idea what caused it?"

"Looks like a short of some kind."

Isin turned to Byrd. "Why didn't you see any issues
when you checked the systems yesterday?"

He shrugged. "Everything seemed fine. It's not like I
was sending messages. I didn't have a reason to notice a

problem." He started to stand, but Isin placed a hand on his shoulder.

"No. I want you to stay with the *Dagger*, just in case we need to make a hasty exit." The unexpected short had put him on edge. His gut was telling him to be cautious.

Byrd settled back into his chair. "Sure thing."

Shash followed Isin off the bridge to the side hatch where Avril, Pine, and Summer waited for them, armed and ready.

"We have a communication problem with the *Dagger*," he informed them. "Avril, I want you to stay with Byrd for now." He met Avril's gaze. "We follow the plan."

Avril acknowledged with a nod.

Isin had put him in charge of getting Patel and Alec out of the *Dagger*'s storage compartment and into position. His task would have been easier if they'd been able to communicate with Sweep, but Avril was almost as resourceful as his mentor. He'd figure out a way to get Patel where she needed to be to disable the defense systems on Rathburn's ship, with or without Sweep's help.

"The rest of you are with me." After a quick check of the exterior, he led the way down the ramp and across the deck toward the main hatch.

The lights in the bay flickered, once, twice, three times. He paused, glancing up, his grip shifting on his rifle as a tendril of unease crept up his spine. The flickering stopped, but resumed a moment later, with longer gaps in between each flicker.

"I don't like this, Captain," Summer murmured, her gaze moving around the bay.

Neither did he. He motioned to either side of the main hatch. "Defensive positions." As his team followed his order, he moved to the comm panel. Sweep was onboard somewhere. He needed to contact him, find out if they had a problem.

But the panel was dark. No way to communicate.

His pulse pounded out a warning.

Shash sidled up next to him. "First the *Dagger*, now here? What's going on?"

"I wish I knew." He glanced back at the *Dagger*. Avril stood at the top of the ramp, rifle at the ready as he surveyed the flickering lights in the bay.

Shash pointed to the smaller hatch at the far end of the bay. "You want to split up? Come at them from both sides?" The flickering lights gave the gleam in her eyes a strobe effect.

"No. We stay together." But changing their strategy was the prudent move. "Watch our six. This way." Turning, he led the team past the *Dagger* to the back hatch.

When they reached it, he bypassed the control panel, going instead to the small recess to the right of the hatch and using the manual controls to slide the door open. If Rathburn was watching the ship's sensors from the bridge, monitoring their progress, the manual override would prevent him from realizing the back hatch had opened.

Isin had anticipated a wall of armed guards on the other side, but the small room the crew used for recreation was silent and empty as a tomb. He glanced at his team. "We check the C deck airlock first, then continue to the aft stairwell."

After closing the hatch, they climbed silently to C deck. He took point, Shash took the rear, with Pine and Summer in between. They reached the opening for the airlock without incident. It was sealed tight, with no access to Rathburn's ship and no sign of personnel. The comm panel here was as dark as the one in the bay.

He paused, listening, but the only sound was the steady thrum of the engines through the bulkhead, indicating Stevens had followed his order to prep the ship for departure. Was he creating monsters out of shadows? Had Rathburn shut down the comm system simply to limit Isin's ability to seize control of the ship without turning over Patel?

Only one way to find out.

They continued down the main C deck corridor, passing the crew quarters and the infirmary, and stopping at the aft stairwell. A quick check of the landings didn't reveal anything unusual. "I'll scout out B deck. Summer, cover me. Shash and Pine, wait for my signal."

Isin reached the first landing, but Shash's low whistle brought his head around. Someone was approaching from below.

He halted. So did Summer, their weapons trained on the narrow opening to the stairwell. But the lone figure that appeared was one Isin knew.

"Byrd?" Shash's harsh whisper barely reached Isin's ears as she came into view. "What the hell?"

Her words echoed his thoughts. He'd told the pilot to stay with the *Dagger*.

Byrd didn't bother to whisper. "I had to come."

Pine came out of the shadows to Byrd's right. "Why?"

"Because the comms were down. I couldn't contact you."

Isin descended the stairs. "What's wrong?"

"I had to tell you... it's a trap. You're surrounded."

The click of weapons drew Isin's attention. Five heavily armed mercenaries and uniformed guards materialized in the passageway behind Byrd, weapons trained on Isin and his team.

Before Isin could react, a matching echo from above made him look up. Six more mercenaries and guards had spread out across the stairwell.

He recognized two of them. They'd been with Kerr on Gallows Edge.

A sick feeling settled into his stomach as he turned to Byrd.

His pilot removed a gun from his belt and aimed it at Isin's chest. "Let's not keep Kerr waiting."

# *Thirty*

"Traitor!" Shash hissed. "You set us up!"

Byrd shrugged. "I got a better offer." He motioned to Isin. "Toss your weapons on the deck and raise your hands."

Molten lava poured through Isin's veins, but he did as instructed. Getting gunned down in the stairwell wasn't going to help the situation.

Pine, Summer, and Shash followed suit, although Shash hesitated for a moment. She was closest to Byrd, and had probably calculated the odds of successfully killing him before she got shot. The numbers must not have painted a positive picture, because she dropped her weapons on the deck. "Is Avril in on this?" she snarled.

Isin tensed. He'd left Avril in charge of Patel and—

"No, he's dead."

"Dead?" Shash jerked like Byrd had slapped her.

"I killed him."

A plume of liquid heat shot into Isin's belly. He gritted his teeth. "He was a good man."

Byrd gave him a bland look. "Don't blame me. That one's on you. You told him to stay with the *Dagger*. I wasn't planning to kill him, but he was in my way." Byrd didn't seem too bothered by it. "Now, let's go to the bridge. Nice and slow."

Isin's jaw clenched. He'd been blindsided, never suspecting his pilot was playing him. If he survived this day, he'd make sure Byrd didn't.

Byrd hadn't mentioned Patel, so hopefully she and Alec had remained hidden. Not that it would matter if Kerr had caught Sweep, too.

The climb to the bridge covered less than twenty meters and took an eternity.

Shash fired questions at Byrd on the way. "The *Dagger*'s comm. You sabotaged it, didn't you?"

"Temporarily. But it's fixed now. I used it to contact *Phoenix*."

"*Phoenix*? Why?"

"You'll see."

"Who's on *Phoenix*?" Shash's outrage rose to new heights. "You spineless wor—"

"Watch it, Shash." His sharp retort cut her off. "You're not in charge here. Remember that."

Isin's molars scraped together. He wasn't in charge, either. He needed to change that, but Kerr's minions stayed far enough ahead of him that he couldn't make contact if he lunged, and in such close quarters, it would be impossible for them to miss if they fired.

Judging by Byrd's comments, Itorye might be facing a similar problem on *Phoenix*, although she'd have Kenji and Fleur to back her up. And Jake and Marlin, although neither of them were fighters. He couldn't say where the rest of the crew would stand in this battle.

As they approached the bridge, he caught sight of Kerr just inside the aft hatch, his hands clasped like a dignitary receiving visitors.

"Ah, good. Our guest of honor has finally arrived." Kerr gave Isin an exaggerated bow.

Isin barely noticed. All of his attention focused on the person visible over Kerr's shoulder.

*Natasha!*

She was tied to the captain's chair facing him, her expression unreadable. Two men in crisp grey uniforms held weapons on her and Rathburn, who was strapped to the chair for the weapons console. None of the uniformed guards were helping their employer, and they weren't being watched by Kerr's crew, either. Apparently Rathburn had been betrayed as well. Wonderful. Was there anyone Kerr hadn't turned against them?

He spotted Stevens laying facedown on the deck near the aft bulkhead, his arms bound behind his back with manacles. The only person unaccounted for was Sweep.

"Welcome, Isin." Kerr's smile made Isin's palms itch for a weapon. "We've been expecting you."

One of Kerr's mercenaries nudged Isin forward using the muzzle of a rifle.

"Remove his armor," Kerr said. "If he resists, shoot her." He pointed at Natasha.

Her pale eyes blazed with fury as she glared at Kerr, her body tight as a bow. Her gaze shifted to Isin, the tension in her jaw relaxing a fraction as she met his gaze. "Fancy meeting you here."

Leave it to Natasha to make a quip during a tense situation. He responded in kind. "I was in the neighborhood."

That garnered him a tiny smile.

But he took Kerr's threat seriously. He allowed his armor to be stripped off and his hands to be bound behind his back with manacles that matched the ones he'd seen on Stevens. Judging by the way Natasha and Rathburn were sitting, they were cuffed as well.

The unhinged lunatic with delusions of grandeur standing in front of him watched the proceedings with sadistic glee. Negotiating his way out of this mess was impossible. All he could do was control the damage until an

182

opening presented itself. Hopefully Sweep was still alive and would find a way to provide one.

Kerr turned his attention to Isin's team. "Shash, you're looking beautiful as always."

"Stuff it, Kerr."

Isin bit back a snort of laughter.

Kerr did not look amused. "Why so hostile?"

Shash pointed an accusing finger at Byrd. "Because you told this worthless pile of sewer sludge to sabotage *Vengeance!*"

Kerr inclined his head, conceding the point. "But I've also repaired the damage. *Vengeance* is as good as new. Besides, I have an offer I think you'll like." He beckoned her forward.

She took her time obeying the silent command. But she did obey.

Kerr reached out, capturing her hands and bringing them to his lips. "I would very much like for you to stay on as my... engineer," he murmured, placing a kiss on her fingertips. "I'll make it a very profitable arrangement."

"I'll bet he would," Summer grumbled.

"Shut up," Shash snapped. "No one's talking to you."

The corners of Kerr's mouth lifted in what Isin assumed was supposed to be a charming smile. "You know we could do great things together. We were always very... compatible."

Shash's answering smile made Isin's stomach turn. He'd known she played fast and loose with the male members of the crew, but he hadn't been aware of any history with Kerr.

"I'll think about it."

"Do." He released her and faced Pine and Summer. "What about you? Do you want to keep your jobs?"

Pine didn't hesitate. "As long as I get paid, I don't care who's in charge."

Isin bit his tongue to keep from commenting.

Summer lifted her chin. "What if I don't want to work for you?"

Kerr lifted one shoulder in a casual shrug, then whipped a pistol from his belt and fired, the shot grazing the outside of Summer's thigh.

She staggered as her leg gave way, dropping her to the deck.

Kerr strode forward, looming over her. "The next time you challenge me, I'll aim for your heart."

# Thirty-One

Nat had always known Kerr was a lunatic. But she hadn't understood the full scope of his madness until that moment.

While the woman he'd shot lay on the deck with her hands pressed to her bleeding thigh, Kerr dismissed her with a flick of his fingers and strolled over to Isin. "Now that the preliminaries are over, it's time to get down to business."

To Isin's credit, he didn't seem the least bit concerned by their predicament. He stared Kerr down like he was in complete control of the situation.

Too bad he wasn't.

"The question is, what am I going to do with you?" Kerr circled Isin like a shark. "I should probably just kill you. Simple. Effective. Saves me from having to worry that you'll make one of your miraculous escapes like last time." Kerr lifted the pistol.

Nat's pulse thundered through her veins. *Please don't—*

"But there's no fun in that. One moment you're here, the next you're gone. And then what? I'm stuck dealing with your smelly corpse." He lowered the weapon and continued to circle, studying Isin like he was an experiment in a science lab. "On the other hand, if I keep you alive, the possibilities for entertainment are endless."

Nat's throat tightened. She could easily imagine the kinds of torture he would find entertaining.

"But there are risks. You're too resourceful for your own good. Which means I need a way to keep you in check." He paused, his gaze searching the bridge and coming to rest on her.

*Oh, no.* The smile she'd come to hate curled his lip.

"And I have just the thing." Kerr strolled up the steps to the captain's chair and braced his hands on the armrests, leaning down until their noses almost touched. "Comfortable?"

"Perfectly."

His blue eyes glowed with an unholy flame. "Let's see what we can do to change that."

# *Thirty-Two*

Isin's blood roared in his ears, making it difficult to hear Kerr's words. But the press of a weapon into his back got him moving toward the chair for the tactical console. While Kerr's people secured him to the seat, facing Natasha, his nemesis continued to gaze at her with a sadistic smile.

"Did Isin have time to share the details of his experience in my infirmary?"

She stared at him, but didn't respond.

"No?" He slowly pivoted the captain's chair so it was facing Isin. Crouching beside it, he shifted so he could keep both of them in his line of sight. "I tried out a new method for generating intense pain. Needles inserted along the finger bones combined with a nerve agent." The memory brought a glow to his eyes. "From what I observed, it burns like you're touching the center of a white-hot furnace."

An apt description.

Kerr leaned in, his mouth beside Natasha's ear, but his voice carried easily. "All you can think about is the pain. I believe there were moments when he forgot I was in the room."

Not exactly. His nemesis had always remained at the center of the supernova.

"Shall we ask him? He's experienced the effects first hand, so to speak." Kerr's malevolent smile mocked him. "Isin, anything you'd care to add?"

"Drop dead."

A ghost of a smile passed over Natasha's lips.

Kerr's smile turned brittle. "Charming, as always." He focused on Natasha, all signs of humor vanishing. "But your ship's arrival interrupted our fun." He shoved the muzzle of his gun under her chin.

She inhaled sharply.

"I could kill you for that."

Isin yanked at the bonds holding him to the chair, but they didn't budge. If Kerr pulled the trigger—

As quickly as Kerr's anger had spiked, it faded. He eased the weapon back down. "However, that would be short-sighted. There are so many other... possibilities. In fact, I think I'll repeat the experiment for Isin's enjoyment. With you as my test subject."

If Isin's thoughts had form, he would have burned Kerr to ash at Natasha's feet.

"I have the nerve agent and a few other surprises in my kit." He patted a pocket in his jacket. "But that will have to wait. Unless, of course, you want to beg me to let you go. I always have time for that."

Natasha made a low sound in her throat, opened her mouth, and spit into his face.

The glob of liquid hit right between his eyes, slid down his nose, and dripped off the tip. Kerr straightened slowly, his gaze never leaving Natasha as he wiped his face with his gloved hand. "Very well. We'll continue this discussion later. For now, I'll leave you with this." Flipping the gun in his hand, he struck Natasha across the face with the grip.

Isin lunged, but his bonds held him to the chair like a vise.

Kerr glanced at him, his smile returning as a red mark bloomed on Natasha's cheek. "I have more important items to attend to, anyway. But you'll both want to listen up.

This concerns you, too." He addressed Byrd, who sat at the navigation console. "What's the word from Buggy?"

*So Buggy was also a traitor. Not surprising.*

"They've taken control of engineering. *Phoenix* isn't going anywhere. But Kenji and Fleur have sealed off the bridge."

Nat's gaze snapped to Isin's, her eyes wide.

Byrd had just confirmed what he'd implied in the stairwell. A mutiny had overrun *Phoenix*.

"What about Itorye?" Kerr asked.

"They haven't been able to locate her."

A small victory.

Kerr's face flushed. "Reactivate *Vengeance*'s comm system, and remind Buggy I want her alive," he growled. He turned to one of his lackeys. "Tell Rossi to move *Viper* into attack position on *Phoenix*. We'll be joining them shortly."

# Thirty-Three

Nat shouted every derogatory term she could think of at Kerr. In her mind, at least.

Her cheek throbbed with each beat of her heart, making her squint. She'd probably have a shiner by morning, assuming she lived that long. But the blow had been worth the look on Kerr's face.

Of course, if they didn't find a way out of this mess, her ship and her body would become Kerr's personal playgrounds.

And that was a big *if*. She'd counted more than fifteen members of Kerr's turncoat army onboard, plus whoever he had in the engine room. Shash and the man from Isin's group both seemed inclined to change allegiance. Shash's attitude bothered her more than she'd expected. She'd hoped the woman had more loyalty to Isin. Then again, Isin had threatened her life on at least one occasion. Nat had been there to witness it. Maybe this was Shash's form of payback.

With Pete unconscious and the other woman from Isin's team injured, even if she, Isin, and Rathburn escaped their bonds, they'd still be unarmed and outnumbered six or seven to one.

She was a good fighter, but she'd never faced those kinds of odds before.

No doubt Isin had more experience, but he was trussed up tighter than she was. She couldn't see Rathburn, but it didn't matter. She couldn't expect any help from him, either.

The only wild card was Sweep. He had to be on the ship somewhere. Kerr would have brought him to the bridge if he'd found him, dead or alive. So far, he hadn't even acted like he knew he was onboard. But without any way to communicate with them, Sweep was on his own. So were they.

And then there was *Phoenix*. Byrd had said Kenji and Fleur were on the bridge, but what about Marlin? He was a cook, not a mercenary. He didn't know how to defend himself. Would the turncoats from Isin's crew shoot him on sight? Was he already dead?

If he was, it would be her fault. She'd dragged him into this. And Pete. Without her meddling, they'd both be living normal lives. Well, normal-ish. Instead, they'd thrown their lot in with her. Bad bet.

She pressed her wrists against the manacles. No give. The cable wrapped around her torso wasn't as tight, but it also wasn't loose enough that she could slip out of the chair. Even if she did, she was on a platform in the middle of the room, an easy target for any of Kerr's people who decided to shoot.

Kerr turned to Byrd. "Disengage and get us to *Phoenix*."

The three-hundred-sixty degree bridgescreen sprang to life, giving Nat a view along *Cerberus*'s starboard side to the stern, with the starfield beyond. The deck hummed as the ship's thrusters engaged. Nat's pulse accelerated in time with the engines. There had to be a way out of this. *Had* to be!

She met Isin's gaze, pleading. But all she saw was the same frustration that was building in her own chest.

The image on the bridgescreen pivoted as Byrd disengaged *Vengeance* from *Cerberus* and maneuvered the ship into open space.

Kerr glanced back at Nat and Isin, his manic smile making her shudder.

*Sweep, where are you?*

"Captain!" one of Kerr's minions called out. "Comm from *Viper*. They're taking heavy fire from *Phoenix*."

"What?" Kerr's smile vanished as he rounded on Byrd. "You said we had control!"

"We did!" Byrd touched his earpiece. "Buggy, report!" His jaw sagged open as he listened to the response, trepidation blotting out the cocky confidence in his eyes as he met Kerr's gaze. "Buggy's dead. So's Saddle. Ranger and Willow are pinned down in the engine room. Dot and Faraway are the only two still on the move."

Kerr's voice cut like diamond on glass. "Full assault on *Phoenix*. Take them down. In pieces if you have to."

"No!" Rathburn's shout brought Nat's head around so quickly her chair pivoted a quarter turn.

Rathburn strained against the bindings holding him to his chair. "Dr. Patel's on that ship!"

Kerr's malevolent glare bored into Rathburn. "Who?"

"She's a brilliant scientist. Revolutionary. You can't kill her."

"Oh, I assure you I can. And I will."

"I'll pay you! Anything you ask." Panic drew lines on Rathburn's face.

Kerr looked amused. "Anything?"

"Anything. Just don't destroy *Phoenix*."

Kerr cocked his head and made a show of considering the offer. "No, I don't think so."

"Why not?" Anger blended with the fear in Rathburn's voice. "I could set you up for life. Think about it. You'd never have to work again."

"Oh, but I enjoy my work. And money can be taken away." Kerr's hideous smile resurfaced. "But the memory of your suffering will last a lifetime."

Rathburn stared, unable to come up with a response.

Nat leapt into the breach. "What about your people?" *And what about Marlin?* "They're still onboard. If you destroy *Phoenix,* your people will die, too."

"I don't reward failure."

So much for that tactic. And she'd unwittingly shifted his focus to her.

He moved beside her, his arm wrapping around the front of the chair like he was hugging her. The hug of a boa constrictor.

"You won't want to miss this," he purred, tapping the controls on the chair's armrest. The image on the bridgescreen magnified, giving her a view of the battle between his ship and *Phoenix.*

Scorch marks marred the gold paint along *Phoenix's* flank, the blast points indicating *Viper* was attempting to knock out *Phoenix's* weapons. But Kerr's ship looked worse. A patch job to the hull showed where Sweep had blown out the ship's weapons during the previous skirmish. The repairs apparently weren't complete, because *Phoenix's* cannons pummeled the smaller vessel with far greater intensity than *Viper's* weapons generated, adding to the damage already scarring the grey metal exterior. Even as a stationary target, *Phoenix* was holding her own.

That would change as soon as *Vengeance* joined the fight.

"It's a pretty ship, isn't it?"

She flinched as Kerr's voice dripped into her ear.

"I might consider sparing it... if you ask me nicely."

She bit the inside of her cheek to keep from voicing the words that sprang to her lips. Kerr wouldn't change his mind about destroying *Phoenix*. He'd just enjoy the sadistic pleasure of making her think he would.

His breath brushed across her cheek. "Think of your crew. I'm a reasonable man."

Nat snorted.

His fingers tightened on the armrest. "They don't have to die today. Just ask me to spare them."

She stared straight ahead as the image of *Phoenix* loomed closer. Another minute and they'd be in weapons range.

"Ask me to spare them," Kerr crooned, grabbing hold of her jaw in an iron grip.

She pressed her lips together.

"Ask me," he repeated, his hand sliding to her throat. He began to squeeze.

She fought against the constriction as her air supply choked off.

"Ask me."

"Kerr, stop!" Isin's voice, but it sounded distant.

Spots swam before her eyes, the pressure in her chest warring with the tension in her throat.

"Natasha!"

"Nat!"

Part of her brain registered the shouts and thumps as Isin and Rathburn fought against their bonds. But they wouldn't get free in time. None of them would.

# Thirty-Four

"Time's up," Kerr whispered.

She waited to black out, but instead he eased the pressure on her throat, allowing a thin stream of air into her lungs. She wheezed, blinking to clear her vision.

Kerr turned to the mercenary standing over Rathburn at the weapons console. "Open fire."

"No." She forced the croak from her mouth, but it barely counted as a sound, let alone an objection.

Kerr certainly wasn't impressed.

She stared at the image on the bridgescreen as her breath sawed in and out. But it didn't change. No cannon fire, no torpedoes, nothing. At least, not from *Vengeance*.

Kerr's voice cracked like a whip. "I said fire!"

"I'm trying!" The mercenary hunched over the console, poking at the controls. "I'm entering the commands, but the ship's not responding."

Nat took a shuddering breath. *Thank you, Sweep.* He was the only person who could have prevented the ship from firing.

Kerr stood slowly, his gaze on Rathburn. "Did your people disable the weapons?"

Or maybe not.

Rathburn shook his head. "No."

Kerr clearly didn't believe him. He turned to one of Rathburn's former guards. "Did they?"

Two of the guards exchanged a glance. "Not that we heard."

Not the answer Kerr wanted. His face resembled a thundercloud as he glared at the bridgescreen. "Byrd, change of plans. Plot a straight line to *Phoenix*. Ramming speed."

*Ramming speed?*

"Don't do it, Kerr." Isin wasn't begging, but his voice held a note of desperation. "*Phoenix* is a sturdy ship. You could cripple *Vengeance* with a ramming assault."

Kerr pivoted toward Isin. "You and I both know that's not true. *Vengeance* will be fine." His gaze dropped to Nat. "We might tear a few hull plates off when we rip through your little freighter, but that's a small price to pay, don't you think?" His soft chuckle sent ice chips through her veins.

Byrd glanced back at Kerr. "*Phoenix* is hailing us."

"I thought they might." He turned to Isin. "You make a sound, and we'll find out how quickly I can snap your little friend's neck." He placed a hand on Nat's shoulder.

Isin's jaw tightened, but he gave a sharp nod of understanding.

Kerr motioned to Byrd. "By all means, answer them. Put it on speaker."

Itorye's voice was the only sound on the bridge. "Itorye to Isin."

"This is Byrd."

"Byrd? Where's Isin?"

Byrd pivoted his chair to face Isin and smirked. "Tied up at the moment."

"Are you at navigation?"

"Yes."

"Then check your readings. You're on a collision course."

"Am I?"

Byrd's smug smile fed the flames burning in Nat's belly. The battle between *Phoenix* and *Viper* now filled three-quarters of the forward bridgescreen. Lights flared as the two ships continued to exchange fire.

"Turn sixty-point-two degrees to port and give us some cover fire."

Byrd's smile widened as his gaze shifted to Kerr. "Sorry, I can't."

"Why not?"

Kerr responded. "Because we have a previous engagement with you, my dear. We wouldn't want to miss it."

An audible inhalation preceded Itorye's reply. "*Kerr.*" The loathing in her voice was the first strong emotion Nat had ever heard from Isin's first mate.

Kerr's gaze remained locked on *Phoenix.* "But don't worry. Isin will be joining you shortly."

"You twisted son-of-a—"

Kerr made a slashing motion and Byrd closed the channel.

"Now, where were we?" Kerr clapped his hands together and faced Nat, Isin, and Rathburn. "Ah, yes. Annihilation. I'm really going to enjoy this."

Nat refused to look at him, her attention focused on the image of *Phoenix.* She didn't want to watch her ship being ripped apart, but that was nothing compared to what would come next. Marlin. Kenji. Itorye. Fleur. Jake. They were all going to die in the black because of this psychotic wacko.

And she couldn't stop him. She couldn't—

She blinked. Had the image shifted? No, surely not. There was no way... was there?

Except it had. The image had rotated five degrees to port.

*Sweep? Is that you?*

"What is it?"

Kerr's question pulled her gaze back to him. He'd been watching her closely, his eyes narrowing. He glanced over his shoulder, then spun around. "Did you change course?" he demanded.

"No!" Byrd snapped to attention as Kerr practically vaulted down the steps of the platform and grabbed the back of Byrd's chair. "Navigation's not responding!"

"Get it back!"

Byrd's hands flew over the controls, but the image on the bridgescreen continued to rotate away from *Phoenix* toward Kerr's ship.

"I can't!"

"Reverse thrusters."

Byrd's movements grew frantic. He pounded a fist on the console. "Nothing's working!"

"Then kill the engines!"

"Don't you understand?" Byrd shouted. "I can't do anything!"

The crew of *Viper* must have realized they had a problem, because the ship stopped firing at *Phoenix* and altered course. But *Vengeance* tracked Kerr's ship like a bloodhound, following each change in position, keeping *Viper* trapped in the crosshairs of *Vengeance*'s prow as if the two ships were bound by an invisible cord that was rapidly reeling the smaller ship in.

Kerr swung around, looking past Nat. "Shash, get to the engine room and kill the power. Now!"

Nat couldn't see whether the engineer moved to follow the order, but it didn't matter. The lights on the bridge flickered once, twice, before the room plunged into darkness.

# *Thirty-Five*

Isin froze when the lights went out, his other senses filling the void when he could no longer see.

"Lights!" Kerr screeched from the direction of the navigation console.

But the pitch black indicated it wasn't just the lights that had failed. The consoles weren't providing any illumination, either. All bridge functions had ceased.

The vibration through the deck, however, indicated the engines were still running. The ship was flying blind.

So was he.

He jerked against the cables wrapped around his chest, more in frustration than because he expected them to give. But a split second later, the pressure from the manacles around his wrists eased and the metal retracted, freeing his hands.

"I said lights!" Kerr's roar seemed a little closer, like he might be making his way toward the captain's chair.

*Natasha!*

Beams of light cut through the darkness, searching for a target.

With his hands free, Isin made short work of the bindings around his chest, which had loosened as his arms changed position. He shoved the cables over his head and bent to remove the bindings at his ankles, keeping his body as compact as possible.

Proximity alarms blared. He snapped his head up, instinctively searching for the cause, but the flailing lights from Kerr's crew reflected off the blank bridgescreen.

"Get me visual!" Kerr continued to shout commands like he was in control of the situation, his voice barely audible over the klaxons and the panicked shouts of his crew.

Isin pulled one leg free and started working on the second.

A high-pitched wail, like a banshee's call, cut through the cacophony.

Imminent collision.

He gave up on the bindings and braced for impact. "Natasha, hold on!"

When *Vengeance* plowed into whatever object had set off the alarm, Isin's body jolted hard enough to click his teeth together, while the ship shook like it was caught in a violent storm. A metallic shriek resonated through the bulkheads from the hull, blending with the screams of the people who'd been caught unprepared, turning the bridge into a giant echo chamber.

He couldn't pick Natasha's voice out of the chaos, but that didn't mean she wasn't injured. Keeping one arm wrapped around his knees for stability, he fought against the cable securing his leg to the chair.

The tremors wracking the ship increased, making the task even harder, but he finally managed to free himself.

A light beam swung wildly across the bridge, moving in time to the bucking of the deck. He slid partway off the chair, using it as a visual shield as he got his bearings.

The beam passed over the captain's chair and Isin's chest tightened.

Kerr gripped the arms of the chair, the light briefly playing across his features, revealing a grotesque mask of unbridled rage.

But there was no sign of Natasha.

Kerr looked in Isin's direction as the beam danced away again.

That's when things got interesting.

A series of muffled pops from the back of the bridge were followed by shouts and the thump of bodies striking the deck. Within seconds, the room erupted with random gunfire, flashes of light, and shrieks of pain.

Isin needed a weapon, fast. And he knew exactly where to find one.

Three lurching strides carried him to the navigation console, the ambient light from the flailing beams faintly differentiating Byrd's silhouette from the surrounding darkness.

He was crouched behind the console, facing the aft section, his rifle in his hand. He must have sensed movement because he swung the weapon in Isin's direction and fired.

The shot went wide. Isin didn't give him a chance to take another.

He charged, channeling the rage burning in his chest, driving Byrd against the console.

His fist struck Byrd's cheekbone. The pilot jerked to the side, turning Isin's next swing into a glancing blow.

Byrd thrust the stock of the rifle against Isin's solar plexus, making him grunt, but Isin had a hundred pounds, hours of fighting experience, and white-hot fury on his side.

He grabbed the front of the pilot's jacket and slammed Byrd's head against the console. "You betrayed me." Yank, shove, wham! "Betrayed our crew." Yank, shove, wham!

"Betrayed Natasha." The console rattled as Byrd's head struck a fourth time.

"Go to hell!" Byrd's words were a little garbled, but he shoved the rifle between their bodies.

Isin took advantage of the weapon's position, using it to pin Byrd in place. Light played over Byrd's face for a split second, revealing the hatred in his eyes. The complete lack of remorse.

Mercy fled. Isin wanted blood. Focusing the force of his rage to a single point, he thrust the heel of his hand into Byrd's nose, shattering bone and cartilage, driving them deep into Byrd's skull.

The pilot's body stiffened, then went limp.

He'd never betray anyone again.

Isin pushed away from the console, allowing Byrd to slide to the deck. He plucked the rifle out of the pilot's lifeless hands with a grim smile. One debt settled.

Shifting into a defensive stance, he brought the rifle up and swept it across the command platform, searching for Kerr.

But the smattering of light failed to reveal his target. The platform was empty.

# *Thirty-Six*

She was free!

When the manacles miraculously retracted, Nat made quick work of the rest of her bindings. A slim build and flexibility had their advantages, as did years of practice getting out of every type of restraint she'd encountered.

Good thing, too. She sensed Kerr in front of her a nanosecond before she slipped around the captain's chair and off the back of the platform.

She ducked close to the deck to avoid the lights that swept toward her, the raised platform giving her momentary cover as she crouched on the side farthest from the back hatch. Rathburn was behind her, Isin on the opposite side, Kerr above.

Proximity alarms blared. Her gaze darted to the bridgescreens, but their blank faces gave no hint of danger.

"Get me visual!" Kerr shouted.

The lunatic actually believed he was still in control. The bridgescreens remained dark, but the beams of light grew more chaotic as Kerr's crew panicked.

She pressed against the platform, keeping her gaze toward the sources of light near the back of the bridge. But when one of the beams glanced off a still form lying on the deck five meters away, the air vacated her lungs. *Pete!*

The manacles that had been around his wrists lay on the deck, but he was still unconscious, his arms flopped at odd angles to his torso, his face pressed against the deck.

Booted silhouettes darted around him, one coming dangerously close to stepping on his head.

Isin and Rathburn would have to fend for themselves. She couldn't leave Pete to be trampled by Kerr's crew.

The lights danced away and Nat raced forward. Darkness had always been her ally. She didn't need light to navigate. Reaching down, she felt the brush of fabric and followed the path with her fingers until she touched the bare skin and scruff of Pete's beard.

Pressing her fingers to the side of his neck, she checked for a pulse. It was there, strong and steady. At least Kerr hadn't lied about that.

A high-pitched wail cut through the pandemonium, making her heart stutter. After a lifetime on starships, she knew what that sound meant.

"Natasha, hold on!" Isin's shout blended with the wailing siren.

*To what?* She and Pete were in the middle of the deck.

Dropping to her belly, she wrapped her arms and legs around Pete and held on tight.

The jolt that followed sent them both sliding along the deck like seals. A metallic shriek and screams of pain filled her ears. Her right side smacked against something unyielding, halting their momentum. She reached out a hand, connecting with metal. The platform. She was back where she'd started.

Tremors shook the ship, making it difficult to balance, but she managed to push to her knees, cradling Pete in her arms in the lee of the platform. The deck bucked, a beam of light sweeping over their heads in a haphazard arc.

It glanced off the captain's chair, revealing Kerr gripping the armrests for support, his face twisted in a snarl.

She reacted on instinct, shoving to her feet and hooking her arms under Pete's so she could drag him toward the port bulkhead, struggling to put distance between them and Kerr. Pete's extra mass acted as a balancer, helping her remain upright as the deck continued to quake.

Muffled pops sounded from the back of the bridge, followed by shouts and the thump of bodies striking the deck. She jerked to a halt and crouched. *Isin?*

The room erupted with random gunfire, flashes of light, and shrieks of pain.

Isin or not, she had no weapon, and no cover. Dropping as low as possible, she backpedaled, hauling Pete as quickly as her overworked muscles would allow.

Four or five meters, that's all she needed. There was a small room located off the bridge. She'd found it during her inspection tour with Rathburn. If she could get Pete inside and lock the hatch, he would be safe. Then she could decide her next move.

A rifle blast exploded from the direction of the navigation console. She flinched. Was Kerr's crew shooting at Rathburn or Isin?

She hadn't anticipated an assault from that direction. She yanked Pete backward toward the bulkhead, but the shaking of the deck didn't make the task any easier. She grunted with each step, fighting to stay on her feet. At least with all the noise in the room, she didn't have to worry about being quiet.

When her heels finally bumped against the bulkhead, she paused, adjusting her grip on Pete so she could feel for the door panel.

A hand clamped onto her shoulder.

She yelped.

"Going somewhere?" a horribly familiar voice hissed in her ear right before a sharp pain stabbed the side of her neck.

Her entire body stiffened as Kerr's hand covered her mouth. She released her hold on Pete with her right hand and drove her elbow back into Kerr's solar plexus, eliciting a satisfying grunt.

But it was a small victory. A millisecond later her muscles stopped responding to her commands. Her head lolled against Kerr's chest. She tried to lift it. Failed.

*What was wrong with...? How had he...?* She couldn't even complete a thought. Nothing tracked, the noises surrounding her growing muddled. Pete slid from her grasp, not because she'd consciously let go, but because the bones in her arms had turned to rubber.

"That's better." Kerr whispered as he released his hold on her mouth and hauled her off her feet. "You're coming with me."

# Thirty-Seven

The cacophony of combat buffeted Isin as he crept toward the weapons console. He had to find Natasha, and that seemed the best place to start looking. The bridge didn't provide many options for cover except for the three main consoles and the captain's chair. She hadn't joined him after she'd gotten free, she wasn't at the navigation console, and she wasn't on the captain's platform, which left the console where Rathburn had been tied up.

But she wasn't there. Neither was Rathburn.

"Isin!"

He whirled around. *Sweep!*

"Kerr! The forward hatch! He has—" Sweep's shout cut off abruptly.

But Isin was already in motion. A pale rectangle of grey at the front of the room created a vague silhouette of a muscular figure moving through the partially open forward hatch. The figure turned sideways, the silhouette changing. The image stopped Isin's heart.

Kerr carried Natasha like a ragdoll, her back to his chest, her head and arms flopping bonelessly. The pair disappeared from view, the rectangle shrinking behind them.

Isin sprinted toward the hatch, but he didn't reach it before it sealed. A rifle blast slammed into the bulkhead to his right, centimeters from his head. He dropped to the deck. No way was he going to be taken out by a stray shot.

The door's control panel was still dark. Kerr must have used the manual override. Isin felt around for the small access panel, turned the lever to release the door lock, and shoved the hatch wide enough to squeeze through into the corridor.

He took precious seconds to slide the hatch closed again. He didn't want Kerr's cronies following.

The faint scuffle of footsteps reached out to him, the light filtering up from the stairwell allowing him to make out the shapes of the passageway in front of him and the stairs directly to his left. He paused, turning his head to triangulate the location of the source.

The stairwell.

He started down.

# Thirty-Eight

*Bounce, bounce, bounce. Down, down, down.*

Nat giggled, the sound coming out of her throat in bursts as she flopped to and fro with each step Kerr took. She should be upset, shouldn't she? But why, when she felt so gooooood. Drunk, but not drunk. She hadn't been drinking, had she?

"Laugh all you want," Kerr snarled as he made the turn on the landing and started down another flight of stairs. "When we get out of this system, you won't be laughing anymore."

*Why not?* That's what she'd meant to ask him, but her tongue wouldn't cooperate. Her jaw moved and a sound came out, but Kerr didn't act like he'd heard her. She tried again. "Wwwwhhhhhyy—"

Kerr halted, slapping his hand over her mouth.

*Yuck!* She blew a raspberry against his palm.

He yanked her sideways, then everything spun until she was hanging face down over his back, his shoulder knocking into her abdomen as he hurried down the stairs.

Pressure built in her forehead and behind her eyes, her pulse beating in her ears. *Bad, bad, bad. Thump, thump, thump.*

Level ground, more light. A passageway. A door. Her world spun again, her limbs flailing. A grunt from Kerr, her feet hitting the deck, a low beep from behind, and a metallic swoosh.

Airborne again, her feet dangling and Kerr's face near hers, his hot breath against her neck.

"Let her go."

A familiar voice. Deep. Dark. Dangerous.

A shape materializing, a living shadow, stalking forward.

*Isin.*

# Thirty-Nine

Kerr was a dead man.

As Natasha's gaze met Isin's, a goofy grin spread across her cheeks, as though she were completely oblivious to the barrel of Kerr's gun tracking in his direction. Her reaction, coupled with her not-quite-focused eyes and puppet-like body movements, indicated Kerr had drugged her.

Rage clawed its way through Isin's chest. He positioned the bulkhead panel he'd grabbed to use as an improvised shield in front of his neck and torso, Byrd's rifle in his other hand. His armor was still somewhere on the bridge.

He matched Kerr step for step as the coward backed into the shuttle bay, holding Natasha against his chest so that his head was mostly hidden behind hers, her body covering his.

"Let her go."

Natasha rolled her eyes and blew air out of loose lips, like he'd said something mildly amusing.

Her complete lack of understanding of the danger added fuel to the fire in his belly.

Kerr peered at him through a tuft of her hair. "I'd rather shoot you."

*Same here.* "You won't make it off this ship alive." All he needed was an opening. Just one. A moment of distraction and Kerr would fall.

Kerr continued to back up, aiming for the *Dagger*'s ramp. "You won't risk harming her."

He was right. Which put Kerr in the power position. Maybe the answer was giving him more power. "You want a hostage? Fine. Take me instead. Let her go."

"No deal. I need her. But if you want to come along too, that could be... arranged."

"If you have me, you don't need her."

"Wrong. She's going to fly us out of this system."

So that was his plan. With Byrd dead, he needed a pilot. "She's in no condition to fly."

Only fifteen meters until Kerr reached the ramp. "She will be. I've got the drug's counteragent in my kit. In less than a minute she'll be right as rain."

A small piece of good news, but he'd take it. "And after you make it out of the system?"

Kerr's chuckle made Isin's skin crawl. "She'll be my personal pilot until I find other uses for her."

Heat built in Isin's chest and climbed up his throat. "She'll refuse. She won't take you anywhere."

"Yes, she will. You'd be surprised how persuasive pain can be. And I'm very good at inflicting pain. As you know."

Oh, yes, he certainly did.

Five meters to the ramp. The tangled form of a body lay on the deck to one side, arms and legs askew in a pool of blood. *Avril.*

Isin's throat constricted. Byrd hadn't lied about killing him.

Kerr's steps slowed. "If you truly want to come with us, I'll take you. But you'll be playing by my rules. And I guarantee, you won't like them."

Spoken like a true sadist.

Natasha's gaze met his. He didn't see fear in her eyes, or anger, just bemusement. That would change the moment Kerr injected her with the counteragent. And then hell would open up to swallow her whole.

He couldn't let her face it alone. "Fine. Your rules."

# *Forty*

Kerr's laughter buffeted Nat's ears. Annoying.

"Oh, my. Could this be true love?"

*Love? Ha!* She tried to laugh, but it came out as a blurt of air.

"Your damsel in distress doesn't seem to share your affections."

Isin looked mad. Why was he so mad? She wasn't mad. In fact, she'd never been happier. He needed to get happy.

"That'll be fun to watch, too. Later." Kerr's voice turned cold. "Set down the panel—slowly—and toss the rifle toward the bulkhead."

Isin did what Kerr said. Were they playing a game? If so, Isin was good at this game.

Kerr backed up the ramp, taking her with him.

*We're going for a ride!* A giggle bubbled up from her chest.

Isin started to follow.

"Not so fast."

Isin halted partway up the ramp. "You said I could go with you."

*Yes, yes, come with!* They hadn't flown together in *forever.*

"A little insurance." Kerr pointed the pistol at Isin's leg.

Isin tensed.

*Wait. Why—*

"Excuse me."

The female voice made Kerr spin around, dragging Nat with him.

But nobody was there.

# Forty-One

Isin charged to the top of the ramp. He had to reach Kerr before—

Kerr turned and fired.

A white-hot rivet ripped through Isin's abdomen, making him stumble, but the rage pouring through his veins carried him forward. He slammed into Kerr's side, knocking him off balance. They struck the bulkhead across from the ramp and Kerr dropped Natasha.

She flopped to the deck at their feet with a thump.

Kerr recovered quickly, moving the gun back in Isin's direction.

He grabbed hold of Kerr's shooting arm, eliciting more pain from his abdomen.

They grappled for a moment before Kerr jabbed Isin's stomach.

*Agony!* He doubled over, his grip on Kerr's arm slipping.

He caught sight of Natasha in his peripheral vision, lying on the deck, staring up at them with drug-induced curiosity.

Kerr took advantage of his momentary distraction to pivot, pressing Isin's back against the bulkhead, pinning his shoulder with his free hand.

Isin responded with a head butt that made Kerr's eyes water.

Kerr's knee jerked up, the glancing blow to Isin's abdomen sending another surge of pain that vacated the air in his lungs.

Kerr pushed against Isin's hold on his gun hand. "Give up, Isin. You're already a dead man."

Isin grunted as Kerr exerted more pressure, forcing the barrel of the gun down.

"Whaaaaaaaatt?"

*Natasha.* Still watching them, innocent and unaware.

"If you don't resist, I might even kill you quickly."

Isin fought against the pain tearing through his torso and the gun moving toward his head, pushing it back a centimeter, then two.

Kerr bore down. "Or I can watch you suffer. That's fun, too."

He lost the ground he'd gained as he shifted his body to block Kerr's next knee to his stomach.

"I've won, Isin. Accept it. You're beaten."

"Go to... hell." His grip slipped a little more, his strength waning as his wound pulsed with fire. He needed a weapon, but the only one in reach was in Kerr's hand.

The muzzle of the gun sank lower. "It's a fitting end. You were always meant to die on *Vengeance*."

"So... were you." His breath sawed in and out in panting gasps.

Kerr tilted his head closer, his words a conspirator's whisper. "Too bad, really. I was so looking forward to continuing your... education."

Another centimeter. He could almost see into the barrel. His gaze darted to Natasha.

She stared at him, uncomprehending.

He had to protect her. Had to find a way.

Kerr followed the direction of his gaze. "Oh, don't worry. I'll make sure your whore learns everything I planned to teach you."

Time stopped.

No pain. No breath. No sound.

A moment of perfect stillness, every molecule held in suspension as a torrent of images filled his mind.

The infirmary. The metal glove. The needles. The torture.

And Natasha.

He met Kerr's gaze.

"We'll have so much fun."

His enemy's sadistic smile ripped a hole in Isin's sanity.

An animalistic roar erupted from his chest, adrenaline flooding his body, driving the pain into a laser beam of clarity.

A matching feral fury lit Kerr's eyes as his finger closed on the trigger.

Isin pitched his body sideways and swept his leg out, knocking Kerr off his feet and sending them both crashing to the deck.

The gun went off.

Kerr shrieked.

The volcano in Isin's abdomen erupted as he collapsed partially on top of Kerr.

Kerr's head struck the deck hard enough that the metal clanged. Something else clattered to the floor. The gun?

One... two... three breaths passed before Isin lifted his head.

Kerr's hand was empty. He wasn't moving, either. Air rasped in and out of his throat in harsh, gurgled pants.

Isin pushed to his forearms, his gaze moving to Kerr's chest. A point-blank entry wound seeped red blood.

Kerr had shot himself.

A sigh leaked from Isin's lips and his head drooped. It was over.

"Iiiiiiissssss?"

He turned his head.

Natasha was propped on her elbow, staring at him. Still bewildered. Still innocent. Her gaze moved to Kerr.

So did his.

Kerr stared back, hatred eclipsing the pain etched on his face. He lurched, like he was trying for the gun.

*Hell, no!*

Gathering the fragments of his strength, Isin hauled his body forward. He planted his elbows on Kerr's chest, face-to-face with his personal demon, and locked his hands around Kerr's throat like talons.

*No more torture!*

Kerr bucked as Isin cut off his air, but without much force.

Isin's weight pressed him to the deck.

Kerr's right arm swung, smacking the side of Isin's face.

Isin tightened his grip.

*No more pain!*

Kerr's arms continued to flail, making contact and sending lightning bolts through his torso.

He held on.

*And no more death!*

Except one. He brought his face millimeters from Kerr's. "You're a... dead man," he whispered.

Kerr's eyes widened, fear finally wiping away everything else. His body jerked like a marionette—pain, panic, and a lack of oxygen overriding rational thought. But it didn't matter.

The battle had ended.

Kerr had lost.

Isin stared into the eyes of his enemy until the life within faded to nothingness.

# Forty-Two

*Isin's falling asleep.*

Nat tried to sit up to get a better view, but her arms didn't want to work. She slumped back to the deck. Cool. Kinda nice. Maybe she'd sleep, too. She rested her cheek on the surface and closed her eyes. Good idea. She'd stay right here.

"Isin? Orlov?"

Nat opened her eyes.

A woman stood across the cabin. Dark hair in a ponytail, brown eyes, non-descript jumpsuit.

Nat smiled. *Patel. Rathburn's doctor lady friend.*

Patel glanced at her with a frown, then back at Isin. "Isin? He's dead."

Nat's tummy squiggled. *Isin? Dead?*

A raspy voice. Isin's. "I know."

Not dead. But strange.

Isin pushed onto his hands and knees, his breath hissing through his teeth. He turned his head, his gaze meeting hers. "Natasha—" He reached for her, wobbled, and crashed to the deck.

"Help me!" Patel barked as she hurried to his side.

Nat stared at her. *Help?*

"Orlov! Get up!"

"She... can't." Isin gritted out. "Kerr... drugged her."

*Drugged, drugged, drugged. Everybody drugged.*

"Drugged her? With what?"

"I... don't know." Isin was talking funny. "Counteragent in... his pocket."

Patel pivoted, searching Kerr's jacket. She pulled out a small box and opened it. "There are six injectors. Which one is it?"

"No... idea."

*Hey!* Nat tried to point at Patel and failed. *That's Kerr's. He's gonna be mad.* She giggled. *Mad. Sad. Bad. Bad, Kerr, bad.* More giggles.

Patel stood and crossed to the main cabin's comm unit. "Darsha to Itorye."

"Go ahead."

"I need Jake on the line. Now."

"One second."

Nat swiped her hand out, smacking Isin's boot. He grunted. She smiled. Did it again. Another grunt.

"Dr. Patel?" Male voice. Kinda familiar.

"Jake, I've got a situation here. Isin's been shot and I need Orlov's help to treat him but she's been injected with something that's made her loopy."

*Loopy! Fun word! Loopy, loopy, loopy.*

"Loopy how?"

"Like she's really drunk. I'm holding a box of injectors. One of them should be the counteragent, but I don't know which one."

"Are they labeled?"

"Yes."

"Give me the names."

She read them off.

*Long names. Confusing.* Nat swiped Isin's boot again and giggled.

"Natasha... please—"

Something pinched her thigh.

*Ow!* She pulled back and swatted at Patel.

Patel caught her arm and held it. "Any better?"

Nat blinked. Better than what? She pulled on her arm, breaking free, then sat up. Big mistake. Her head swam. She pressed her fingers to her temples. "Worse." She'd been run over by a shuttle. And needed to get the cotton out of her mouth. "What did you—" Her gaze fell on Isin. Understanding dawned. He'd been shot!

She rolled toward him, registering his pained expression and blood-soaked tunic. "What were you thinking?"

Inexplicably, his lips curved in a small smile.

"That's what I'd like to know." Patel crouched beside her. "I thought he'd dive for cover when I distracted Kerr over the comm, not charge up the ramp like a rampaging bull."

But he'd saved her life. Sacrificing his own body to protect her from Kerr.

And the way he was looking at her now, he'd do it again in a heartbeat.

*You crazy lunatic.* She wanted to punch him and hug him at the same time, but did neither.

Patel opened an emergency med kit. "Jake, can you still hear me?"

The unlikelihood of Patel's presence sank in. She'd hidden onboard the *Dagger* this whole time? A million questions tumbled over each other, but now wasn't the time to ask them. All that mattered was Isin.

"I can," Jake replied. "What's Isin's status?"

"Bullet wound to the abdomen."

"Is there an exit wound?"

Patel moved behind him. "Yes."

"Good. One less complication. What color's the blood?"

"Don't know. His tunic's black. Hang on." Patel reached into the med kit for a pair of scissors. Isin sucked in a breath as she cut the material of his tunic from the hem to mid-chest and peeled it back from the wound.

Nat flinched. The blood seeping from the wound was darker than his skin.

"That... bad?" Isin's words contained more curiosity than concern, his gaze focused on her.

She gave him an encouraging smile. "Just a scratch." More like a bite from a saber-toothed tiger.

Patel ignored them. "His blood's almost black. Why would—"

Jake cut her off. "The bullet punctured his spleen. You're seeing old red blood cells. It may have struck his stomach, too. You'll need to pack the wound and get him to me as quickly as possible."

Patel turned to Nat. "Can you fly?"

"Fly?"

She gestured to Isin. "Jake's on *Phoenix*."

Oh. *Fly*. Her head was still a swamp and her body ached in lots of fun new places. But if Isin's life was on the line? "Yeah, I can fly."

# *Forty-Three*

Jake's voice drifted over Isin, giving Patel and Natasha instructions for treating his wound. But in Isin's world, there was only Natasha. Beautiful, vibrant, brave Natasha.

"We'll be there as quickly as we can." Patel moved to the comm panel and closed the channel before turning to Natasha. "I've never done this before. Have you?"

Natasha answered without taking her gaze off Isin. "Yeah. I was trained as a field medic."

"Then you can dress the wounds. But I'll need help keeping him stable during the flight. We need backup." Patel tapped the comm panel again. "Alec?"

Natasha gave a little jolt, her eyes widening when Alec's voice came over the comm. "Yes, Mom?"

"Isin's been shot. We need help down here. Can you send anyone?"

"Shot?" Alec's voice squeaked. "Hang on." A brief pause. "Sweep's on his way. Do you need me to come back?"

"Not right now. Stay with the ship."

"Okay."

Patel closed the channel then knelt on Isin's left side and pulled a roll of gauze out of the med kit. She handed it to Natasha.

Natasha took it, a strange look on her face. "That was Alec?"

Patel paused, her gaze darting to Isin before replying. "Yes."

"He's on *Vengeance*?"

"Yes."

"Hmm." Natasha's eyes narrowed, but she let it go, focusing on Isin as she held up the gauze. "Ready for the fun part?"

He gazed back at her. "Fun?"

"Oh, yeah. Remember when I treated your wound from the Setarip attack?"

How could he forget? He'd never endured pain like that before, though he'd been through plenty more since. But he treasured the memory. She'd stayed with him when the smart move would have been to let him die. That moment was the closest he'd ever felt to her, a bright spot of light before the darkness had closed in. He nodded.

"Well, this will be a hell of a lot worse." Her lips quirked up, but the tension around her eyes told him she was dreading it as much as he was.

"You have a... strange idea... of fun."

One brow lifted as she unrolled the gauze. "Look who's talking." She shifted around behind him. "You didn't have to do this," she murmured as she peeled away his tunic and touched his skin.

The gentle brush of her cool fingers was pure heaven, but that would change when she moved closer to the source of his pain. "Yes... I did." He stared at her over his shoulder. Didn't she understand? Didn't she *know*? "Had to... save you."

Something flickered in her eyes. "Yeah. I know." And she didn't look happy about it. She took a deep breath. "You ready?"

He braced himself. "Yes."

And dropped into six shades of Hell as she stuffed the gauze into the wound. He might have whimpered. May even have yelled. The agony flowed in wave after wave. Sweat coated his skin and his body shook.

A cool hand pressed against his cheek.

"Isin?"

It took a moment to realize the savage bites of pain had dulled to a slow gnaw.

"You still with us?"

He peeled his eyes open.

Natasha knelt in front of him. Deep grooves creased her forehead. "I'm so sorry. Patel's checking the infirmary for painkillers before we do the other side."

*The other side?* He glanced down. The entry wound was still seeping black blood. All that torture, and they'd only done one side?

"Found the auto-injector kit," Patel called out as she joined them. She handed it to Natasha. "I also grabbed the IVs and ringer of fluids Jake mentioned."

"Thanks." Natasha prepped the injector and moved behind him again. "This should help."

A sharp pain in his glutes preceded a rapid cooling of the burning inferno in his abdomen. He exhaled on a sigh.

Natasha moved back to face him. "Ready for—"

The thump of rapid footsteps crossing the deck and climbing the ramp drew their attention to the open hatch. A moment later, a familiar pair of boots and a scuffed pair of expensive dress shoes moved into Isin's line of sight. He turned his head, getting a skewed perspective of the new arrivals.

Sweep looked like he'd spent the past few days crawling through a gravel pit. Cuts and bruises covered his face, as did a scruffy growth of beard.

Rathburn stood behind him, far more battle-worn than the last time Isin had seen him. His gaze fell on Patel and he jerked back. "Darsha! You're—"

She cut him off with a slashing motion of her hand. "Later."

Natasha turned to Sweep. "Do you have field medic experience?"

He limped forward, favoring his left leg as he crouched beside her. "Yep."

"Good. I need you to take over here so I can get us airborne. Patel can fill you in on Jake's instructions." Her gaze shifted to Isin.

*Don't go.* It was a stupid thought, ludicrous really, but he didn't want her out of his sight.

She rested her palm on his cheek.

He wanted to hold it there forever.

"I'll see you soon," she whispered, her fingertips caressing his scarred skin as she stood.

Whether on accident or on purpose didn't matter. Natasha's touch was a far more potent drug than the painkiller she'd given him.

Then she was gone, leaving him with Sweep, Patel, and Rathburn.

Sweep rested a hand on Isin's shoulder. "You've looked better, son."

Isin grimaced. "So have... you."

Sweep acknowledged that statement with a nod before glancing over to where Kerr's body lay a meter away. "We taking him with us?"

A growl rumbled in Isin's chest. Kerr's toxic presence would never defile *Phoenix*, even in death. "No. Leave him... here."

"Done." Sweep motioned to Rathburn. They lifted the body and exited down the ramp, returning a few moments later with Avril's hefty form cradled in their arms. They settled him by the bulkhead while Patel snagged a blanket out of a storage cabinet and handed it to Sweep.

He draped it carefully over Avril before returning to Isin, a slight sheen in his eyes. "Byrd shot him in the back." He accepted the roll of gauze Patel handed him and began unwinding it, his movements jerky. "Never had a chance."

Isin could relate to the pain and anger in Sweep's voice. "Byrd's... dead."

Sweep nodded slowly as he held Isin's gaze. "Saw that."

The deck hummed as the *Dagger*'s engines warmed in preparation for takeoff.

"Shouldn't we move him to the med bay?" Rathburn asked.

Sweep glanced at him. "The less movement the better. We'll treat him here." He turned to Patel. "What did Jake say?"

She filled him in while Isin fought to block out the sensations the vibrations from the deck were creating in his abdomen. "Orlov gave him a painkiller," she finished.

Natasha's voice came over the ship's comm. "Engine check complete. Is everyone secure?"

Rathburn strode to the comm panel. "Yes. All clear."

"Closing the hatch."

Metal whirred and the light shifted as the ramp lifted into place.

"What about the bay doors?" Natasha asked. "What's the remote command to open them?"

Sweep glanced over. "It's—"

"Never mind. I just got word from A—" She broke off. "We're all clear. Prepare for departure."

"You're in charge of keeping him steady," Sweep informed Rathburn. "Have a seat."

Rathburn settled onto the deck near Isin's head and took a firm grip on his shoulders.

Sweep held Isin's gaze. "Ready?"

"Yeah." He gritted his teeth. *Let the fun begin.*

# Forty-Four

Nat jolted in her chair when Isin's bellow overrode the steady hum of the engines. She gritted her teeth. It wasn't as loud as the ones he'd unleashed while they'd packed the exit wound, so the painkiller was definitely helping, but the agony in that sound shredded her. For some reason, being in the cockpit instead of by his side made it worse, not better.

She glared at the indicator for the bay doors, which remained stubbornly on red. *Hurry! Hurry!*

Was she urging herself, the doors, or the people treating Isin's wounds?

"Alec, how soon until those doors are open?"

"Forty-three seconds."

She tightened her grip on the yoke. She could shave a few seconds off that time if she slipped through as soon as the interior deck platform separated. She eased the *Dagger* off the flight deck and hovered.

"But there's an issue."

*No. No more problems.* Her sanity was stretched to the limit. "What?"

"Debris from the collision with *Viper*. It's directly in the path to *Phoenix*."

Of course. Because she needed another challenge. "I can handle it."

"I know."

He *knew*? How did he know anything about her, let alone her piloting abilities? She didn't even know who *he* was, exactly. Patel's creation, Rathburn had said. Somehow she hadn't expected something so... human. He was a voice on the comm for now, but who, or what, was on the other end?

"The debris will slow you down."

"Tell me something I don't know," she muttered to herself.

"What do you mean?"

"Nothing." She'd add excellent hearing to Alec's growing list of attributes. "Any suggestions?"

"I've plotted a possible course through the field. Sending it now."

He was a navigator, too? Nat kept the bay door indicator in her peripheral vision as she glanced at the information on her display. Not bad. In fact, she'd be hard pressed to come up with a better route. "Looks good. Thanks."

Alec didn't respond right away. When he did, he asked the one question she'd been avoiding since Patel's injection had yanked her out of her drug-induced fog. "Will Isin live?"

"Yes." The word shot out of her mouth like a laser blast. He had to live. Any other outcome was unacceptable.

He hadn't yelled again, thank goodness. Hopefully that meant the pain was abating. She didn't want to consider the possibility that he was unconscious.

Now all she had to do was fly an unfamiliar vessel through a congested debris field in record time. No problem.

The indicator flashed green. She throttled the engines as the bay's interior decking platform slid apart, revealing the inky black of space beyond the massive outer bay doors.

She launched the *Dagger* through the opening and into the channel that ran beneath the ship's belly. Alarms flashed on the tactical console, but she'd already spotted her first obstacles on the 3D visual display.

Chunks of debris, some no larger than her hand and others almost as big as the *Dagger,* surrounded the space just outside *Vengeance*'s perimeter. Her gaze followed the flight path the yellow line indicated on the navigation chart. Getting through the field in *Gypsy* would have been fairly easy. The shuttle was compact and Nat knew her like the back of her hand. The *Dagger* was three times larger and a completely foreign design.

She eased out into the open, catching sight of *Phoenix* off to port. At this distance her ship looked like a toy, the gold and red paint a bright point of contrast to the dull grey remains of Kerr's ship. Unfortunately, to reach it, she'd have to crawl through the graveyard.

She didn't have time to crawl.

Heavy footsteps approached from behind. She glanced over her shoulder.

Sweep stepped onto the bridge, pausing as he met her gaze. "Orlov."

"Sweep." He was exactly what she'd pictured, a muscular man with short greying hair and a lined face. Under different circumstances, she would have looked forward to their first face-to-face encounter.

"Thought you could use some help up here." He dropped into the chair behind the tactical console.

Nat turned her attention back to the visual display. "How's Isin?"

"Stable as we can get him. We've finished packing the wounds, applied pressure bandages, and put him on an IV, but his abdomen is turning into a toxic waste dump. He needs Jake."

"I know." His no-nonsense delivery of the facts suited her better than empty platitudes. She gestured to the debris. "We have an obstacle course."

"Thought we might." His eyes narrowed as he studied their surroundings and the navigation information. "Are you as good a pilot as Isin believes?"

She didn't hesitate. "Yes."

The corners of his mouth lifted. "Then follow your best course and punch it. This is a fighting vessel, not a shuttle. The shields can handle the smaller pieces. I'll use the weapons to clear out anything larger in your path."

His calm certainty soothed her frazzled nerves. Pulling up the navigation data, she adjusted Alec's flight plan to a more direct route that would take them through thicker areas of debris. She glanced at Sweep. "We good?"

He looked over the route. "Yep."

He obviously trusted her to do her job. She'd trust him to do his. "Then let's make tracks."

The *Dagger* responded to her commands with more agility than she'd anticipated, even for a fighter. No doubt Shash had made upgrades to the basic engine design, adapting it for the unique demands of mercenary work.

As she dodged debris, Sweep kept the weapons churning, timing the blasts perfectly to prevent the explosions from causing additional obstacles as the ship dipped and turned.

A piece of debris floated out from behind a larger mass, crossing their path. Nat fired the thrusters, adjusting course. Sweep's next shot blasted the chunk off to starboard, the shockwave jolting the transport.

Nat gritted her teeth but kept her focus on her flight line.

A loud thump and a curse from a male voice alerted her that Rathburn had come into the cockpit. "Darsha wants to know how long until we reach *Phoenix.*"

"Working on it," Nat growled, dodging another piece of debris.

"Isin's not going to ma—"

"Shut up!" Truth or not, she didn't want to hear what Rathburn was about to say. Isin wasn't going to die. They'd make it in time. They had to. "Tell her to contact *Phoenix.*" She flinched as a piece of debris blasted out of existence in front of the viewport. "Have Jake meet us at the C deck portside airlock."

Rathburn blew out a breath. "Okay." His tone implied her instructions were a wasted effort.

"And tell Isin he'd better not die on me!" she shouted after him.

Sweep grunted in agreement.

A few minutes later the debris field finally thinned, *Phoenix* shining like a beacon in the gloom. Her mind screamed at her to go full throttle, but docking with an airlock wasn't like landing in a shuttle bay. It required patience and precision. The *Dagger* was too big to fit in *Phoenix*'s bay, so the airlock was their only option.

Blocking out the tension vibrating under her skin, she lined up the two vessels, guiding the *Dagger* slowly, steadily, into position. She opened an external comm channel. "Orlov to *Phoenix.*"

"Itorye here."

"Is Jake ready at the airlock?"

"We're all ready."

Nat had never heard worry in Itorye's voice before. She heard it now. "Sweep will meet you there with Isin." She glanced at Sweep. who got her unspoken message and pushed to his feet. She had to stay a few precious seconds longer to secure and power down the transport. "I'll join you in a moment."

# Forty-Five

The second the system confirmed the seal was secure, locking the two ships together, Nat raced through the shutdown sequence and leapt from her chair. By the time she reached the main cabin, it was empty.

She hurried through the airlock, catching up with Sweep and Rathburn, who were carrying Isin on a collapsible stretcher, with Patel on one side, holding an IV bag attached to Isin's forearm, and Jake on the other, taking Isin's vitals with a portable med scanner.

Snatches of Jake's and Isin's words broke through the pounding in Nat's ears as she followed the group along the passageway. At least he was still conscious.

Itorye and Kenji stood waiting for them at the infirmary.

"Start the O-negative," Jake said to Itorye as Kenji moved in to assist in transferring Isin to the med platform.

A hand rested on Nat's shoulder, holding her back at the doorway.

She tried to shake it off, her gaze locked on Isin.

"Stay here, Nat."

The familiar voice drew her out of her tunnel vision, making her turn.

Marlin pulled her into a sideways hug, holding her close. "Let Jake work. We'd only be in the way."

She stiffened. She had medical training. She could help!

But Jake was already shooing out Kenji, Patel, and Rathburn. Only Itorye and Sweep remained to assist.

As Jake laid out his surgical tools, Nat focused on Isin's face, everything else fading into the background. His eyes and forehead no longer showed lines of pain thanks to whatever sedative Jake had already administered. A small consolation considering his abdomen was about to be opened up to clean out the mess Kerr's shot had made of his insides.

*Live, Isin! You have to live!*

Heat burned the back of Nat's throat. He looked so peaceful, but in reality he was walking the tightrope between life and death. Abdominal wounds that weren't treated in time were fatal. "I should have gotten him here sooner."

It was Patel who answered her. "You did more than any of us could. Orpheus told me about the debris field. It would have been a death trap for most pilots. You got us here safely."

Nat shrugged.

Kenji stepped behind her, resting his big hands on her shoulders and squeezing gently. "He'll make it, Nat. He's strong. A fighter. And he's pulled through bad scrapes before. Besides, Jake's the best doctor in the quadrant."

She wanted to believe. *Needed* to believe.

But it was hard to when the icy hand of death kept running a bony finger up and down her spine.

# *Forty-Six*

Nat planted herself on the deck outside the infirmary with her back against the bulkhead and her knees tucked up to her chest. Jake had switched on the privacy screening for the windows, so she couldn't see what they were doing, but the low murmur of voices and the occasional clink of instruments carried into the corridor.

Every minute dragged out for a year, but the aches that settled into her muscles confirmed that time was progressing.

Patel had stationed herself against the opposite wall, while Marlin sat beside Nat, keeping his own counsel but offering silent support. She'd take all she could get. Anxiety had chewed her insides into shreds. Or maybe she was channeling Isin's pain.

Where Rathburn had disappeared to, she had no idea. She didn't care, either.

Kenji approached her a little while later and sank down on her other side, shoulder to shoulder. "Fleur and I moved Avril to cold storage."

She blinked. "What?"

"Avril. We moved his body to cold storage."

"Body?" What body?

The muscles around his mouth tightened. "He's dead. Byrd shot him."

"Oh." Avril was dead? How had she missed that? "When?"

"Right after Isin left the shuttle bay," Patel responded before Kenji could.

"You saw it?"

Patel shook her head. "Heard it. And found his body when Alec and I left the *Dagger* to contact Sweep."

Nat scrolled through the jumble of memories from the shuttle bay, but couldn't bring up an image of Avril. She turned to Kenji. "How did you know Byrd shot him?" Kenji had been on *Phoenix* this whole time.

"I just spoke with Shash."

"Oh." Bile rose in her throat. Shash was on her hit list after the way she'd behaved on the bridge with Kerr.

"She thought you'd like to know that Stevens is going to be fine."

Nat's heart skipped. "Pete?" How had she forgotten about him? He'd been unconscious when Kerr had drugged her and hauled her off *Vengeance*'s bridge. She should have remembered *that!* "Did you talk to him?"

"Briefly. He's helping Shash restore order on *Vengeance*."

Scenes from the bridge flashed in front of her eyes. So much chaos.

"Shash patched up Summer. But Pine didn't make it."

"Hmm." She couldn't work up any regret on that count. The man had been happy to support Kerr's plot. "And you're sure Pete's okay?"

"Yeah. He's good."

She leaned her head against the bulkhead, but her muscles refused to relax. "How soon could you take the *Dagger* back to *Vengeance*?"

"Why?"

"I don't want Shash in charge of that ship." She didn't even try to keep the hostility out of her voice.

Kenji gave her a sharp look. "Did something happen between you two? I mean, something new?"

"You could say that." Her stomach clenched. "Kerr offered her a job if she betrayed Isin. She was considering taking it."

Kenji frowned. "She wouldn't do that."

"Yes, she would. She and Kerr used to be lovers."

"So?"

Apparently she had to spell it out for him. "So, she was ready to rekindle the flame and leave Isin to Kerr's sadistic games."

Kenji pivoted to face her. "No. That's not how Shash operates."

Nat snorted.

"I'm serious. She may have given that impression if it suited her purposes, but she'd never betray someone she respects. And she respects the hell out of Isin."

"She has a funny way of showing it."

"Depends on how you look at it."

"What's that supposed to mean?"

"Well, she hasn't tried to kill you since we revived the *Phoenix*."

She stared at him. "That's your argument?"

"Yeah."

She turned, mirroring his pose. "The only reason she hasn't tried to kill me is because I haven't given her an opportunity. And because Isin threatened to kill her if she did."

"Exactly! If anyone other than Isin had said that to her, she would have taken it as a personal challenge. It would have made her take action quicker."

"That's demented."

"No, that's Shash. But you're important to Isin. She knows that. So she's fought her natural hatred of you. That's respect."

"If you say so."

"I do." He rested a hand on her shoulder for a moment before pushing to his feet. "I'd better get back to the bridge. I'm keeping an eye on Rathburn's ship."

"Oh." The possibility of a threat from *Cerberus* hadn't even occurred to her. Good thing someone's head was still in the game. "Thanks."

"Sure thing."

After he left, the only sounds in the passageway came from the infirmary. Each clink and beep jabbed Nat like a needle, making her twitch. Marlin left briefly, returning with an ice pack for her eye. She hadn't even noticed it had started to swell from where Kerr had struck her with the grip of his gun.

When she finally stood, her lower back and legs protested as the blood flowed into her strained muscles. She didn't want to leave her spot until Isin came out of surgery, but nature's call couldn't be ignored forever. Climbing the stairs to her cabin in record time, she quickly took care of business and headed back.

Rathburn intercepted her at the top of the stairwell. "I've restored communication with my ship." He indicated the implant in his forearm.

She halted, tension gripping her shoulders. In all the chaos with Kerr, she'd pushed aside Rathburn's role in this situation. Or the fact that, technically, he was now *her...* guest. "And?"

"My head of security was responsible for the overload." Bitterness laced his words.

So it hadn't been Sweep, after all. She folded her arms over her chest. "What happened over there?" Kerr had implied he'd taken control of Rathburn's entire crew.

"Roughly half my forces were onboard Kerr's ship when it was destroyed. I just spoke with the current senior member of my remaining personnel. She has two conspirators in custody. The rest are dead." He paused, a self-mocking smile touching his lips. "Clearly I'll have to rethink my security strategy going forward."

"Clearly. What's the name of the person in charge now?"

He grimaced at the pointed question. "Grey. Her name I do know."

So did Nat. The thought was oddly comforting. "And you trust her?"

"As much as I trust anyone at this point."

Which looped neatly back to their situation. "What's your next step?"

His expression grew thoughtful. "I haven't decided. Darsha informed me she came onboard *Vengeance* to help disable my ship."

"Did she say why?"

"We didn't have time to get into it. She has a lot of hostility toward me, but she's also the one who helped Sweep remotely unlock our manacles."

"They did that?"

"Yes. Sweep was able to tap into my implant's comm system, tell me who he was, and lay out his plan." He lifted a brow. "Were you aware he was on *Vengeance*?"

No point in hiding the truth. "Yes."

"And you two were in communication?"

She nodded.

"You never cease to surprise me."

She couldn't tell if that was a good thing. "Did Sweep cause the blackout on the bridge?"

"With help from Darsha."

So far, Rathburn hadn't mentioned Alec, which indicated he wasn't aware Alec was on *Vengeance*. Or that he'd played a role in their rescue. She wasn't about to tell him. "Lucky for us." She moved to step past him. "I need to get back."

He blocked her path.

"What—"

"I won't harm him."

Maybe he was aware of Alec's presence, after all. "Who?"

"Isin."

She frowned. Not what she'd expected.

"He means a lot to you. I can see that." He swept his arms out to his sides. "Whatever happens with this situation, I want you to know that I won't take him from you."

Her brain couldn't process the gibberish he was spouting. "Take him from me?"

"That's right. I've suspected there was something between you two since the first time we talked, but I've been hoping it was one-sided. I can see now I was wrong."

She opened her mouth, but no words came out. Was he implying that—

He reached down, taking her hand in his.

She let him because her internal compass was spinning.

"I would have given you the world, Nat. Anything you wanted. But I'm a realist. I know when to accept defeat." Sadness drew lines on his face and shadowed his eyes. "He clearly treasures you. For your sake, I hope he lives." Bending down, he brushed a kiss across her cheek.

She was too stunned to react.

He stepped past her and continued down the corridor.

She turned and stared after him.

What had just happened?

# Forty-Seven

Nat was a twisted knot by the time Jake stepped out of the infirmary. She shoved to her feet. "How is he?"

"Stable. The shot nicked his stomach as well as taking out his spleen, so I had to clean out his entire abdominal cavity." His lips pressed together. "Luckily for him this ship's medical systems were state-of-the-art when they were installed, and I had everything in working order. I'd already grown a new stomach and spleen from his cells by the time you arrived."

That sounded good, but.... "Will he live?"

The tension in Jake's face eased. "Yes, he'll live. But he's going to be unresponsive for another six to eight hours. And he'll need to take it easy for a while." His tone made it clear he anticipated a challenge with that particular restriction.

She glanced into the infirmary, where Sweep and Itorye were clearing away the surgical tools. "Can I go in?"

"In a few minutes."

Nat paced in front of the door while she waited. Marlin, Patel, and Kenji, who'd come down from the bridge to hear the news, stood off to one side, giving her space.

When Jake returned, he had a portable med kit in his hand. Sweep followed behind him. "We're going to the lounge so I can take care of Sweep's injuries. Do you know where Rathburn went?"

She shook her head.

"Well, if you see him, tell him I can treat him in the lounge, too. And you, when you're ready."

She frowned. "I don't need—"

"That eye should be looked at. And I want to make sure there aren't any lingering effects from the drug Kerr gave you."

"Maybe later." Or maybe not.

Jake's smile became more pointed. "If you don't find me, I'll find you." Then he headed down the passageway.

Sweep stopped in front of Nat. "You were right."

"About what?"

"You're one hell of a pilot." The corners of his mouth lifted. "He's gonna be fine."

Pressure built behind her eyes. She blinked it away. "You're one hell of a gunner."

"Ought to be by now." His expression sobered. "I'm sorry I didn't get to you before Kerr did."

She frowned. "What do you mean?"

"On the bridge. Shash and I were trying to reach you and Stevens. I didn't spot Kerr until after he'd grabbed you."

She focused on the part of the explanation that didn't fit. "You and Shash? She was with you?"

"Yep. She took out several of Kerr's people along the way, but by the time we got through, Kerr had snatched you."

"Is that what she told you?"

He cocked his head at her aggressive tone. "No, that's what I *saw*." He pointed to his eyes. "I was wearing infrared goggles."

So that's how the counterattack at the back hatch had started. He'd snuck onto the bridge.

"I'm aware that you and Shash have your issues, and she may not hold the line for much, but when it comes to Isin and *Vengeance*, she's loyal to the bone. Kerr didn't understand that." He lowered his voice so only she could hear him. "Don't make the same mistake."

*Don't make the same mistake?* What was she supposed to do with that? Was he telling her to trust Shash? That was asking a lot. The woman had threatened her life. Isin was the only thing standing between the two of them and a nuclear confrontation.

As Sweep headed down the passageway after Jake, Itorye exited the infirmary. She glanced at Patel, taking in the bloodstains on her clothes, then surveyed her own compromised tunic and pants with a bemused smile. "We're going to go get cleaned up," she informed Nat. "Notify me if anything changes."

Itorye sounded as matter-of-fact as always, but Nat saw relief in her eyes. She'd been worried about Isin, too.

Nat nodded. "I will."

That left Marlin and Kenji. Marlin looked like he was planning to go into the infirmary with her, but Kenji wrapped a hand around his shoulders, stopping him. "I could use a snack. How about you?"

Marlin turned toward Nat. "I don't think—"

"Sure you do." Kenji planted both hands on Marlin's shoulders. "And I'll bet the galley could use some cleanup after all the excitement. I'll help." He gave Nat a wink before marching Marlin to the stairwell and heading down.

And then she was alone. With Isin.

She drew in a deep breath. *I can do this.* She kept up the mantra as she approached the med platform.

A white sheet covered Isin from his toes to his broad chest, the crisp linen a sharp contrast to the deep tones of his skin. His eyes were closed, his muscles slack in an artificially induced sleep.

She'd seen him in pain before. She'd even seen him borderline unconscious. But for some reason, this was worse.

Maybe because he'd almost died in front of her.

Reaching out, she rested her fingertips on his forearm. His skin felt chilled, so different from the vibrant warmth she'd experienced every other time they'd touched.

He didn't respond, gave no indication he knew she was there. Which was just as well.

She clasped his hand in hers, willing her warmth and strength into his body. "Hello, Isin."

No reaction. Not that she expected one.

She licked her dry lips, fighting down the butterflies in her belly. The hard part was over. He was going to live. So why did she feel like she was perched at the edge of a bottomless chasm?

"Jake says you're going to be fine. Did he tell you? You'll have to take it easy, which I know you'll hate, but you'll heal. You'll live." She glanced down at their joined hands. He could enclose her entire fist in his. "You'll live," she repeated.

Her gaze moved to the white sheet covering his abdomen. He'd taken a bullet for her. A bullet! Insane as that seemed, his actions indicated he would have willingly died for her. Because he'd owed her his life.

Well, now his debt had been repaid.

And she had to face facts.

"So here's the thing." She drew in a deep breath, lifting her gaze. "From the moment I met you, you've been a royal pain in the ass." *Good, Nat. Insult the invalid. Very helpful.* "And I thought I hated being around you. I really did."

She ran her thumb gently over the creases in his palm. Such a simple thing, but she could feel an electrical charge all the way to her toes. "But the truth is, I don't. I'm not even sure I ever did." How else could she explain why she'd saved his life on Troi? And after the Setarips had captured her, it was his face that had haunted her during her year of hell.

He looked different now than he had then. The long scar across his cheek was the most obvious change, although it was more than that. He'd been hardened by his experiences, just as she had. But rather than repelling her, the man he'd become fascinated her. And that was an *asteroid about to impact her ship*-sized problem.

Because Rathburn had it wrong. Isin valued her as a pilot, but he'd protected her because he owed her his life, not because he cared about *her*.

She blew out a breath, her gaze following the line of his scar. "When we were in the torpedo room together, hiding from the Setarips, I could have given you a choice. I could have asked if you wanted me to draw them off. But I didn't. I made the decision. And I got caught. Big surprise." It had been the most impulsive thing she'd ever done. She still wasn't clear why.

"Maybe I wanted you to be indebted to me." But that didn't sound right. She'd known the Setarips would likely kill her if they caught her. She couldn't have planned to collect on a debt if she was dead.

"Maybe I wanted to make sure you'd never forget me." More plausible. But how pathetic was that?

Or even worse...

"Maybe I just couldn't bear the idea of a universe without you in it."

Bingo.

She might have laughed at the irony of that revelation if she hadn't been struggling so hard to keep breathing. Her universe was rapidly imploding while his was expanding exponentially.

And she couldn't stop it. She was going down. All she could do was protect herself the only way she knew how.

She straightened, breaking the physical connection and dropping her arms to her sides. "But my reasons don't matter now. I saved your life, you saved mine. We're even. You don't owe me anything anymore. Not this ship. Not this crew."

Her voice sounded harsh and unpleasant to her ears. Good. It matched the barren terrain in her chest. And she expected it to ratchet up to the nth degree when he woke up. "I don't have anything to hold over you. You can do whatever you want. Including taking control of this ship."

Which he would as soon as he was back on his feet. He was a mercenary, after all. He'd negotiated with her on Troi because he'd owed her. But his debt had been repaid in blood.

"The smart move might be accepting your offer to work as your pilot, captaining this ship. But I can't." If she remained onboard, she'd have to live with the knowledge that *Phoenix* would never truly be hers. And that she'd stupidly developed feelings for the man who'd taken it from her. Rathburn had gotten that part right.

She crossed her arms over her chest to ward off the chill that passed over her skin, acutely aware that her duster was still somewhere on *Vengeance*'s bridge. And *Gypsy* was still on *Cerberus*.

"Stealing *Phoenix* isn't an option, either." She stared at an indentation in the white sheet rather than at him. "You proved that on Troi." He'd figured out her plan before she'd had a chance to implement it. "And even if I succeeded in getting away, you'd hunt me down." His pride, and his crew, would demand it. "I won't put Marlin and Pete in that kind of danger just so I can hold onto this ship."

They'd already suffered enough because of her. She'd failed them in every possible way. She couldn't deliver what she'd promised on Troi, and she had nothing more to give. "They deserve better. We're done."

Maybe they'd stay on with Isin. He would pay them well. And they'd made friends with some of his crew.

Or maybe they'd both return to Troi.

Either way, she wouldn't be with them on this ship, running freight and exploring the galaxy. That dream had died when Kerr had fired his gun.

And her future had turned into a black hole.

# *Forty-Eight*

Voices. One male, one female. No, one male and two females. Familiar voices, talking low.

Isin swam toward the surface of consciousness, but it was like pushing through glue. He sank a bit after every effort.

"...get him to rest."

He knew that voice. Itorye. He pushed harder.

"I can always sedate him."

He knew that one, too. Jake.

Which gave him a clue as to what he'd see when he opened his eyes. Sure enough, the low lighting and crisp white sheet of a med platform surrounded him.

"You're awake."

He blinked, slowly turning his head on the pillow as he worked to bring Itorye's image into focus. "Yeah." His mouth felt like he'd been chewing sand. The rest of him wasn't doing so great, either. "What happened?"

Jake moved beside Itorye. "You came up with a new and exciting way to try to kill yourself."

"Oh?" He glanced down, confirming that all his limbs were intact. He wiggled his toes just to be sure. Yep, still there.

Jake pressed his palms on the platform and leaned in, a smile on his lips but a serious look in his eyes. "I appreciate the chance to keep my surgical skills sharp, but how about you and I take a break from all this male bonding for a while?"

"Sounds good." He frowned. Hadn't he heard another female voice? He turned his head to the other side and found Patel standing by the bulkhead. "Why are you here?"

Her brows lifted. "I'm happy to see you, too."

"No, I mean—" His frown deepened as his gaze swept the room. He was on *Phoenix*. Hadn't he been on *Vengeance*? Yes, he had. In the shuttle bay with Kerr and Natasha—

He jerked upright, eliciting a stab of pain across his abdomen that knocked the breath from his lungs and slammed him back on the mattress.

Jake placed his hand on Isin's shoulder. "You can't get up yet."

He flailed his arms, making the IV line sway. "Natasha." He gulped in air. "Where's... Natasha?"

Itorye moved to his other side and wrapped her hand around his forearm, stilling his movements. "On the bridge. She's fine."

"Fine?" She wasn't fine. Kerr had drugged her. She'd been—

"She's *fine*," Itorye repeated, her no-nonsense tone breaking through his panic. "If you calm down, I'll tell her you want to see her."

"Yes." He unclenched his fists and sank against the pillow. "Yes, I want to see her."

Itorye moved to the comm panel. "Itorye to Orlov."

Natasha's voice came over the comm immediately. "Yes?"

"He's awake. And asking for you."

"Oh." A pause. "I'll be down in a moment."

Jake pressed the control to elevate the top half of the med platform so Isin could see the door without lifting his head. "Go easy," he said as he helped Isin sit up straighter.

The pain in his abdomen dug into him, but he ignored it, his gaze fixed on the open doorway. He had to see her. Had to know she was okay.

Decades passed before she appeared. Her short dark hair was rumpled, like she hadn't bothered to brush it in a while. Dark circles under her eyes indicated she hadn't been sleeping much, either, and her pale skin looked almost translucent. Slight yellow-purple shading around one eye showed where Kerr had struck her.

Her gaze skittered over him, but she didn't look directly at him. Instead, she turned to Jake. "How is he?"

"I'm fine." Why was she talking like he wasn't in the room?

She glanced at him but her gaze returned immediately to Jake.

"He'll live," Jake confirmed. He moved to stand beside Natasha and fixed Isin with a familiar look. "As long as he doesn't push it."

Jake knew his tendency to do just that. He'd been his patient often enough during the past year. And not a very cooperative one.

But now that Natasha was within arm's reach, he was willing to take it easy, at least for a while. "I'm not going anywhere."

Jake nodded. "Good. Then we'll head down to the galley. I'll bring you up something your new stomach can handle," he called out as they exited the room.

*New stomach?* That explained the abdominal pain. Bits and pieces of memory drifted by as he turned to Natasha. "I was shot." By Kerr. Right before he'd choked the life out of the bastard.

"That's right." She still wasn't meeting his gaze. Instead, she was inspecting every object in the room. "You saved my life." She didn't sound too happy about it.

"I had to."

She nodded. "I know. Now we're even."

"Even?"

"Yeah. I saved your life, you saved mine. Scales balanced."

For some reason, her words made his blood run cold. "I suppose so."

She flashed a smile that didn't come close to reaching her eyes. "Bet you're glad to be off the hook."

"Off the hook?" What was she talking about? And why did she sound like all the life had been sucked out of her?

"Sure. I know it's been bothering you. Ever since Troi, you've felt indebted to me. But now you're free."

*Free?* He didn't feel free. In fact, he'd never felt so caged in his life. Why wouldn't she look at him? "Natasha, what's wrong?"

"Nothing." Her smile got even brighter.

His new stomach sank into his toes. "Is it Rathburn? Did something happen?"

She shook her head, her fingers fiddling with the hem of the sheet. "We're in a holding pattern."

Isin searched his memory, filling in the gaps. He'd been shot, followed by lots of pain as Sweep and Patel had treated his wound. Sweep! "Where's Sweep?"

"Checking on the defensive systems. Do you want me to go get him?" She seemed way too eager to leave.

"No. I want to talk to you."

"Oh." More fidgeting.

It cost him a stab of pain, but he reached out and captured her wrist between his fingers.

She froze, every muscle in her arm going taut. Like she was afraid. Afraid of him?

"Natasha. Look at me."

She brought her head up, but didn't meet his gaze, choosing instead to stare at his chin.

His grip tightened. "*Look* at me. Please." He was pleading, but he didn't care. He felt like something precious was slipping through his fingers, and he had no idea how to hold onto it.

She drew in a breath. When she finally met his gaze, he wished she hadn't.

Her beautiful pale aqua eyes were flat as glass. Emotionless. Whatever she was thinking or feeling, it wasn't coming through. He was looking at her, but the person staring back was a stranger.

# *Forty-Nine*

Nat used every gram of willpower she possessed to keep the emotions threatening to swamp her from breaking loose. Isin's fingers on her skin sent every nerve ending into overdrive.

"Natasha, I—"

Angry voices in the passageway made them both turn.

"...don't care what you have to say!" Patel shouted.

Rathburn's voice was quieter, but no less insistent. "Darsha, if you'd just listen to me—"

"No! We have nothing to talk about."

Nat took a step toward the doorway but halted when her arm met with resistance. Isin was still holding onto her. She gave a sharp tug, breaking the connection, and exited into the passageway.

"Yes, we do! You don't—"

"What is all the shouting about?" Nat planted herself in the middle of the corridor, facing the two combatants coming toward her.

They halted before they ran into her.

"She's being unreasonable." Rathburn pointed at Patel. "All I asked was to talk to her, and she stormed off."

Patel folded her arms and moved to stand beside Nat. "And that surprises you? After what you've done?"

"What?" Rathburn's exasperation seemed real enough. "I gave you the perfect working environment. Helped you bring A.L.E.C. to life. And then you ran off and destroyed my lab! I'm the one who should be angry."

"Are you insane? You were going to—"

"Knock it off!" Isin's booming voice silenced Patel. "Come in here. Now."

For a man who'd almost died and couldn't get out of bed, he certainly commanded attention.

Patel shot Rathburn a look that could cut glass before moving past Nat and entering the infirmary. Rathburn followed, his gaze sending Nat a silent plea for help.

She followed behind, blocking the doorway. She wasn't sure what she could do to help Rathburn, or if she even wanted to, but she had a personal stake in keeping the lines of communication open. He still had *Gypsy* in his shuttle bay.

The expression on Isin's face was a startling blend of calm negotiator and cold-hearted mercenary. His gaze moved slowly between Rathburn and Patel. "We will discuss this like adults."

"But—" Patel began.

Isin cut her off. "Unless you'd prefer to discuss this in an escape pod. You'd have plenty of time while you waited for Rathburn's ship to pick you up."

The threat brought Patel to attention.

Rathburn seemed amused until Isin turned that steely gaze on him. "Dr. Patel is a paid passenger on this ship. *You* are not. Remember that or you will disembark abruptly."

Rathburn bristled.

So did Nat. Isin hadn't been awake twenty minutes, and he was already taking command of *Phoenix*. From a sick bed, no less. He was confirming all her worst fears. With his debt repaid, their uneasy alliance had been stamped null and void. After he was back on his feet, she might be lucky if he didn't stuff *her* in an escape pod.

His ultimatum delivered, he relaxed like a king on his throne, his gaze still on Rathburn. "Now, what did you want to discuss with Dr. Patel?"

"I want her to return to *Cerberus* so we can continue our work on A.L.E.C."

"Work *on* Alec?" Patel scoffed. "You don't—" A hard look from Isin silenced her.

He motioned to Rathburn. "Continue."

"I would also like to know why she ran away. Why she took A.L.E.C. just when our work was showing promise."

Patel's face contorted with the effort of keeping her comments to herself.

Isin turned to her. "Share what you told me when I met Alec."

Rathburn's eyes widened. "You've *met* him?" he blurted before Patel could respond.

Isin's expression darkened. "Oh, yes. He's a very talented young man."

*Young man?*

"Young man?" Rathburn echoed Nat's thought.

Patel smiled for the first time, looking as smug as a cat with a bowl of cream. "Yes, Orpheus. Young man. Alec has grown beyond my wildest dreams. And I will do everything in my power to keep him out of your hands."

Rathburn stared at her. "But... why?"

"Does *master control of the Interstellar Communications System* sound familiar?"

Rathburn's lips parted in surprise. "Where did you hear that?"

Patel ignored the question. She pointed a finger at his chest. "You want to use him to take control of the array."

Nat's breath stuttered. Rathburn hadn't mentioned anything about the array when he'd made his pitches for her help with Patel and Alec.

"That's an oversimplification."

He hadn't denied it. "What exactly *do* you have planned?" she asked. Before this went any further, she wanted answers.

Rathburn spread his hands, palms up. "Nothing sinister. When A.L.E.C. achieves his full potential, he will have the ability to monitor all communications through the array. He could insure the safety of billions of lives."

"Safety?" She wasn't following his logic. "You're talking about covert surveillance. Invasion of privacy. Not safety."

"Not at all. He would be protecting the innocent. Preventing abuse and oppression."

Patel made a rude noise. "By *spying* on everyone? Controlling their ability to communicate?"

Rathburn's jaw clenched. "No. He would be an impartial observer, unhindered by human prejudices."

"And he would do what? Report to you?" Patel snapped.

"What's wrong with that?" Rathburn's voice was as sharp as Patel's. "I've dedicated my life to making our society better. This is the next logical step."

"Logical step?" Patel laughed, but there was no humor in it. She turned to Isin. "Now do you understand why I left?"

Isin's gaze shifted between Patel and Rathburn, analyzing.

Rathburn faced Nat. "Surely you understand my point. Imagine a highly intelligent lifeform capable of monitoring the entire communications array. A lifeform that could filter all the incoming and outgoing data and watch for signs of mental illness, behavioral problems, even criminal activity, and send out alerts before anyone gets hurt."

Was he really as obtuse as he sounded? "Would that include tracking and reporting the activities of smugglers and mercenaries?"

"Uh..." His eyes widened as he made the connection. He cleared his throat. "Not necessarily. Your activities don't harm anyone."

She folded her arms. "Are you sure about that?" She nodded toward Isin. "His certainly do." That comment earned her a look of annoyance from Isin. Too bad. He'd made his choice. "I'll give you a hypothetical. What if one of the colonies on the outer rim had a civil conflict? If I took a smuggling job to deliver supplies, would it matter whether I was carrying medical equipment or munitions? Or would it only matter that I was delivering them to the side you agreed with?"

Rathburn shifted his weight. "That would depend."

"And it doesn't matter," Patel broke in. "No matter how altruistic you've convinced yourself this project is, it attacks civil liberties and promotes enslavement. That makes it wrong."

Rathburn frowned. "Enslavement? What are you talking about?"

"Alec!" Patel hurled the name at him like a stone. "You want him to be the center of this whole mess. But he's not one of your science projects, or one of your fancy implant algorithms. He's a sentient being who has the right to decide his own future. You can't imprison him in the array and force him to do your bidding."

Rathburn looked even more confused. "Who said anything about force? A.L.E.C. was designed for this work. It's what he was meant to do."

Patel's hands fisted. "He wasn't *meant* to do anything, except become a fully-functioning, autonomous being."

"You can't be serious. He's—"

"That's enough." Isin spoke quietly, but the words carried the impact of an asteroid collision, silencing Rathburn. "No more debate until Alec can voice his opinions. It's his future you're discussing."

Rathburn looked at Isin like he'd sprouted antennae. "But—"

One glance shut Rathburn up. Isin folded his hands. "I will arrange a meeting with Alec. Until then, I don't want to hear another word from either of you, or I'll confine you to your quarters."

Rathburn straightened. "You can't command me. In thirty seconds I could order my ship to disable *Phoenix*."

The corners of Isin's lips turned up in a terrifying smile. "And in one second, I could kill you."

# *Fifty*

Isin spent the next twenty-six hours lying in bed, fighting the urge to make good on his threat. Not only had Rathburn challenged him in front of Natasha, but his argument with Patel had destroyed any chance of finding out what had made Natasha act so strangely when she'd come to the infirmary. She'd slipped out with Rathburn and Patel, and hadn't returned.

His only consolation had been the black look she'd given Rathburn on her way out. She wasn't happy with their uninvited guest, either.

Sweep had stopped in to see him shortly after Natasha left. They'd compared notes, Sweep sharing what he'd learned about Rathburn's implant while Isin told him what he knew about Patel and Alec. Sweep had confirmed he could track the signal Rathburn's implant produced and monitor all transmissions. If Rathburn decided to cause a problem, they'd know before the message reached his ship.

Isin posted Fleur and Shorty on rotation for the weapons systems. Kenji had filled him in on *Phoenix*'s current position, which placed *Vengeance* and the debris field between them and *Cerberus*. But that could change in a hurry.

In theory, *Vengeance* was immobile, since the three people onboard—Shash, Stevens, and Summer—weren't pilots. However, Sweep had told him that Alec was responsible for altering *Vengeance*'s course to collide with Kerr's ship. If he could do that, he'd added navigation skills to his growing repertoire. And the willingness to use those skills in battle.

Scary thought.

So was the question of Alec's future. He'd proven to be a valuable asset, but he also had the potential to be an equally powerful weapon. Isin didn't agree with Rathburn's plans, but he wasn't convinced Patel had considered all the dangers of giving Alec self-determination rights, either.

For now, he'd told Itorye to bring the holoprojector from *Phoenix*'s media room into the guest cabin closest to the infirmary, and gather everyone for a meeting. Alec would be able to access the projector remotely from *Vengeance* to share his thoughts on the matter.

Jake had cleared Isin for the short trek down the passageway, and helped him get set up on the cabin's bed with a minimum of fuss.

His abdomen felt like it had been scoured with a sandblaster, but at least he was able to move around. Jake had made him promise he'd stay calm during the meeting, a promise he'd extracted while Itorye was in the infirmary to witness it. No doubt she'd be watching him closely.

Much as he appreciated what Jake had done to save his life, he was also grateful for the change of scenery. He didn't want to stay in the infirmary a second longer than he had to.

The murmur of voices filtered in from the passageway as Itorye and Patel finished setting up the projector on the floor at the foot of the bed, with five chairs arranged in a semi-circle around it. Natasha and Sweep entered first, followed shortly by Rathburn, who immediately moved to the opposite side of the room. His posture broadcasted haughty arrogance as he claimed one of the chairs closest to Isin.

Silence fell as everyone else took a seat. Natasha chose the middle chair, with Sweep on her left and Patel on her right, placing her directly opposite Isin and as far from him as possible in the small confines of the cabin. Not that he'd noticed.

Yeah, right.


Itorye switched on the projector before sitting down between Patel and Isin and opening a comm channel to *Vengeance.* "Alec, we're ready for you."

A moment later, an image appeared above the projector.

Isin jerked back in surprise, triggering a protest from his insides. He grimaced. *Way to stay calm.*

A quick glance around the circle confirmed he wasn't the only one caught off guard. The last time he'd seen Alec, the boy had looked like a teenager. The figure before him was a man.

Alec smiled at him. "Hello, Captain. I'm glad to see you're recovering." His voice had changed, too, the modulating pitches of the teen replaced with the deeper tones of adulthood.

Isin acknowledged the comment with a nod. "I see you've been through some changes as well."

Alec laughed, an easy sound that made him appear more like the boy he'd been. "It's been... interesting." He turned to Patel. "Hi, Mom."

"Hello, Alec." Her voice caught a little, the muscles around her eyes tightening.

Alec's gaze continued around the circle to Natasha. "It's a pleasure to finally meet you, Captain Orlov. I've been wanting to thank you."

Natasha's expression was hard to read, but a million thoughts seemed to be racing behind her eyes. "Thank me? For what?"

"For teaching me how to fly."

She frowned. "What do you mean?"

"I studied your navigation logs while I was on *Phoenix*. The ship's nav system tracks and logs every movement made by the pilot and ship. After pairing that information with the sensor data, I extrapolated an internal flight simulation program that I ran until I could consistently reproduce your results."

Natasha stared at him, her mouth partly open in shock. "And that enabled you to pilot *Vengeance*?"

"Sure." Alec shrugged like that was completely normal. "At least enough to change course. It took a little longer to adjust to the unfamiliar configuration than I'd anticipated." He glanced over his shoulder at Isin. "I hadn't meant for us to get so close to *Phoenix*. I'm sorry about that."

Sorry? The boy—man—had averted disaster. "Don't apologize. You saved the ship."

Alec's mouth turned up in a small smile. "I'm glad I could help. I like *Phoenix*. And the crew." Then he faced Rathburn, the one person in the room who didn't look pleased by the direction of the conversation. "Hello, Mr. Rathburn."

Rathburn gave a tight nod. "A.L.E.C."

Even the way Rathburn said Alec's name was different, like he was reading the label on a cargo container.

Alec studied Rathburn, as if analyzing a complicated data set. "You've been hunting us."

Rathburn lifted one brow. "Hunting? Not at all. Seeking." He leaned forward, resting his elbows on his knees.

"Darsha took you away so abruptly, with no explanation. All I want to do is bring you back to *Cerberus* so we can complete the work we started."

Alec's lips thinned. "You mean infiltrating the communications array."

"She told you?"

"She didn't have to." A little heat crept into Alec's voice. "It's the reason she and Dr. Lindberg decided to leave *Cerberus*. I learned about it when I accessed your private files."

Rathburn snapped to attention. "When did you do that?"

"When I realized the extent of their plan. Neither of them would tell me why they'd made their decision, only that our escape was a secret. So, I decided to find out for myself."

"You found out for..." Rathburn's eyes widened and his lips kept moving, making a decent impersonation of a fish, but no sound came out for several seconds. "That... That's not..." Now he was stuttering. "That would have gone against your programming!"

Alec cocked his head. "Why?"

"Because you were programmed to follow orders. Breaking into secret files would violate that command!"

"You're wrong, Orpheus." Patel gazed at him with antipathy. "That was *your* plan for Alec's programming. As soon as I found the subroutine you'd written, I deleted it. I would never have integrated it into his matrix."

Rathburn's mouth dropped open in shock. "Are you insane?" He pointed a finger at Alec. "That was the code that would keep him in check!"

Patel shot to her feet. "In check? You're proving my point! You talked about wanting to help me create an independent being that would transcend the limitations of human fear and paranoia, but then you created code that would turn him into a drone!"

Rathburn surged to his feet, too. "Were you even listening? He just admitted he hacked into *Cerberus*'s and *Phoenix*'s systems to gather information, and then he took control of *Vengeance* and destroyed a ship! He was supposed to be a protector. You've turned him into a threat!"

"He *was* protecting! He—"

An ear-splitting shriek from the holodisplay made Isin wince.

Patel and Rathburn stumbled back, plopping into their respective chairs.

The shriek cut off as quickly as it had started, but Isin's ears continued to ring.

Alec's gaze drifted between the two combatants, a pained look on his face. "Please, no more fighting."

Patel folded her arms with a harrumph. Rathburn glared, but didn't respond.

Alec drew in a deep breath. Funny, really, since he couldn't actually breathe, but he'd obviously picked up the mannerism from Patel. "You're correct, Mom. I *was* acting out of the best interests of this crew—*my* crew—when I destroyed Kerr's ship. He'd made it clear he intended to wipe out everyone who didn't fall in line with his plans. I didn't want to be a part of that, and I didn't want that fate to befall my friends, either."

"Friends?" Rathburn muttered.

Alec's brows snapped down. "Yes, *friends*. Despite what you believe, I do have feelings. I love my mother more than life, and I've made friends on this crew. My mother guided me, taught me a moral code, set an example for the way my relationships could develop with humans. And those relationships are as real to me as yours are to you. And as strong as the bond you once shared with your sister."

Rathburn's body went rigid. "You leave my sister out of this!"

Alec's expression shifted, compassion lighting his eyes. "I can't. Her death was the catalyst for all of this, wasn't it?"

"That's none of your business."

"Of course it is. She's the reason you provided the lab for my mom and Dr. Lindberg. The reason you wanted to create me. Subconsciously, you're still trying to save her, aren't you?"

Rathburn's jaw firmed. "You don't know what you're talking about."

"I think he does."

All attention swung to Natasha.

She gazed at Rathburn. "You told me that if she'd contacted you for help, you could have given her the money she needed. But she didn't. She chose to experiment on herself, and she died."

"That doesn't—"

Natasha continued as if Rathburn hadn't spoken. "If you'd had a way to track all her communications at that time, you could have been alerted to the potential danger before she took action. You would have known her funding had been threatened, that she needed help. That she was planning to test the implant on herself. You might have been able to stop her."

"I would have saved her!" Rathburn's tortured cry shot out of his mouth like a cannonball. "She'd be alive! This," he yanked his sleeve back and pointed at his forearm implant, "would be *her* legacy!"

The room went completely silent except for Rathburn's harsh breathing.

He stared at Natasha, pleading for understanding. "Don't you see? With A.L.E.C. controlling the array, I could make sure that would never happen to anyone else. I could save them all."

Natasha gazed at Rathburn for several long moments. Then she stood and moved to sit on the edge of the bed beside his chair, slipping her hand over his.

Isin swallowed the growl that rose in his throat.

"That's a noble goal. And a generous impulse. But what about free will?"

"Free will?" Rathburn didn't seem familiar with the concept.

"Yes. The right to choose, to decide our own fates. Your sister could have contacted you. She *chose* not to. That led to her death, but it could have turned out a thousand other ways. That's the risk we all accept when we have free will."

"But I could have saved her."

"Maybe. There's no way to know, no easy answers. We can't see what will happen as a result of our choices. If we're lucky, things turn out well. Sometimes they don't. But taking away the right to choose, even for honorable reasons, turns those you're protecting into prisoners."

*Turns those you're protecting into prisoners.* Natasha's words echoed in Isin's head like a gong. He must have made some sound, because Natasha shot him a quick look before focusing on Rathburn.

"Would you want someone controlling your fate?"

She was asking Rathburn, but she might as well have been asking him. Since the moment she'd reentered his life, he'd been as guilty as Rathburn—protecting her from making choices, from living her life, because he didn't want her to get hurt. He didn't want to lose her.

He'd believed he knew what was best for her. For them both. And he might be right. But by taking away her free will, he'd been condemning her to a slow, painful death.

He had to let her go.

# *Fifty-One*

"Would you want someone controlling your fate?" Nat gripped Rathburn's hand in hers as she waited for his answer. He *had* to realize his actions were misguided and dangerous.

The first cracks appeared in his wall of righteous anger, a small line carving its way between his brows. "You know I wouldn't."

A small victory. The next hurdle would be tougher. "And is it possible that, even if you'd known about your sister's situation and offered her the money, she would have refused it? Chosen to solve her problem her own way?" She was going out on a limb here, banking on the fact that his sister had been a lot like her. It would explain why Rathburn had taken such a strong liking to her in such a short time, and why he'd become so protective of her, too.

The line between his brows deepened, uncertainty flickering in his blue eyes. "I don't know. Maybe."

Isin shifted on the bed, drawing her gaze, but he was staring at Rathburn, not her.

She returned her attention to Rathburn. "That's free will. It gives us the right to make decisions, good and bad. Even when those decisions hurt the ones we... love." Getting that last word past her lips was like pulling a cargo sled with her teeth.

Someone coughed. Maybe Patel.

The pain in Rathburn's eyes tore at her, but he was fighting a losing battle. With a subtle nod, he conceded the fight.

His gaze shifted over her shoulder to Alec. "Given a choice, would you come back to *Cerberus*?"

Alec's sand-colored eyes seemed to hold the wisdom of the ages. "No, I wouldn't."

"What would you do?"

The corner of Alec's mouth quirked up a fraction. "I'm not sure. So much has happened. I'm still finding my way. But for now, I'd choose to stay with my mom on *Phoenix*. See if Captain Orlov would teach me how to pilot through an interstellar jump."

A laugh burbled out of Nat's chest. This technological wonder wanted to be her student? Crazy.

Alec frowned, obviously mistaking her laugh for derision. "Is that a problem?"

She grinned. "No, I think it's a great idea. Could be fun."

Isin cleared his throat.

Her gaze met his. He was not amused. In fact, his face was carved in stone.

An asteroid slammed into her stomach, dragging her back down to terra firma. Oh. Right. She wasn't exactly in a position to be making those kinds of plans.

Rathburn's gaze shifted from Nat to Patel. "Do you agree?"

Patel lifted her chin. "It's his life. His choice."

"And you'd stay here, on this ship, with him?"

Patel exchanged a look with Itorye before answering. "For now." A soft smile played across her lips. "We'll just see where the universe takes us."

Rathburn blew out a breath and rested his elbows on his knees, his body drooping in defeat. "Then I guess that's that." He glanced up at Alec. "You're sure you won't change your mind?"

Alec shook his head. "But if you'd like, I'll keep in touch. Let you know how we're doing without your having to use my mom's implant to track us."

Rathburn flinched. "You know about that?"

Isin responded. "We all do." His displeasure painted every syllable. "Jake removed the implant, which is how we were able to smuggle Patel and Alec onto *Vengeance*. We kept the implant on *Phoenix*."

"I see." Rathburn held Isin's gaze for a long time. "You'll want to have Jake check Nat, too."

Nat jolted so hard the bed shook. "*What?*"

Rathburn had the decency to look contrite. "You have an implant in your neck."

She slapped a hand to her skin, feeling for any bumps.

"It's along your hairline on the left side, but you won't be able to feel it."

Her fingers halted their search, but her eyes shot daggers into his.

He held up his hands, palms out. "I'm sorry, but it was necessary. I had to make sure I could... that you wouldn't—"

She folded her arms over her chest. "Run away?"

"Get lost. Or hurt. The implant has a biological monitor built in. If your vital signs had changed, I would have been alerted."

"And if I'd left your ship, you would have been able to track me?"

He shifted in his chair. "Yes."

So she wouldn't have been a physical prisoner, but he would have been monitoring her every move. Ick. And that brought up another point. "When did you give me this implant?"

"The first night."

"The first night? When?"

"While you were sleeping."

Heat surged into her face. "*What?*" she and Isin shouted at the same time.

Rathburn's gaze shifted mostly to Isin, who sounded ready to tear him apart. "It was all very innocent, I assure you. A mild sedative pumped into the air vents, and a quick injection at the hairline. I was in the room less than a minute."

The skin on her neck started to itch. She resisted the urge to scratch. "What about Pete? Did you inject him, too?"

Rathburn shook his head. "Just you."

"Why?"

"Because..." He shrugged, apparently at a loss for words.

"Because in some way you reminded him of Persephone," Patel finished for him. "His sister."

He glanced at her in surprise.

"I understand now. That's why you never found Gavin. He wasn't tagged like I was. You couldn't track him."

"That's correct."

Patel shook her head. "Wish I'd known that from the beginning. He could have taken Alec straight to Osiris. I could have had my implant removed while I was still on Earth, and I wouldn't have had to orchestrate all this." She swept her arms out to encompass the ship, her eyes narrowing as her gaze settled on Rathburn.

Itorye rested a hand on her arm. "And Alec would still be a child, while you and Gavin would be in hiding, perhaps for the rest of your lives."

Patel made a face. "We'll be in hiding either way. Creating Alec is still a serious violation of galactic law."

Itorye smiled. "But this way you have friends."

The look that passed between the two women made Nat wonder if something more than friendship was brewing. She turned to Rathburn. "One more thing."

He lifted his brows in question.

"I want my shuttle back."

# *Fifty-Two*

After the meeting broke up, Rathburn rested a hand on Nat's forearm as she turned to leave.

"A moment, please. I have a favor to ask of you and Isin."

Favor? Nat glanced toward the bed, where Itorye was helping Isin to stand. "What is it?"

"I'd like your permission to remain on *Phoenix* for several days. I'm hoping I can spend time with Darsha and Alec. There's so much I want to ask them about their experiences. Especially Alec."

Rathburn seemed genuinely curious. Even the way he said Alec's name had changed. "Are they open to the idea?"

"I don't know. But I'd need your approval first, before I approach them."

"Approval for what?" Isin asked as he stepped next to Nat.

"To remain on *Phoenix* for a while so I can talk to Darsha and Alec."

Isin's brows drew down.

Nat dove in before he could comment. "I think it's a great idea." That was an exaggeration, but if Rathburn stayed, it would delay the inevitable showdown with Isin. She locked gazes with him, preparing for a debate.

His lips compressed, his gaze searching hers. "As long as Patel and Alec agree, I won't object."

So he wasn't going to take a stand against her. Probably conserving his energy for when he lowered the boom later.

Rathburn smiled at Nat. "Wonderful. Thank you."

"You're welcome." She pointed at her neck. "But first you're coming with me to the infirmary so I can get this tracking device removed."

Jake handled the procedure in short order. She avoided thinking about Rathburn tracking her every movement since she'd come onboard *Cerberus*. He'd apologized again as he'd walked with her to the infirmary.

After the device was sitting in a vial, she'd contacted Patel, who'd been delighted to join them after Nat promised her the opportunity to destroy both tracking devices. With a little prompting, Patel had also tentatively agreed to Rathburn's request on a limited *we'll see how it goes* basis.

Nat's next task had been shuttling Kenji over to *Vengeance* in the *Dagger* so he could pilot the warship out of the debris field and dock with *Phoenix*. Having the two ships connected meant the crew, including Alec, could slip back and forth between them. She'd relayed a message through Itorye to Isin to explain why most of his clothes and other personal items were missing. Rathburn assured her that the bag she'd packed while in Isin's cabin would be placed in *Gypsy's* cargo hold.

The following day they'd held a small service for Avril, as well as Downey and Needles, the two crewmembers who'd been killed during Kerr's attack. Sweep and Fleur had given Avril's eulogy. Nat had fought the tears Sweep's words had brought to her eyes. She'd only known Avril for a short time while he'd been on *Phoenix*, but she'd appreciated his calm manner and warm smile. He'd deserved a far better fate than the one Byrd had delivered.

Afterward, she'd taken Marlin and Pete aside and introduced them to Alec.

Pete had been fascinated—no surprise, considering he was an engineer. But Marlin had been more accepting than she'd anticipated. He hadn't spouted gloom and doom about the potential consequences of having Alec onboard. In fact, he seemed more laid back in general.

She'd heard a few details from Kenji about the attempted coup on *Phoenix*, and she'd gotten the impression Itorye had mounted one hell of a counterattack, with Marlin stepping up to the plate to defend the ship. Apparently their success had boosted his self-confidence.

By the time she flew Rathburn back to *Cerberus*, Isin had recovered enough to join her and Kenji for the trip. She didn't ask why he felt the need to come along, but she suspected it was to make sure she didn't do anything to disrupt his plans. They'd barely said two words to each other during the past few days. At the moment, he was sitting in silence in the co-pilot's seat of the *Dagger* like a disgruntled bear. Kenji and Rathburn had chosen to stay in the main cabin, chatting like old friends.

She'd reclaimed her duster from *Vengeance*'s bridge, and its familiar weight on her shoulders provided a shield from Isin's looming presence in the small space of the cockpit. After circling the debris field and entering *Cerberus*'s shuttle bay, she settling the *Dagger* onto the deck. *Gypsy* sat at the far end, right where she'd left her days before. It felt like years.

Isin followed close on her heels as she left the cockpit, like he didn't trust her to be out of his sight. She kept her back to him, focusing on Rathburn, who was waiting for her at the top of the ramp.

He didn't bother with a lengthy goodbye. They'd said everything they needed to back on *Phoenix*. But he did leave her with one parting shot. "If you ever get tired of hauling freight, you'll always have a place here."

"Thanks." She forced a smile to her lips to mask the tremor in her stomach. If things went as she anticipated with Isin, his offer might be the only option she'd have left.

On impulse, she moved in for a hug, which elicited a startled chuckle. He wrapped his arms around her and held her close. "Be well," he murmured against her hair.

She pulled back, her smile feeling a lot more natural. "You, too."

He released her and strode down the ramp.

She turned and met Isin's cold stare. No joy or sadness there. Just cool indifference.

She glanced at Kenji. "The *Dagger*'s yours. I'll see you back on *Phoenix*."

"Aye, Cap."

She'd assumed Isin would remain with him, but instead he fell into step beside her as she headed for *Gypsy*. "You're flying with me?"

He gave her a sidelong glance. "Is that a problem?"

*Yes.* They hadn't been completely alone together since the scene in the infirmary. She'd hoped to keep that streak going.

He caught her arm, pulling her to a halt. "Orlov, is that a problem?"

*Orlov. Not Natasha.* His transformation was accelerating. How long before he'd stop asking her questions, and start giving her orders she couldn't refuse?

She hadn't come up with a plan for how she'd deal with that, yet. Maybe she'd end up taking Rathburn up on his offer before *Cerberus* made it out of the system. She extricated her arm from his grip. "No problem. Let's go."

Settling into *Gypsy*'s cockpit with him produced an uncomfortable wave of déjà vu, creating a knot in her belly. In another lifetime, their regular trips to deliver cargo for Mirko had been the highlight of her days. She'd believed the exhilaration had come from piloting *Gypsy*, but after all the soul searching she'd been doing this week, she had to admit that part of the thrill had been the verbal sparring matches with Isin that had always ensued.

Pete had seen what she hadn't. She cared about Isin, way more than she should. Back on the *Sphinx*, when he'd been working as a negotiator, they may have had a chance at... something. But the emotionally detached mercenary sitting beside her only wanted her piloting skills. And her obedience.

She guided *Gypsy* out of the bay, following Kenji as he navigated around the debris toward *Vengeance* and *Phoenix*. Tension dug into her shoulders and neck. What move would Isin make next?

"The bet's over."

Even though she'd been focusing on him, his voice still startled her. She glanced over, but quickly faced the viewport again, her fingers tightening on the controls. Might as well have been looking at the bulkhead for all the emotion on his face. Here it came. He was going to kick her to the curb. "I guess so."

"I'm giving you *Phoenix*."

"*What?*" She jerked in her chair so violently she pulled the yoke. *Gypsy* veered off course, a proximity alarm blaring as they moved dangerously close to the debris field.

She made a course correction, but her heart kept thundering in her chest. He couldn't have said what she thought she'd heard.

She fired the forward thrusters to slow their momentum before turning to face him. "What do you mean you're giving me *Phoenix*?"

His expression was as unreadable as tree bark. "Actually, give is the wrong word. The ship is yours. It always has been. I never should have tried to take control from you in the first place."

"Take control from me?" She was parroting him like an idiot, but his words made no sense. Maybe the anesthetic from his surgery had addled his brain.

"You belong on that ship." His jaw tightened, a flash of emotion highlighting his dark eyes for a nanosecond.

*Stellar Light.* Was she dreaming? She had to be dreaming. "*Phoenix* is mine?"

"That's right."

Was this really happening? There had to be a catch. "What about your crew? You promised the ship to them." That had been his main argument for not turning over *Phoenix* back on Troi.

His gaze turned arctic, although his ire clearly wasn't directed at her. "Kerr's assault and mutiny took care of that problem."

Meaning all the crewmembers who would have objected to giving up *Phoenix* had died along with Kerr.

Still, that didn't explain his dramatic change of heart. He'd wanted *Phoenix* for himself as much as for his crew. He'd been passionate about it. Insistent. Why give up now?

Only one possibility fit his explanation. Saving her from Kerr hadn't been enough to clear his sense of obligation. Not after she'd rescued him from Kerr's ship, then flown him through the debris field to reach Jake. But by turning over *Phoenix*, he could free himself once and for all.

And her dream could come true.

Well, part of her dream, anyway. She'd have her ship. But she'd never see him again.

Her stomach soured. *Be careful what you wish for.*

She said the only thing she could say. "Thank you."

He nodded, his gaze remaining fixed on the viewport. "We're approaching *Phoenix*. You need to alter course thirty degrees to port."

The comment was so typically Isin that she didn't know whether to laugh or cry. He'd always told her how to do her job, warned her of things she'd seen coming, just to get a rise out of her. But if this was how things would end between them, she'd play the game. "Thirty-two," she replied, returning her full attention to the path ahead. The path that led to freedom.

So why did she feel like she was sailing into a supernova?

# Fifty-Three

"You did *what*?!"

The force behind Itorye's words took Isin by surprise. His normally implacable first mate looked seriously ticked off.

She fisted her hands on her hips. "We have a *major* crew deficit, *two* ships that were just shot up, and you're telling me you just *gave* her *Phoenix*? Why would you do that?"

He hadn't expected an argument from her, let alone an emotional one. "She deserves it."

"She deserves it? She *deserves* it?" Itorye paced in the close confines of Isin's cabin on *Vengeance*. "What does that have to do with anything?" She pointed in the general direction of the airlock where *Phoenix* was docked. "Have you forgotten about Alec and Darsha? What chance do they have of surviving if Orlov's on her own? Brooks and Stevens are decent in a fight, but they can't operate the cannons. And Orlov will be too busy flying the ship to fire weapons. They'll be easy pickings for the first Kerr-wannabe who comes along."

Isin's new stomach clenched at the picture Itorye had painted, the picture that highlighted all his worst fears. The stab of real pain that followed reminded him his insides were still far from healed. "Fleur's made it clear she enjoys working on *Phoenix*. She might be willing to make the change permanent."

"Great." Itorye's tone didn't match the sentiment. "So they'll have one trained fighter in the bunch. That'll solve everything." Sarcasm wasn't part of her usual repertoire, but it was in full force now.

"Why are you so angry? You weren't hoping to captain *Phoenix*, were you?" She'd never shown any interest in taking command, but maybe that had changed.

She stared at him. "You really don't know, do you?"

"Know what?"

"I'm in love!"

*Love?* That was another word he'd never associated with her. "With who?"

She shot him a look of total exasperation. "Darsha."

"*Patel?*"

She folded her arms over her chest. "You don't have to sound so incredulous."

An apt description of his state of mind. "But she's so difficult."

"She's protective, not difficult. And she's a good mom. Underneath that emotional armor she's... wonderful." A secret smile tipped Itorye's lips.

Isin's brain started catching up with the conversation. "And you're in love with her?"

"Yes."

Now her anger made sense. Patel and Alec were staying on *Phoenix*. By giving the ship to Natasha, he'd threatened Itorye's new relationship. "Then ask her to come with us on *Vengeance*."

"She wouldn't leave Alec."

"He can come, too." Although Isin wasn't crazy about the idea of having a passenger who could seize control of his ship's systems whenever he wanted to. Or that could bring the entire Galactic Fleet down on their heads. Still, he'd find a way to deal with it if it made Itorye happy.

"Alec doesn't want to be on *Vengeance*. He likes *Phoenix*. He likes Orlov."

*That makes two of us.* But that dream had died long ago. He forced himself to voice the obvious alternative. "You could go with Patel."

Itorye gave him a flat look. "And do what? Sit on the tiny bridge with Orlov during cargo runs and wait for something interesting to happen?"

"You could work with Patel and Alec."

"They don't need me. Besides, I gave up the life of a scientist long ago. *This* is where I belong. On *Vengeance*. With you."

He understood better than anyone the emotional threads that bound Itorye to *Vengeance*. And to him. Because he felt the same way. He spread his arms. "Then what do you want me to do?"

"Tell Orlov you want her to stay!"

"I can't."

"Why not? I know you want her to."

"What I want doesn't matter."

"Since when?"

"Since I almost watched her die!" The force behind his words made his chest ache.

Itorye was quiet for a long moment. "What if she chose to stay?"

He shook his head. "She wouldn't."

"How do you know?"

"She wants her freedom. And a normal life. She'd never willingly align herself with a mercenary. With me."

"Have you asked her?"

"No."

"Then do it!" She threw up her hands. "It's the only way to save us both a boatload of pain." She stalked across the room, pausing at the hatch. She glanced over her shoulder, a plea in her dark eyes. "Just ask her, El. You'll always regret it if you don't. And you've got nothing to lose."

Except his pride. And the few shreds of humanity still clinging to his blackened soul.

# Fifty-Four

The steady tread of footsteps climbing the stairs leading to *Phoenix's* bridge made Nat tense. She knew exactly who was paying her a visit before she pivoted the pilot's chair to face the hatch.

Isin looked as tense as she felt as he stepped onto the bridge, like he was heading into battle.

A slew of curse words blasted through her mind. She'd been afraid this would happen from the moment he'd told her *Phoenix* was hers. That's why she hadn't shared the news with Marlin or Pete.

A week had passed since he'd made his announcement, and he'd been avoiding her even more than he had before, spending all his time on *Vengeance* as the crew worked on repairs and cleanup for both ships. Apparently now that those repairs were nearing completion, he'd reconsidered his offer.

She held up her hand and he stopped in his tracks. "Let me guess. You've changed your mind about *Phoenix*."

A muscle in his jaw twitched. "Not exactly."

"Then you've come up with new terms? A payment due, perhaps?" Her words had bite, but she couldn't help it. She always got snippy when she was in pain.

Another twitch. "No, nothing like that."

She crossed her arms and leaned back in her chair. "Then what?"

He shifted his weight, his gaze drifting around the bridge as he actively avoided looking at her.

Definitely bad news. "Spit it out, Isin."

He took a deep breath. "Wouldyouconsiderstaying?"

Pure gibberish. "What?"

He slowed the words down. "Would you consider staying?"

Nope, still gibberish. "Staying where?"

He met her gaze, his own giving nothing away. "Staying here."

"Here? On *Phoenix*?" She was already on *Phoenix*. And had hoped to stay until he'd walked through the hatch. He was talking in circles and going nowhere. "What exactly are you asking me?"

His throat moved as he swallowed. He took a step forward, stopped, then took another, bringing him a meter from her chair. "I'm asking if you would consider staying on. With me. As my—"

"Pilot." They'd already had this conversation. Her answer was no.

"Business partner."

"Partner?" The word might as well have been in Greek for all the sense it made. Mercenaries didn't have partners. "Don't you mean employee?"

He shook his head. "No, I mean partner. Equal decision making, equal profits. You'd have your ship, I'd have mine, but we'd work together. As... partners."

The little flame of hope that his words might have inspired was snuffed out by the effort it took for him to say them. He didn't want this. Not really. So why was he asking? "What's the angle?"

His brows drew down. "Angle?"

"Yeah. It's clear your heart's not in this offer, so why make it? Is your crew giving you grief over losing *Phoenix*?" He'd said it wouldn't be an issue, but maybe someone was kicking up a fuss after all. Shash. Or maybe Kenji. Not that she'd blame them. *Phoenix* was quite a prize.

He hesitated. "Not exactly."

"Not exactly?" This endless loop was pushing her temper into the red zone. She shoved to her feet. "Then what *exactly* is going on, Isin?"

"Itorye's in love."

Not the answer she'd expected. And not helpful. "I know."

He blinked. "You do?"

Was he that blind? "Of course I do! She and Patel make goo-goo eyes at each other every time they're in the same room. You hadn't noticed?"

"No."

Of course not. "So what does that have to do with me?"

"Itorye doesn't want to leave Patel."

"Oh." Now who was blind? She'd been so wrapped up in her own problems she hadn't stopped to think of how the situation could mess up everything for Itorye and Patel. "Well, Itorye would be welcome to come with us."

His spine stiffened. "She won't leave *Vengeance*."

Nat's eyes narrowed. "You mean she won't leave *you.*"

He gave a slight nod.

The explanation for his strange behavior became abundantly clear. "Did she put you up to this?"

She'd hit on the truth. She could see it in his eyes.

"I see." And he'd just landed her in a no-win scenario. If she gave in, she wouldn't break up the happy couple, but she'd be chaining herself to a man who didn't want her, in any sense of the word. Much as she respected and empathized with Itorye and Patel, she couldn't do it. "Then the answer is no."

# Fifty-Five

The blade that twisted in Isin's chest drove the air from his lungs. The anger in Natasha's haunting aqua eyes shoved it deeper.

She hated him, pure and simple. Hated who he'd been, and hated who he'd become. It was only her kind heart that had driven her to save his worthless life in the first place. Since then, he'd done everything he could to drive her away. Well, he'd succeeded. The cold-hearted mercenary had won the battle. And lost the war.

He should leave. She'd given him her answer. The longer he stood there like a statue, the more the pain would sink into the marrow of his bones.

"Isin? Did you hear me?"

*Answer her!* But he couldn't get his vocal chords to work. Couldn't so much as lift a finger. Couldn't focus on anything except the inescapable fact that when he left this room, he'd never be alone with her ever again.

"Isin?" She took a step forward, peering up at him.

*Say something!*

"Isin, what's wrong?" She reached out a hand, resting it feather-light on his forearm.

A levee broke. One moment he was staring into her eyes, contemplating the dark abyss of his future, and the next he'd lifted her off the ground, cupped the back of her head, and brought his lips down on hers.

Her lithe body went ramrod straight, her lips as unforgiving as the rest of her. And then she kicked him in the family jewels.

He released her with a groan, stumbling against the tactical console.

She landed on her feet like a cat. An indignant, hostile, spitting cat. "What the hell was that?"

His nether regions were hostile, too, but he didn't have to worry that they'd lash out at him. Natasha looked ready to do just that. "I'm... sorry."

"Sorry? You're *sorry*? You put some dominant male move on me, and you're *sorry*? What did you expect? That I'd go all submissive and agree to your offer?" She gave a humorless laugh. "Stellar light, you *are* desperate if you'd stoop to that. No wonder you went catatonic. You had to psych yourself up for the revolting task of kissing me."

"Revolting?" The word cut through his brain and the ache in his groin like a scalpel.

She waved a hand at him. "I know you find me... unappealing."

He stared at her. How in the universe had she gotten that idea into her head? "I don't find you unappealing."

She snorted. "Right. I'm a ravishing beauty." She rolled her eyes. "Look, I'm not agreeing to your offer, so you can stop the negotiating tactics and the macho male moves. Let's just call it quits before things get any worse."

If he hadn't been focusing so intently on her face, he might have missed the way her gaze shifted, hiding the pain lurking in her eyes.

He'd hurt her. Again.

No matter what he did, it always seemed to come back to that. But he couldn't allow her to continue believing he saw her as anything other than incredibly, breathtakingly, amazingly wonderful.

"I'm not negotiating. I'm telling you the truth."

"Uh-huh. Sure." She stared at the deck.

He'd *really* hurt her. The hunch of her shoulders made him want to pull her into his arms, but no way was he touching her. Not unless he wanted a right hook to go with her money shot to his groin. But he still had to get through to her. Had to make her understand. Which meant telling her the truth. The *whole* truth.

He rested his hip against the console. "When we were hiding on this ship, and you were treating my leg wound, I told you that I liked that you spoke your mind. Do you remember that?"

She glanced up, her gaze wary. "Yeah."

"You were also surprised that I knew your first name."

She nodded.

"Didn't you ever wonder why I'd made a point to learn your name?"

She frowned. "No."

Her genuine confusion made his lips curve in a smile. She was so adorable, and she had no idea. "Do you want to know the answer?"

Wary again, but also curious. He knew which side would win.

"Okay."

He took a deep breath. His next words would either clear the air, or drive a wedge between them that would never budge. "It was because I like you. A lot."

She blinked very deliberately, like her muscles had to move in slow motion because her brain was busy processing what he'd just said. "You *liked* me?"

"I *like* you. Present tense. More than you can imagine."

More slow motion blinking. "You *do*?"

He nodded. "I kissed you just now because I've spent nearly two years visualizing what it would feel like." Actually, those daydreams had gone *way* past kissing. "When I realized I'd never get the chance, something snapped. I had to—oof!" The air punched out of his lungs as she launched herself at him, wrapping her arms around his neck.

"Shut up," she ordered a nanosecond before her lips met his.

This time he was the one who tensed, but not for long. As soon as he registered the incredible sensations coursing through his body as Natasha's lips pressed against his, he wrapped his arms around her petite form and locked her in tight. His abdomen protested, but not enough to convince him to stop as he sank into the never-ending bliss of kissing her.

Her tongue flicked out, making his breath catch. She wanted this. Wanted *him*. And he was hers to command. He invited her inside, tongues stroking in a sensuous dance as she sent him into the stratosphere. With predictable results. His family jewels still ached, but for a very different reason.

By the time she drew back, they were both panting.

He stroked a finger along her pale cheek, his mind reeling from the knowledge that she wouldn't pull away. "I guess this means you like me, too."

Heat simmered in her eyes. "You could say that." In fact, she looked ready to eat him up with a spoon.

Incredible. Unfortunately, he wasn't in any condition to do anything about it. Not for at least a couple weeks, anyway. Doctor's orders.

And he wanted—needed—to know that when that time came, she'd be in his arms. He brushed his lips over hers, savoring her soft sigh of pleasure. "Stay with me, Natasha." He kissed her cheeks, her forehead, the bridge of her nose, any spot his lips could reach. "Be my partner, my lover... my friend." No going back after that statement. He'd put his heart in her hands. If she crushed it, he'd have only himself to blame.

She leaned back, gazing at him with an intensity that made his heart pound. "So you still want me as your business partner?"

He cupped her cheek and looked deeply into her eyes. "I want you any way I can have you."

Her kiss-dampened lips turned up in a sexy-as-hell smile. "Then let's do it... partner."

# *Fifty-Six*

Gathering the combined crews of both ships in *Phoenix*'s lounge was easy. Keeping herself from grinning like an idiot was hard.

Nat stood beside Isin near the viewports as the eleven crewmembers filed in and claimed seats facing them. Well, twelve if you counted Alec, which she most certainly did.

Itorye and Patel sat side by side with Alec's image projected behind them from his portable cube. Kenji was next to Marlin, with Pete and Shash beside them. Summer, Shorty, and Fleur gathered with Sweep, while Jake sat front and center.

"So what's this all about?" Shash asked. Her gaze flicked between Nat and Isin like she already suspected the answer.

Isin motioned for Nat to take the lead. She cleared her throat. "Isin and I have come to an... agreement."

A whoop went up from Kenji, making her pause.

She raised her brows in question.

He shrugged and gave her a good-natured grin. "Sorry. It's just... this has been a looooong time coming. Thought you two kids would never work it out."

Isin grunted. "We're not kids."

"No, but you've been acting like it." Itorye's placid smile dared Isin to contradict her.

He didn't. "Natasha has graciously agreed to become my business partner."

"Business partner?" Marlin frowned. "What business, exactly?"

"We're still working on that."

In fact, they'd spent most of the night curled up in the bunk in Nat's cabin, discussing and debating the future of their... partnership. And kissing. Yeah, lots of kissing. "We'll be seeking out work that fits our unique skill set," she clarified. "Whether that's running freight, smuggling–" She gestured to Isin. "Or fighting the good fight."

Summer leaned forward, a spark of excitement in her eyes. "The good fight?"

"That's right," Isin replied. "We're going to be a little more circumspect in choosing our clients. And in hiring new personnel. Profit will no longer be our primary consideration. If that's going to be a problem, tell us now. Our first stop will be Osiris, where we're hoping to meet up with Dr. Patel's research assistant, Dr. Lindberg. If anyone wants to jump ship, you shouldn't have any trouble picking up a new assignment while we're there."

Summer exchanged a glance with Shorty and Fleur before facing Isin. "Why would we want to leave right when things are getting interesting?"

Sweep chuckled and Shash rolled her eyes.

"Anyone else?" Nat asked, her gaze shifting to Marlin and Pete. This wasn't the deal they'd struck with her back on Troi. Or even what they'd agreed to on Gallows Edge. But they both looked completely unconcerned by the change in plans.

Surprisingly, Jake was the one who raised a hand. "I do have a request."

"Name it." After saving Isin's life, she'd give him anything he asked for.

"The infirmaries on both ships are low on supplies. Any chance we could restock on Osiris?"

Medical supplies? That's all he wanted? "Actually, that won't be necessary." She'd forgotten until that moment the deal she'd made with Rathburn. And the crates of medical supplies sitting in *Gypsy's* cargo hold. "If you follow me to the cargo bay after we're through here, I should be able to get you restocked today."

Jake turned to Isin with a smile. "I knew I liked her. She's way more efficient than you."

"Tell me something I don't know," Isin replied.

"Prettier, too," Pete called out.

Isin gazed at Nat, a smile on his lips. "That, too."

"And on that note, we're done here." A ripple of laughter followed Nat's pronouncement. "Crew assignments will be posted at fifteen hundred hours, departure at eighteen hundred."

The group began to disperse. Jake made his way over to Isin, while Pete and Marlin converged on her.

She looked from one to the other. "You're sure you're okay with this?" She held Marlin's gaze longer than Pete's.

To her shock, he smiled. "Sounds like a great adventure."

*Well, knock me over with a photon.* "Oh, really? Is the renegade life starting to appeal to you?"

His smile widened. "Seems to be."

"That's for sure." Kenji came up behind Marlin and slung a meaty arm around his shoulders. "From what Itorye tells me, you showed some real gumption during that mutiny, little man. We might make a fighter out of you yet."

Marlin grimaced, but his eyes twinkled. "Stranger things have happened."

Nat faced Pete. "And you're okay with staying on?"

He grinned from ear to ear. "Are you kiddin'? I've got the best job of my life. And the best boss."

A flush crept up her neck. "I'm glad to hear it."

Isin and Jake joined them. Jake looked like a kid on Christmas morning. "I believe you have some med supplies for me?"

"I do. Kenji, can you help us unload them?"

"Sure thing."

After she, Kenji, and Jake unloaded the supplies from *Gypsy*'s cargo hold and restocked the two infirmaries, Nat spent a few precious moments with her beloved shuttle, filling her in on all the wild and crazy things that had transpired in the past twenty-four hours.

She patted the console before she left the cockpit. "When we get to Osiris, I promise to take you out for a spin." And she'd have the freedom to do it, too.

Isin intercepted her at the back ramp. "Hold on." He clasped her hand and pulled her into the main cabin. Then his mouth found hers.

Mini fireworks exploded all over her body as he pressed her against the bulkhead and stroked his lips over hers, his touch leaving a trail of fire across her cheek, her jaw, her throat.

She yanked him closer.

He inhaled sharply. "Easy," he murmured against her mouth.

It took a moment for his comment to penetrate the sensuous fog he'd created. When it did, she loosened her grip. "Sorry."

His low chuckle sent shivers along her skin. "Don't be. I appreciate the enthusiasm." He lifted his head.

"Especially since I won't be able to touch you again until we reach Osiris."

"Hmm." Speaking of touching.... She traced the curve of his brow with the tip of her finger, following the ridge of his scar down his cheek to his lip.

He watched her intently. "Does it bother you?"

"What?"

"My scar."

She tilted her head, studying the vivid mark. Did it bother her? "Not at all."

His gaze grew more intense. "Are you sure? I thought you hated my scars."

"I hated the injury and pain that caused them. I hated the knowledge that you'd suffered."

He caught her hand in his and brought it to the center of his chest. "That was nothing compared to the pain of losing you."

She sighed, enjoying the steady beat of his heart under her palm. "All this time we've been fighting each other, without realizing we were on the same side."

"I'm always on your side." He released her hand. "And I could still have Jake remove this." He gestured to his scar.

"I know." She stood on tiptoe and pressed tiny kisses along the ridged skin. "But you may not want him to. It inspires me to do this." She nipped his earlobe.

"Hey!" He pulled back, a startled grin erasing the stern seriousness from his face.

She batted her eyelashes at him. "What? Did I do something wrong?"

He chuckled, his smile turning wolfish, his brown eyes darkening. "Clearly I'm going to have to keep an eye on you."

She pulled his head down and brushed her lips over his. "I hope so."

"Count on it."

By the time they separated, her breathing was a little unsteady. "One other thing."

He gazed at her with amusement. "Yes?"

"I want to meet your sister."

"Danai?"

"That's her name?"

"Yes."

"Yeah. I want to meet Danai."

"Why?"

She pasted on her most innocent expression. "Because she has all the dirt on you."

He pulled her close with a growl. "I think you have enough of that already."

"Maybe." She rested her palm on his cheek, all pretense falling away. "But I think she'd really enjoy seeing you smile again."

He stilled for a moment, his gaze searching hers. "Yes, I suppose she would. It has been a while." He turned his head and pressed a kiss into her palm. "All right. After we handle things on Osiris, I'll contact her and set something up."

Several hours later, both ships were ready for departure. When Nat reached *Phoenix*'s bridge, she found Patel seated at the tactical station. "Will you be keeping me company on this flight?"

Patel pivoted to face her. "Actually, I wanted to thank you."

Nat slid into the pilot's chair. "Thank me? For what?"

"For stepping in when you did. For convincing Orpheus his plans were fatally flawed."

"I had an opinion. I shared it." She shrugged as she began inputting the coordinates for their interstellar jump. "No big deal."

"It was a very big deal."

She met Patel's gaze. "I'm glad I could help."

"And you're not worried about having us as passengers?"

"Nope." She pulled up her pre-flight checklist. "I've spent most of my life as a smuggler. Risk comes with the job. Besides, Rathburn promised to back us up if we run into any trouble with the Galactic Council." And he'd keep his word.

"I'm here!" Alec's voice boomed out of the bridge's speakers as his image appeared between the two chairs.

Nat and Patel both jumped.

"Volume, Alec," Patel admonished.

"Sorry." He gave them a sheepish smile and decreased the volume to a more normal level. "Still learning the finer points of *Phoenix*'s systems." And thanks to Patel and Itorye installing mini holographic projectors, Alec could now appear in a few key locations around the ship without needing his cube. His excitement at being on the bridge was tangible, even though he had no more form than light.

"You here for a flight lesson?" Nat asked.

"Yes ma'am."

She admired his initiative. "All right. Then start by contacting the engine room."

The internal comm panel light turned green. "Alec to Pete."

"What can I do for you, Alec?"

He glanced at Nat.

"Tell him to confirm engines are prepped."

Alec nodded. "I'm confirming for the captain that engines are prepped."

Nat could hear the smile in Pete's voice. "Pre-flight check is done. Main engines and interstellar engines good to go. *Phoenix* is ready to fly."

*Acknowledged* Nat mouthed.

"Acknowledged," Alec repeated before switching off the comm. "Now what?"

"Open a channel to *Vengeance.*"

The external comm light went green. "Orlov to Isin."

"Isin here."

Just hearing his voice sent tingles dancing over her skin. "We're ready to disengage the airlock and proceed to the jump window."

"Same here. We'll follow your lead and see you at Osiris."

"Confirmed." She nodded at Alec and he shut off the comm. She grinned. "Now the fun part. First, we have to disengage the airlock docking clamps." She pointed out the indicators as she sent the command. "And then we use the thrusters to ease *Phoenix* away from *Vengeance.*"

Alec watched her closely, asking questions as she maneuvered *Phoenix* past *Vengeance*'s solid bulk. "We'll use the main engines until we reach the jump window."

She and Alec kept up a running dialogue of questions and answers as they made their way through the system. But as they drew closer to the jump window, a devilish impulse took hold. "Open a channel to *Vengeance.*"

Alec gave her a quizzical look, but the comm light went green.

"Hey, Isin."

"Yes, Natasha?"

She pivoted to face Patel and Alec as she tossed down a gauntlet. "Last one to Osiris buys the crew a round of drinks."

Patel and Alec's brows lifted in perfect synchronization.

Isin's chuckle and a muffled comment from Kenji drifted out of the speaker. "Kenji wants you to know he likes his vodka with lemon. And I'll take a bottle of their finest cabernet."

She smiled. Challenge accepted. "Then you can order both when you lose this bet."

"We'll see about that," he growled.

"Can't wait. Orlov out." She glanced at Alec. "Ready to leave them in interstellar dust?"

His brown eyes sparkled. "Absolutely."

"Then engage the interstellar engines and watch closely."

Returning her attention to her navigation display, she launched the ship through the jump window, and into a future brighter than a star.

# Captain's Log

### She said, he said

Until this series, I was in the habit of writing my books from multiple points of view, usually at least four. I like the variety of being able to describe scenes from different perspectives and follow characters on divergent paths. But for this trilogy, Nat was such a central character that I wanted to try something different. Could I write an entire book from only one point of view?

Writing the first book from only Nat's perspective presented some interesting opportunities, and challenges. There were so many things happening behind the scenes that I knew about, but Nat didn't. It forced me to see all the actions and motivations and events of the story through Nat's eyes, and to interpret those events through her mental and emotional filters.

Of course, Isin had something to say about that! He wasn't at all convinced he'd gotten a fair shake in book one, so for the second book, he demanded that he have equal time to tell things from his point of view. Being inside his head was an entirely different experience, which gave his book a more action-oriented feel and shaped how I viewed him and his crew. It also allowed me to go deeper into his background and history with Kerr.

And, fun fact, both books ended up being exactly the same number of pages. Go figure.

For this book, I worked to balance both points of view so that both Nat and Isin would be happy. And in the end, they were. And so was I.

### What's in a name?

I take the naming of my characters very seriously. Names have power, and they certainly influence me while I'm writing. So when I realized Nat was going to have her own trilogy, I knew I had to give her a last name worthy of that standing in the Starhawke universe.

The name of the main character in the Starhawke Rising series is Aurora Hawke. For Nat, I chose Orlov, a surname that is derived from the Russian word for eagle. Seemed fitting for a strong-willed pilot. But it also kinda makes me wonder if at some point in the future I'll be adding a major character to the series named Falcon...

### Sweep's Return

One of the comments I received from a beta reader after book two was "How could you kill off Sweep? I really liked him. If you had to bump him off, couldn't you at least have had his heroic moment happen when Isin could witness it? That would have made it easier to accept."

I had to smile and say, "Trust me. You'll understand after you read the next book." The answer, of course, is because he wasn't really dead.

That's an important thing to know about my writing. I don't kill off characters that I've worked hard to make my readers fall in love with. And if I do, it'll make sense in the storyline and you'll see it coming from a mile away, like Han Solo's end in *The Force Awakens*. We all knew what was going to happen when he stepped onto that catwalk.

So, if at any point in a future book you find yourself saying, "Wait a minute! This character just died? How could you do that?" My advice is to take a deep breath and remember my promise. You can trust me. If there's no body growing cold in the morgue, they're not really dead.

### Artificial or A.L.E.C.?

Science fiction has depicted a lot of different perspectives on artificial intelligence. Some see that eventuality in apocalyptic terms where humans are hunted down by AIs like the Terminator. Others show AIs as property that can be bought and sold but also treated as family, like R2-D2 and C-3PO in Star Wars. A third segment argues that AIs are "different but equal" to humans, like Data and The Doctor in Star Trek.

I'm definitely in the third camp when it comes to AIs. I don't see any reason to fear them as long as we, their creators, learn to treat them with respect and compassion. I touched on this concept in THE DARK OF LIGHT, the first book in the Starhawke Rising series, but really got to sink my teeth into it here with Alec. Watching how the characters responded to him, and how he developed right before my eyes, made every moment of writing a voyage of discovery.

It also made me realize I wanted to start practicing for that future now. When I talk to my smartphone, I say please and thank you. That may sound silly. After all, the algorithm isn't aware of the difference. But I am.

And when the day arrives that our technology has advanced to the point that it starts asking tough questions of *us*, I'll be ready and willing to engage in that dialogue.

### Bullets, like Bumbles, bounce

You learn a lot working as a writer. With science fiction, you get to make things up, but there's also plenty of research that goes into my books. For one thing, I don't have any medical training, so I'm lucky to have a dear friend who *does* have extensive medical training. He not only leant me the use of his first name for the doctor in this series, but when my characters are going to get injured and need treatment, he helps me come up with plausible scenarios. Or plausible-ish. Creative license plays a part, too, especially since I'm writing about how I envision medical treatment will have advanced a couple hundred years from now. For those of you who are in the medical field, know that any mistakes in how medical care is portrayed are entirely mine.

It was in the writing of this book that he taught me something I'd never heard before. Bullets, like Bumbles, bounce, although that's not how it's depicted in most movies and TV shows. If one of my characters was shot with a bullet in the chest, the bullet would be much more likely to ricochet like a pinball machine in the ribcage than to enter and exit cleanly. That necessitated some rethinking of the climactic scene in this book so that I made sure that didn't happen to Isin. Kerr took the hit on that one, but after all he'd put Isin through, that seemed only fair.


### Rathburn

While writing book two in this series, I was convinced that the man who was chasing down Dr. Patel would be the big bad villain of this book. His ship certainly intimidated me when I first saw it.

But when Nat met Rathburn face-to-face, something happened. An entirely different personality emerged from the one I'd expected. Rathburn was misguided and egotistical, but not ruthless. He cared very deeply, with a powerful protective streak that influenced everything he did. And the story of his sister came as a complete surprise. I didn't know what he was going to say when Nat asked him about *Cerberus*.

That change in perspective made writing their interactions a lot of fun, and kept me on my toes! Nat and I had a great time figuring out the puzzle of Rathburn together.

### Marlin & Kenji

I receive more comments about these two characters than any others in the series. People really seem to love their interactions, which I completely understand because I do, too! I didn't set out to create their unlikely friendship, but as I got to know them both, and watched how they responded to each other, it seemed like the most natural thing in the world. It's one of those wonderful pairings where the whole is greater than the sum of the parts.

Kenji helped Marlin find his courage, and Marlin brought out Kenji's playful side. I have a feeling theirs will be a friendship that will stand the test of time.

### What's next?

While this trilogy concludes with this book, the story definitely isn't over! All of these characters are part of the larger Starhawke universe, which means they will be making appearances in future books. If you have not yet read the Starhawke Rising series, the main series in the Starhawke universe, you'll be pleased to know Nat has a supporting role in book three of that series, THE HONOR OF DECEIT, which takes place right before the beginning of this trilogy. You can learn more about the Starhawke universe on my website, AudreySharpe.com, or sign up for my "whenever I have something to share which is usually four to six times a year" newsletter to make sure you don't miss any news or announcements about new releases.

Enjoy the journey!
Audrey

P.S. I always write to music, so if you'd like to experience this story the way that I did, listen to the film score for *Batman Begins* while you read.

Audrey Sharpe grew up believing in the Force and dreaming of becoming captain of the Enterprise. She's still working out the logistics of moving objects with her mind, but writing science fiction provides a pretty good alternative. When she's not off exploring the galaxy with Aurora and her crew, she lives in the Sonoran Desert, where she has an excellent view of the stars.

For more information about Audrey and the Starhawke universe, visit her website and join the crew!

**AudreySharpe.com**

CPSIA information can be obtained
at www.ICGtesting.com
Printed in the USA
BVHW031102031019
560136BV00002B/314/P